Praise for the works of K

Virgin Territory

A classic rich woman, poor woman tale, White's story brings together wealthy and successful Elise with her chauffeur Jan, who is from the poorer side of the tracks. Both main characters are great—they each have their flaws, and Jan in particular carries a secret that keeps her quite distant from Elise at times. Elise's attempts to get closer to Jan, and to get her to admit she wants their romance as much as Elise does, are rather poignant in places. I liked that Elise is in her forties—it's refreshing to read a romance featuring a woman older than thirty-five. White's writing style is good—just enough detail and background to allow me to delve into the characters, and great pacing.

-*Rainbow Book Reviews*

Simple Pleasures

When the storm is over, the difficulties of recovery are just beginning... Read it to experience empathy and hope, resiliency, and triumph over adversity—and second chances at love, because in the end, love is the most important simple pleasure of all.

-*Lambda Literary Review*

Taken by Surprise

Kenna White is one of the mistresses of lesbian romance. She definitely knows how to write a love story that grips its readers from start to satisfying finish. *Taken by Surprise* does not disappoint her readers. In this story set in Aspen, with wonderful descriptions of both the charming town and the beautiful

Rockies, White has given us two very lovable characters. ...A great fireside read, which lets you enjoy the mountains, beautiful women, and a great romance while snuggled in your chair.

-Just About Write

Body Language

Kenna White has developed a reputation for writing satisfying romances with strong characters. *Body Language* may be the best she's written so far.

-Just About Write

Worth the Wait

Kenna White

Other Bella Books by Kenna White

Beautiful Journey
Beneath the Willow
Body Language
Braggin' Rights
Comfortable Distance
Confessions of a Dreamer
Romancing the Zone
Shared Winds
Skin Deep
Simple Pleasures
Taken by Surprise
These Two Hearts
Virgin Territory
Yours for the Asking

About the Author

Lambda Literary Award winner for her contemporary romance, Taken By Surprise, multi-published and best-selling author Kenna White resides in Southwest Missouri where she enjoys family, travel and writing with a good cup of coffee by her side. Kenna's historical romance, Beautiful Journey, was a GCLS Finalist and an Ann Bannon Popular Choice Award Finalist. Yours for the Asking was the 2nd Place Winner for the Rainbow Writer's Award of Excellence. After living from the Rocky Mountains to New England, she is once again back where bare feet, faded jeans and lazy streams fill her life.

Worth the Wait

Kenna White

BELLA
B O O K S

2024

Bella Books, Inc.
P.O. Box 10543
Tallahassee, FL 32302

First Edition - 2024

Editor: Katherine V. Forrest
Cover Designer: Heather Honeywell

ISBN: 978-1-64247-591-3

Acknowledgment

I'd like to acknowledge and thank Dr. D for her unwavering assistance and thank her for not laughing at my computer illiteracy. I came away from our conversations enlightened and with a dear friend. And a big hug to Buffie, already a friend, for sharing her knowledge and guidance on a restaurant's inner workings. Thank you both.

And thank you to Cameron, grandson extraordinaire, who also shared his computer knowledge. I'm so proud of you, Bud.

Dedication

This book is dedicated to all those computer nerds who know way more than I do but graciously and patiently shared their knowledge. I appreciate their support and assistance as I created Val and Susan's story. I also appreciate they didn't facepalm at my often trivial and ridiculous questions. Thanks!

CHAPTER ONE

Val Nardi pulled her twenty-year-old green Subaru behind Heidi's Coffee Cabin, or at least what had been Heidi's Coffee Cabin. It had been a drive-thru establishment situated along the business district in Bonney Lake, Washington, thirty-five miles west of picturesque Mount Rainier. Now it was a small vacant building Val would spend part of her day off cleaning in preparation for the next tenant.

Val worked for her older brother, Joe, in his restaurant, Mama Nardi's Pizzeria and Ristorante, usually as a server but occasionally in the kitchen as a cook. She also delivered pizza and acted as hostess when needed. Anything Joe and his wife, Audra, needed her to do. It was steady work and paid the bills although she rarely had days off and if she did, it was usually on Tuesday. Owning and renting out her little building was extra income. She couldn't live off it but she counted on it.

After the loss of her own business due to pandemic restrictions, she had needed a job and Joe needed help as he restructured his restaurant from a strictly dine-in establishment to a delivery and takeout facility. For months, the restaurant's mere survival had been in question, forcing Joe and Audra to reduce the number of employees. Some of the servers had already quit, too afraid to work in the public sector in any capacity. Some were let go when they couldn't agree to the new hours and reduced pay, but Joe had no choice. With other restaurants boarding their doors, he was determined to keep Nardi's open. People, after all, still had to eat. For some, although they couldn't dine in, having a pizza delivered to their front porch represented contact with the outside world. Contactless contact. Working from home was a challenge for many former office workers. For many, balancing work with children's online schooling meant finding time to cook was difficult at best. That created an opportunity Joe wanted to fill. When he, acting as brother protector, offered Val a job, she accepted, both to help pay her bills and to help her brother's family business survive the chaos of the Covid years. And to help Val herself survive her own life-altering losses from the virus. She'd spent many long hours wearing gloves, a mask and a face shield and delivering pizza for her brother. There was no face-to-face contact with the customers, only a thank-you shouted through a crack in the door and a small tip left under a flowerpot. Val did whatever her brother needed her to do, occasionally for less than full wages. Joe and Audra's son, Jackson, also came on board. Fresh out of high school, he needed a job and they needed his help. Jobs for unskilled nineteen-year-olds were few and far between when so many had been laid off. It wasn't Jackson's first choice but it was something.

Val wasn't a large woman. Not like her two brothers, both tall, muscular and imposing. Perhaps that was why they were protective of her and always had been. She wasn't fragile either. In spite of her stature and trim build, she was capable of pulling her weight. And they knew it. As of today, Val had worked ten days straight, a few of them double shifts at the restaurant. She had plans for her day off but first she needed to see how much cleaning her building needed. It had been an investment she steadfastly clung to, refusing to sell it even in the most desperate times. It was her security blanket. Her safety net. She hoped a quick mopping and trash removal would be sufficient. She'd then advertise it and have a new tenant paying rent before the end of the month. Hopefully. It was a great location, right on the main commercial artery of Bonney Lake. Whether another coffee barista or some other entrepreneur moved in, she didn't care. She wanted and needed it occupied and rent rolling in.

Her previous tenant, Heidi, had been in business less than a year and seemed to be surviving, but increasingly when Val stopped by to check on the property the closed sign was in the window during what should be peak hours. Val had had early misgivings about renting to the woman but Heidi paid the deposit and two months' rent up front so Val hoped she would be successful. It wasn't until two months' worth of rent checks were late that Heidi informed Val she was closing the coffee kiosk permanently. This wasn't Val's first tenant to abandon a lease owing her money but it was still disappointing. It meant she had ignored her inner voice and taken a gamble that proved regrettable.

Unlocking the back door, she was greeted by the strong smell of coffee. Not a fresh, appealing, first-thing-in-the-morning coffee aroma but a stale, strong stench of burned reheated coffee mixed with mold and sewage. She stepped back, nose stinging and eyes watering, drew a deep breath of fresh air, then entered. The floor was a speckled mess of what she suspected were coffee grounds, along with dried milk, sticky sugary coffee flavorings all smashed and blended together in muddy footprints. Paper napkins and cups, stir sticks and paper towels, all of them dirty, added to the mess around the room on both the floor and counters. The door to the small bathroom in the back corner stood open. The toilet had overflowed. It looked and smelled disgusting. Val gagged and her eyes watered at the stench.

"You have got to be kidding me," she grumbled as she lifted her sandal from the sticky floor, drawing back a long string of something gooey. If she had known what she was walking into she wouldn't have worn her new capri pants and wedge sandals.

Fortunately, she had a broom, mop, trash bags and everything she'd need in her car, because none of the cleaning supplies she kept in the tiny closet were still there. Anything and everything that wasn't attached to the wall, floor or counter was gone. Even the fire extinguisher from the holder and the toilet paper spindle were missing. From the angle of the refrigerator, Val suspected they might have tried to take it as well. The only spot that wasn't dirty and sticky was a square patch on the stainless-steel counter where the coffee maker once sat.

She pulled her shoulder-length brown hair back into a ponytail and went to work, first clearing the toilet with a plunger, then collecting trash. From the looks of the dried-on mess, she suspected she'd be mopping at least twice, if not more, to clean and disinfect the bathroom and scrub sticky coffee stains off the floors.

She filled three trash bags with litter and refuse. The gentle morning rain added to the sultry atmosphere, making the air heavy in spite of the pleasant temperature. She opened the sliding drive-thru windows to vent the strong odor now mixed with cleanser and to cool the sweat that rolled down her face.

She had just returned from loading the last bag of trash in her car when a thirty-something couple in a shiny new BMW pulled up to the window and honked. Val could hear music from their car stereo even before she came to the window. She leaned out and said, "Sorry. We're closed."

"White chocolate mocha with a double shot and a caramel macchiato. Both venti," the man said through his partially lowered window. He bobbed his head in time with the music.

"We're closed," she said, leaning further out the open window.

"What?" He clearly couldn't hear over the sound of his stereo.

"*No coffee,*" Val shouted and shook her head.

A woman in the passenger seat leaned over the driver and waved a piece of paper.

"We've got a two-for-one coupon," she yelled, as if that made a difference.

"No coffee," Val mouthed, realizing they couldn't hear anything she said. There was no closed sign she could show them. Heidi had even taken that. Val shrugged and shook her head again.

The woman finally lowered the volume and peered up at Val.

"How can you be out of coffee?" she demanded.

"I'm sorry but we're closed. And I'm not a barista." Val didn't want to admit that the previous tenant had gone out of business. Hopefully someone else would be moving in soon and reopen even if not as a coffee shack. She didn't want to discourage future customers from returning, whatever the new business was.

The woman tossed a narrowed scowl at Val and said to her companion, "She's just the cleaning lady. She doesn't know how to operate an expresso machine even if she had coffee. Come on, Jerry. Let's go to Starbucks." She wadded up the coupon and tossed it out the window.

"I may not know how to operate the machine but I know it's espresso, not expresso, you little twerp," Val called after them.

Val closed and locked the window. She wanted to finish cleaning and leave before more would-be customers drove up, demanding service. And if Heidi thought she was getting her security or cleaning deposits back, she had another think coming. The pictures on Val's phone were her evidence of how the building was vacated. She had a feeling she wouldn't see the delinquent rent checks either. It wasn't worth the attorney fees or the aggravation to sue.

It took another thirty minutes of wiping surfaces before she was comfortable the building was ready to show to potential tenants. At least it didn't smell repulsive and her shoes didn't stick to the floor. She'd locked the back door and loaded her cleaning supplies in the car when her phone chimed in her pocket. She checked the ID on the screen and considered not answering but she knew her sister-in-law would keep calling. She had a pretty good idea what she wanted.

"Hi, Audra."

"Val, could you come in?"

"It's Tuesday and I'm not on the schedule. It's my day off."

"Could you?"

Val started the car, turned on the windshield wipers as the drizzle became a full-fledged downpour. She leaned back against the headrest, deciding how to answer. It was 12:30, the prime lunch hour.

"Tony called off," Audra added. "His mother is in town so I bet he's off somewhere with her. And Kathy called off. She's sick. It's getting crazy, Val. We need you to come in."

Val desperately wanted to say no, she was busy and couldn't come in. She owed it to herself to have the rest of the day to herself. She'd cleaned a disgustingly dirty building and had been stiffed on two months' rent. She wanted time to decompress and soothe her anger. And she desperately needed a shower. But she also owed her brother her undying allegiance. Knowing what he had done for her was enough. She couldn't say no. And seldom did. Audra knew how to play her and get what she wanted. Val strongly suspected that the request to come in for a couple of hours meant come in and work until close.

"I'll have to go home first. I need to shower and change."

"Oh, wear whatever you've got on. It'll be all right this time. It'll be covered by an apron anyway."

The customary and acceptable dress code for the servers was black slacks, or black jeans, so long as they weren't ripped or worn. Audra made that quite clear before any applicant was hired. Black shoes were also required. Nardi's provided red T-shirts but each employee was required to have appropriate and clean apparel at the start of their shift. Audra was a stickler for appearance. Val never questioned it, even appreciated Audra's insistence the servers dress neatly. Audra's reassurance that she could wear whatever she had on meant they were severely shorthanded.

"Audra, I can't. I've been cleaning and I'm all sweaty."

"Cleaning what?"

"The drive-thru. They stripped the place clean and left a disaster. They left me hanging for two month's rent, too."

"Give me the phone number. Don't worry. I'll have Joe take care of it."

Audra was taking control and Val didn't need or want her help.

"*No!*" Val exclaimed. "I've taken care of it. I don't want Joe calling her. I've got the security and cleaning deposits. I'm not refunding any of it."

"Hell, yes, you should keep that."

Val didn't like Audra's brand of interference. As helpful as she tried to be, it was invasive and overbearing. But she was family and that was the justification for meddling in Val's business.

"I'll be there but I'll need an extra thirty minutes," Val said, knowing Audra was going to ask why then complain about it. She didn't like being second fiddle to anything or anyone, whatever the reason.

"Extra thirty minutes for what?" she immediately demanded.

"I have a pan of brownies I need to drop off at the center. I promised Nana I'd have them there today."

"Can't you do that tomorrow morning before you come in? I need you as soon as you can get here."

"They're for bingo night. I need to drop them off by six. How long will you need me? Not more than an hour or two, right?"

"Probably all evening. We've got a group coming in."

"Then I'll drop them off before I come in and I won't have to worry about it later. I promised, Audra."

"Bring the brownies with you. I'll drop them off this evening. I need to run an errand."

Val heaved an exasperated sigh, knowing the rest of her day off had been commandeered and no excuse short of death would release her from that fact.

"You'll have them there by six? No later. I promised the activities director," Val reiterated.

"Yes. I'll have them there by six," Audra groaned.

Val wouldn't bet a plugged nickel the brownies would be delivered on time but she'd give Audra the benefit of the doubt.

"All right. I'll bring them and be there shortly. But I *am* taking a shower first."

"Hurry." Audra hung up.

Val pulled into traffic, knowing she had relinquished her day off and probably wouldn't get another one for at least a week, if not two weeks.

"Why do I let myself be talked into this," she muttered and headed home. She knew why. Since she had been shorted on rent payments, she'd be paying the utilities, insurance and taxes on the building without income assistance from a renter.

In spite of the rain, she lowered her window. The stinky bags of trash were filling her car with a disgusting odor. Or did she smell that bad?

"Whew," she gasped, hoping to defuse the gag she felt rising in her throat. "Heidi, I hope you never ask me for a reference because you are *not* getting one."

CHAPTER TWO

As soon as Val walked in the back door of Mama Nardi's Pizzeria and Ristorante, she heard raised voices, the loudest coming from her brother, his voice thunderous and unmistakable. Val stowed her tote bag in the office, retrieved an apron and hoped to avoid whatever chaos had him shouting. She'd considered allowing Audra to deliver the brownies to the senior living facility but thought better of it and dropped them off herself. It seemed a wise decision now with all the commotion in the kitchen. She didn't take time to visit with her grandmother but at least she'd fulfilled her obligation. What would Audra do to her for taking a few extra minutes? Fire her? She'd probably grumble and complain about the delay but the time to cross town and back wasn't a big deal since technically it was Val's day off. Several of the servers frequently clocked in late even though they were on the schedule. Val wasn't on the schedule but she was there and ready to fill in whatever they needed.

"What the hell?" Joe pulled three undelivered pizza boxes from the insulated sleeve and tossed them on the counter. He scanned the order slip then opened the lids. "Two large double pepperoni. One large supreme with extra mushrooms. That's what they ordered and that's what they got."

"The crabby old lady refused the order," Jackson said with a sneer. "She was a bitch.

Not even a tip for my time after I drove all the freakin' way out there."

"Did you check the address?" Joe demanded, stabbing his finger against the delivery slip.

"Why isn't there a phone number on this order?"

"How the hell do I know? I don't write the orders. I just deliver them," Jackson replied loudly.

"Where have you been? You're late," Joe said in Val's direction, ready to lash out at anyone who crossed his path.

"How can I be late? I'm not supposed to be here at all. It's Tuesday. Remember?" Val tied on a pocketed apron and stood at the sink washing her hands.

He grumbled something then turned his scowl back at Jackson.

At fifty-two, Joe was the oldest of three siblings and the patriarch of the family—or at least he thought so. A few pounds overweight, with a barrel chest, he looked every bit the part of an Italian restaurant owner. He wore a white apron over a white T-shirt and khaki pants, all of them speckled with red pasta sauce. Visible were the eagle tattoo on his right forearm and crossed swords on his left. He'd served twenty years in the Army where he learned his food service skills as a mess hall manager. He had gray hair he wore in the same crew cut from when he was a teenager, and a black patch over his right eye, the result of a cooking accident which had led to his early retirement and partial disability. He refused to wear the prosthetic eye provided by the VA, claiming it didn't fit right. He couldn't be convinced, even after multiple refittings, that it took a little time to get used to it. He was hard-working, dedicated and protective of his extended family, which included Val. His crusty edge and feisty disposition were what had made him a successful restaurateur, that and his ability to adapt. Once Covid restrictions were eased and it was safe to reopen for indoor dining, he'd continued to offer the home delivery service. Like many restaurants that survived closings, he had found a new and lucrative clientele. And delivering pizza was the perfect job for Jackson. Now twenty-one, Jackson looked as unlike his dad as he could be. He had long, curly brown hair, wore black jeans perched low on his hips as if they were a size too big, and a hoodie with a red dragon on the back. He also looked like his razor was MIA.

Val waited for instructions on what they needed her to do, suspecting the argument between father and son wasn't over. She didn't have to wait long.

"The old witch was supposed to pay in cash. Mom said so. Seventy-eight bucks plus my tip," Jackson shouted. "I didn't get a fucking dime. She said why the fuck should she pay seventy-eight bucks for pizza she didn't order?"

"Audra, why the hell did you send out an order without payment?" Joe demanded of the woman watching from the doorway to the dining room.

Audra stepped closer and held up her hand. "Calm down, Joe," she demanded. "The online payment went through but after a few minutes it popped up as unpaid. You already had the pizzas made and boxed. So, I sent them out. Besides, you've sent out orders before as cash on delivery. You let that big order go out to your buddies last month and it was over two hundred dollars," she argued.

"That was for the high school. Not some random old lady out in the sticks trying to scam me for free pizza. From now on, if they don't pay first we don't fill the order. Period," he enunciated loudly, ejecting the toothpick from his mouth.

Val turned to Jackson. "Did the woman ask you to leave the pizza without paying for it?"

"Heck no. I didn't give her a chance," he snorted.

"He better not have," Joe snapped.

"Then she wasn't trying to scam you, Joe," Val offered calmly but his nostrils were still flaring.

"Joseph, that's enough. Let it go." Audra's raised voice let everyone in the kitchen know she had taken control. The subject was now closed. Joe wasn't happy. Jackson wasn't happy. Audra wasn't happy. The pizzas didn't get delivered or paid for. The boxes were back and abandoned on the counter. It was time to move on with the business of running the restaurant.

Joe Nardi was the owner and head chef at Mama Nardi's but everyone knew Audra was the dynamo to be reckoned with when it came to problems. Sometimes pushy, sometimes abrasive, sometimes an out-and-out pain the ass, Audra was in charge and Joe accepted that rather than provoke her ire. She was a short woman with dramatically arched eyebrows, salt-and-pepper hair and bright red lipstick. She had fake fingernails she referred to as her claws, often coated with pastel nail polish. Joe and Audra had met literally by accident. She ran a stop sign one rainy night and T-boned Joe's truck. Four months later they were engaged but it was another three years before they were married. Their relationship had best been described as two goats butting heads, but lovingly so. They'd raised one occasionally disrespectful child, survived Joe's many military deployments and kept a business afloat through horrific financial times, so it was assumed they had something going for them. Whatever Audra said, either at the restaurant or at home, was the law of the land.

"What section do you want me to cover?" Val asked Audra once the dust had settled and no one was yelling.

"The back."

The section where tables could be pushed together for groups and where family gatherings were seated.

"Do you have something coming in?" Val plucked an olive from the bin, suspecting this was going to be a long evening and she hadn't had lunch.

"We're supposed to have a tour bus about four thirty."

"How many?" Val braced for the worst.

"Twenty or so."

Val gave her a long look.

This was what Audra meant when she said they were shorthanded. They needed someone to cover a bus full of hungry customers and do it alone. Val had done it before. They trusted she could handle it again but that didn't mean it wouldn't be a nightmare.

"Could be a couple more," Audra said with a shrug.

"Oh, goodie." She checked her watch then blew out an exasperated breath. "Well, don't give me anyone else right now. Let me get it set up."

"I need you to cover that six-top before the bus gets here. You'll have plenty of time." Audra nodded toward a nearby table with two adults and four children, all of the preteens bouncing and fidgeting in their chairs.

Val tended to the family, bringing drinks, taking pizza orders and cleaning two spilled glasses of sticky soda while both parents spent their time texting and ignoring their kids. She was in a hurry to get things ready for the bus's arrival but she didn't rush the family, keeping a cheery disposition until they paid their ticket and left.

"Thank you," she said politely when the man handed her a five-dollar tip on a ninety-three-dollar bill.

Val went to work loading trays with napkin-wrapped silverware and glasses of ice water. She arranged the tables and chairs, doing as much as she could before they arrived. And it was in the nick of time. She had set the last menu and silverware on the tables when a large silver and blue tour bus pulled into the parking lot.

Val allowed Audra to seat the stream of senior citizens, adjusting chairs for those with canes and two with walkers. The group was on its way to Seattle for an overnight in a hotel before boarding a cruise ship, so most were giddy with anticipation. Many laughed and joked like it was old home week. It took several minutes to get everyone settled so Val stepped back and waited. Audra was right. There were more than twenty. Twenty-seven, including the driver and tour director.

"Good evening, ladies and gentlemen," Val announced from the end of the long table once they were all seated. "My name is Val and I'll be your server this evening." She smiled hospitably. "I'm going to do my very best to provide you with an unsurpassed dining experience here at Mama Nardi's." She reached down and touched the shoulder of one of the nearby customers. "I promise, if I fail, it won't be from lack of trying." The group laughed quietly. "I'm sorry, but we don't have toys in the happy meals." They laughed even louder. So far, so good. "Let me get your drink orders while you look over the menu. Spaghetti pomodoro is our special this evening. It's delicious and comes with a side salad and bread."

She moved down one side of the table then up the other, taking orders for everything from decaf coffee to iced tea to an occasional glass of wine. When some of the people insisted on having separate checks, she politely reminded them the tour director was responsible for the total ticket, including the tip. Separate checks for a large group were a pain in the neck. And were ripe for cheapening out on a tip. When Joe decided tour groups had taken advantage of his servers and his hospitality long enough, he'd instituted the policy, giving the tour director the responsibility of paying for the entire group, making sure a suitable tip was included. If they didn't like it, they could make reservations elsewhere.

The group kept Val busy for over an hour serving food and drinks, refilling cups and glasses, returning unsatisfactory orders, usually after most of it was consumed, and wishing they had picked something else altogether. Some were sweet, patient and polite. Some, not so much. There was always one or two who couldn't be pleased, no matter what they were served. That went with the job. But Val kept her smile bright and her service attentive right through dessert. As the group was filing out, one man, well into his seventies if not his eighties and leaning on a cane, waved her over. A small man, he had been quiet throughout the meal, had ordered the special, eating barely half of it. He'd sipped a glass of red wine but like his dinner, left half of it. The serious look on his face suggested he hadn't been pleased with his meal or the service. She smiled pleasantly as she walked over to him.

"What did you say your name was, young lady?" he asked, stooped and relying on his cane for support. He squinted at her as if his eyes couldn't focus.

"Val. Val Nardi," she replied agreeably.

"Val Nardi. I'll remember that. You're a good waitress." He nodded then took her hand as if he wanted to shake it. His grip was weak and his hand shook slightly but Val felt him press something into her palm. He then folded her fingers around it, holding her fist closed. "This is a hard job and I appreciate your kindness." He released her hand, gave it a pat and turned for the door. His cane clicked with each step as he shuffled toward the parking lot and disappeared into the crowd waiting to reboard the bus.

"Thank you," she called. "Have a pleasant trip." Then she discreetly checked what he had placed in her palm. "Oh, my God," she gasped at the neatly folded hundred-dollar bill.

She rushed outside. He was climbing the steps into the bus, struggling with his cane for support. She hurried up to him, locked an arm through his and helped him up the last two steps.

"Thank you, sir," she whispered and kissed his cheek.

"You're welcome. My wife's name was Val. Valerie Rostowski." He looked back at her with a thin, reflective smile as a tear glistened in his eye. He squeezed her arm and moved down the aisle to his seat.

She started across the parking lot, but tossed one last look at the bus and noticed a hand pressed against the window in the last row. It was Mr. Rostowski staring out at her. She smiled and raised a hand, as if pressing her hand to his. She watched as the bus slowly pulled away, his hand never leaving the window. She heaved a contented smile and went back inside.

Val helped a busboy carry the last of the dirty dishes into the kitchen, then separated the tables, once again ready for individual couples and families. She could use a five-minute break to catch her breath but knew she wouldn't get one. She hadn't had anything to eat since breakfast, followed by cleaning the putrefied remnants of Heidi's failed business venture. She went into the kitchen, hoping to find the three undelivered pizzas so she could snag a quick bite before Audra announced she had seated someone in her section. The pizza boxes were on the counter, opened and empty but for a few slivers of cold leftovers and dried cheese stuck to the cardboard.

Joe saw her and held out a fresh slice of sausage pizza. He usually kept one for staff consumption, often a returned order or mistake.

"Here," he said then went back to assembling a family-size pizza order.

"Thanks." She took a bite, expecting it to be sweet Italian sausage, one of her favorites. She coughed and nearly choked on the bite. "Hey," she said, covering her mouth as she coughed again.

"Spicy, huh?" he said with a chuckle. "Table fourteen didn't like it either."

"Yes!" She picked off the chunks of sausage and dropped them in the trash. "That's better. Good old cheese pizza." They both laughed.

"Audra told me what happened with your building." He opened one of the pizza ovens and checked the contents then, slid in a freshly made large pizza. "Why the hell did you let them get so far behind? You should have cracked down when the first month's check was a week late."

"I took care of it, Joe," Val said in an attempt to defuse the conversation before he built up a head of steam.

"You can't let them walk all over you like that. It'll happen again if you don't let them know who's boss right up front. Haven't you had enough crap over that place?"

"I know what you're going to say next and don't. It's mine and I'm keeping it. One way or the other, I'm keeping it."

"I've already told you I'll make you a good offer on it when you're ready to sell. You've had one loser after another in there and they keep taking advantage of you. If you're going to be a landlord, you've got to have balls. Set the rules and stick to them."

"You never know. Someday I may open my own drive-thru business," she joked, knowing how silly that sounded.

"Like what?" he teased, stirring a pot of sauce. "Maid service again?"

She smirked at him and headed back into the dining room.

Jackson made several deliveries throughout the afternoon and evening, keeping him busy, out of the kitchen and avoiding further arguments with Joe. The kitchen staff was careful not to mention the undelivered order. From past experience with Joe's anger, they seemed to know it was better not to poke the bear. It wasn't the first delivery faux pas and it wouldn't be the last.

Jackson held the back door for his mother as she walked out, then he came in and dropped the insulated carrier on the counter as if there was a problem.

"Where's Mom going?" he demanded, looking at the door as if he expected her to reenter.

"Costco."

"Could she wait and do it later?"

"No." Joe glared over at the undelivered pizza. "Why are you back already?"

"Because I've got a flat tire," he sneered, making it sound like it was Joe's fault.

Joe tossed a long look then said, "Well, get out there and change it and get the damn order delivered before it's cold."

"I can't. I don't have a spare."

Val noticed him give her a quick look then lower his eyes as if embarrassed that anyone heard him.

"Why not?" Joe demanded.

"I let Alex borrow it."

"That was six months ago."

"He's still driving on it. What am I supposed to do? Jack up his car and take it off?".

Joe turned on him. "Yes. Get your damn tire back. Call him up and have him bring it back *now*. Your buddy can buy his own tire. Have him come drive you to deliver the order then get your tire back."

"He's in Vancouver until next Saturday."

Joe's jaw muscles rippled as he glared daggers at Jackson. He finally heaved a disgusted sigh then looked over at Val.

"Give the kid your keys," he said, nodding at Jackson.

"What?" She had hoisted the tray over her shoulder, ready to deliver it to the dining room.

"Jackson needs your keys. He's got a flat tire and no damn spare."

"I heard that but why is my car his only option?" She adjusted the tray.

"Just give him the damn keys."

Val tossed a disapproving glare at her brother. She knew she couldn't win this. An emergency was an emergency and it wasn't the first time she had been asked to share her keys. Audra had taken her car to pick up supplies. Jackson couldn't drive Joe's huge truck with the manual transmission, something Joe wouldn't allow anyway. Her Subaru was older, therefore justifiable. Sometimes she thought Joe considered her car community property. She could argue, but she couldn't win. The best she could hope for was a polite request. Or at least one without a cuss word in it.

"You can ask nicely, Joseph. And so can he." She nodded toward Jackson on her way out of the kitchen. When she returned with an empty tray, they were both staring at her impatiently.

"Can I use your car?" Jackson said as if it was an effort to utter the words. "Please."

Val retrieved her keys from her tote bag and slapped them on the counter then fixed him with a please-be-careful-with-my-car stare.

"Thanks." He grabbed the keys, the insulated carrier, and hurried out the door.

"Thanks, Val," Joe said quietly.

"Yep." She clenched her jaw so she wouldn't say more.

Jackson came back through the door, holding the keys. He glared at Val.

"What?" she said.

"I've got to go out to Tehaleh then Buckley then back to Sumner," he said.

"The car only has a quarter tank of gas."

"So, put some in it."

"Have you got some money?"

Val wanted to say no. He was using her car. He could pay for the gas. He had a paycheck and tips, too. But this was another technicality not worth an argument. She balanced the tray with one hand and pulled two ten-dollar bills from her apron pocket with the other, careful not to expose the hundred-dollar bill Mr. Rostowski had given her.

"Put it all in the car, Jackson." She tossed a deliberate stare at him. "All twenty dollars. In the car. In the gas tank. Not in your pocket or in your mouth."

He smirked and went back out the door.

"You should keep your tank at least half full," Joe said, overhearing the exchange.

"I didn't know I was subsidizing Nardi pizza deliveries this evening."

She headed to the dining room to serve her customers. She wanted to ask if she'd have her car back so she could go home at a decent hour but it was fruitless to ask. She knew she'd probably be working the entire evening shift. So much for her day off.

When she returned to the kitchen for her next order Joe looked over at her and said in a hushed tone, "Don't worry. I'll slip you a little extra on your next paycheck." He gave a reassuring nod. "I got you covered, sis."

"Okay." She wanted to ask why they continued to coddle and condone Jackson's immature behavior, a thought that crossed her mind whenever one of these unfortunate and annoying events cropped up, often at her expense. But he was their son, their only child. If they accepted it, she had to as well.

CHAPTER THREE

Jackson returned Val's car sometime after nine thirty. She found an empty Taco Bell sack in the back seat and two empty pop cups in the cup holders. And not surprisingly, the gas tank had barely enough gas to hold the peg off the E. Whether he drove the twenty dollars-worth of gas out or drove his friends around town and spent it on food, she didn't know. She did know she wasn't confident she could get home and back to work in the morning. She stopped for gas, gnashing her teeth.

When she pulled into the parking lot the next day for her afternoon shift, she noticed Jackson pulling out in his car. As promised, Jackson's flat tire had been repaired. Her car and her full tank of gas wouldn't be needed, thankfully.

It was going to be a good day. One of the servers was having her thirty-fifth birthday and Val had made her a pan of the gal's favorite blond brownies. It was Grandma Nardi's special recipe with the dark-brown sugar, a half teaspoon of cinnamon and a *whisper* of orange zest, as Nana had instructed. Val loved to tinker with her grandmother's recipes. Some were dismal failures. Some were delightful successes. She wasn't a master chef. Far from it. She had a plentiful spice cabinet and an adequately stocked pantry of the basics so it was fun experimenting. Her first success had been applesauce pancakes when she was twelve, stuck at home during an ice storm and bored. She still chuckled to herself when she remembered her *science projects*, as the family called them.

"Sweetheart, you don't need to make that again for a while," her mother had said on more than one occasion, her way of politely discouraging a failed concoction.

Val tied on an apron, checked what was ready to take to a waiting customer and plated a pizza when Audra rushed into the kitchen with a gleam in her eye and headed straight for Val.

"There you are," she exclaimed, grabbing the plate from Val's hands. "She's here. Table twelve. I put her in the corner so you'd have some privacy. I'll deliver this. You go say hello. And LeeAnn was right. She is super cute."

"Audra, I'm working. What are you talking about?" She reclaimed the pizza, straightening it on the serving plate. "I'm not going to have a social hour with a customer." She picked up a dish of parmesan cheese and a shaker of pepper flakes.

"Michelle drove all the way down here to see you. The least you could do is be pleasant."

"Michelle who? And why did she drive down here to see me? Is she interested in leasing the building?" Val was only half invested in this conversation.

"She's a real cutie, Val. Gorgeous blue eyes. Nice figure. And she broke up with her girlfriend a couple weeks ago." Audra grinned wickedly. "She's available."

Val threw her head back, closed her eyes and groaned. "Audra, what did you do? Please, please, please tell me you didn't arrange another blind date for me." She glared at her. "I asked you not to do that, especially when I'm at work." Or anytime. She was so not nearly ready for this.

"You work for us. Who's going to care if you spend a few minutes being polite? We'll cover for you."

"I am. I'm going to care." Val picked up the order and headed into the dining room.

"Table twelve. She's wearing a gray jacket," Audra called after her. "She's in your section so check her out when you take her order."

Val was nothing if not professional. Michelle, like all of her customers, would receive her most courteous greeting and hopefully it wouldn't be mistaken for something it wasn't. All she could see of the woman was her curly brown hair and her Seattle Mariners hoodie. If Audra said she was cute, she probably was. Val took a deep breath, smiled demurely and crossed the room to her table.

"Hello," she said, drawing the woman's attention up from the menu. "How are you this afternoon? I'm Val and I'll be taking your order. What can I get you to start off with? Iced tea? Coke? Draft?"

Val did a quick assessment. Thirty, maybe thirty-two, stocky athletic build, short curly hair in need of a good brushing and a pea-size mole on her right earlobe. No, not a mole. A tattoo of a spider.

"Hi, Val. I'm Michelle." She had a deep though quiet voice. The woman did a deliberate, slow scan of Val's body then smiled as if she approved. "How about a beer. Do you have Rainier Summit?"

"Yes, we do. Good choice." It was Val's standard reply to whatever the customer ordered from the bar. Although Rainier wasn't an elite choice, it was popular with the locals. "Have you decided what you'd like to eat? Would you care for an appetizer with your beer?"

"I need a minute," she said as she studied Val's face, a devious smile forming on her lips.

"Okay. I'll get your Rainier and be right back."

Val could feel Michelle's eyes follow her as she walked away. She stepped behind the counter and retrieved the beer from the cooler along with a glass mug. Audra hurried to intercept her.

"Didn't I tell you she was cute? Did you see the dimples?"

"Audra," Val scolded in a hushed tone. "Please!" She returned to the table with the drink.

Sure enough, Michelle was watching as Val approached, her gaze alternating between her crotch and her bustline.

"Have you decided what you'd like?" Val didn't usually need to write down orders for small groups and especially not single customers. But she wanted something in her hands so she looked occupied, busy. She pulled her order pad and pen from her apron pocket.

"What do you recommend?" Michelle leaned back in the booth and draped her arm over the back of the seat.

"Depends on how hungry you are. The special is chicken alfredo and it comes with a salad and bread. One of my favorites." Another standard proclamation for customers who seemed undecided. "The pizzas are all good. We have twenty-six different toppings so you can be as creative as you'd like. Lasagna is excellent. Four kinds of cheese. The bruschetta goes great with the lasagna or any of the pasta dishes."

While Val explained more of the choices, Michelle slowly ran the tip of her tongue across her upper lip and winked, sending Val a message loud and clear.

"How about I work on my beer and think about it a little more?" She winked again.

"Okay. I'll check back with you in a few minutes." Val turned and left. "Oh, good grief," she groaned as she walked away.

Postponing her order so Val would have to stop by the table occasionally wasn't a new game but Val had no intention of playing it with this blatant woman. She would tend to her other customers and return when she had a spare minute.

Val took two tables' orders, refilled drinks, cleared two tables as customers left, and corrected a calzone order. Twice she stopped to ask Michelle if she'd decided. Maybe she had no intention of eating, was merely nursing her beer and ordering another while waiting for some of Val's time. As Val was delivering an extra-large pizza to the round table in the corner, she noticed Audra sitting with Michelle, seemingly carrying on a covert conversation. They looked in Val's direction and smiled.

"Oh, Audra, please don't," Val muttered to herself.

Michelle occupied the booth for over an hour, nibbling bread sticks that came from Audra and two Rainier Summit beers. She spent most of the time, at least when Val noticed, watching her comings and goings as she tended to her customers, and staring at her crotch.

"So, what do you think?" Audra said, following Val into the kitchen and taking hold of her arm.

"You can't judge a book by its cover." Val pulled away and went to wash something sticky off her hands.

"But she is cute, right?" Audra followed her to the sink.

"How old is she? She's a child, for God's sake."

"She is not! She's twenty-eight."

"And I'm old enough to be her mother." Val frowned at Audra, hoping to make her point.

"You said that woman last month was too old. She was forty." Audra perched a hand on her hip.

"What I said was, at least she's older than the children you keep trying to set me up with. And I wish you would stop." She checked the orders ready to be delivered to tables, searching for anything in her section.

Audra took her arm and offered a sympathetic smile. "Val, it's been five years, sweetheart. It's time to find someone again. Kate would want you to. You know she would. Do you want to be single the rest of your life?"

"What I want is to go back to work and for Michelle to go away."

"Val," Joe called from across the kitchen. He placed two plates of pasta on the counter and tucked the ticket under the corner. "Table six."

"On my way." She collected the order, glad to have a diversion. Audra meant well but grief lay in constant ambush and Val couldn't deal with anything that resurrected the heartbreak of losing her longtime companion and business partner. It was devastating when it happened and continued to be, especially since hospital restrictions surrounding Covid patients meant she couldn't be with Kate, hold her hand, tell her she loved her or say goodbye to her beloved.

She noticed Michelle's ticket for the beer had been taken off her table, probably by Audra. When she finally left, Val also noticed she hadn't left a tip, only a business card with the phone number circled and a smiley face drawn in the corner.

"No, thank you, Michelle," Val muttered as she crumpled the card and dropped it in the trash.

Audra tossed her a few disappointed looks but Val ignored them. She had settled into her routine, taking orders, serving customers and doing the in-between chores, all of them with a smile and a cheery disposition. A few customers tested her resolve but she did her best to not let them get under her skin. Some people couldn't be pleased, regardless of how hard she or anyone else tried.

"Val?" Audra called, nodding her over to where she was processing a credit card payment. "I need you to cover the front for me," she said, holding the phone against her chest. "I need to run an errand. It shouldn't take long." She went back to her phone conversation with a worried look on her face.

Val nodded, wondering what was so important that Audra needed to leave during the upcoming dinner rush. Maybe a last-minute supply shortage in the kitchen. Val was already busy but she'd find a way to juggle incoming customers who needed to be seated, wait on tables in her section and process those ready to pay. They trusted she could handle it.

"Excuse me." A woman stood at the register, presumably waiting to be seated. She was tall, dressed in gray slacks, a black button-down shirt and a bright yellow jacket spackled with raindrops. Her brunette hair was short, damp and graying at the temples. Somewhere in her late fifties, early sixties, Val guessed. Many of the customers were familiar to her but not this woman.

Seating guests was Audra's job and she seemed to have a strategy when it came to who sat where. Val suspected she saved the better tables for those she thought were customers who ordered higher on the menu and added alcoholic drinks to their dinner. This professionally though simply dressed middle-aged woman, dining alone, would probably be shown to one of the tables along the far wall without a view out the windows.

Val took a menu from the rack. "Good evening, ma'am. Would you like to follow me?"

"No, I don't want a table or a booth. I want to talk with whoever takes delivery orders."

"Oh, you have an order to pick up?"

"No, I want to talk to the manager. Or the shift supervisor. Or anyone with knowledge about deliveries." She seemed patient enough but she frowned as she searched the room.

"I'm very sorry but she had to run an errand. Can I help you with something? Was there a problem with your order?"

"The problem is, I didn't place an order. A young man tried to deliver pizza to my house yesterday that I didn't order."

"Early twenties, dark hair, probably wearing a hoodie?" Val asked. "That's Jackson, the owner's son."

"Well, Jackson's people skills are sorely lacking. When I told him in no uncertain terms that I didn't place the order he insisted I did, insisted I pay for it, including a tip and he used very colorful language." The woman directed a piercing stare at Val. "And since when do delivery drivers tell the customer how much the tip should be? A tip is a reflection of services performed and at the customer's discretion."

"I'm very sorry. You are absolutely right. We didn't have a phone number for verification of the order sent to you. I'm so sorry for the mix-up. Please accept our sincere apologies. We'd be more than happy to offer you a complimentary pizza."

"No, thank you. I'm not here for a freebie. I was in the middle of an online meeting and he repeatedly rang the doorbell and pounded on the door." She glowered at Val. "Is Jackson allowed to speak disparagingly to your customers in-house or only when he attempts home delivery? Coercing unsuspecting individuals into paying for things they didn't order with crude and disrespectful language sounds suspiciously like a scam. I sincerely hope Nardi's doesn't condone such language or such behavior. Jackson seemed intent on bullying me into paying for your mistake."

"Again, I'm sorry. I apologize for the misunderstanding." Val was getting annoyed with the woman and her tirade. Why stop by in person if she wasn't happy? Why not a phone call? Or why not ignore the unfortunate mistake for what it was, an accident? She wasn't charged for anything. It might have been an inconvenience but nothing earth-shattering. Yes, Jackson's manners were occasionally suspect. But this woman seemed determined to exaggerate the point and the couple waiting behind her was obviously listening.

"Can I assume this won't happen again?" the woman asked, still with an indignant tone in her voice and a challenging arch to her brow.

Val had enough. She had other customers waiting. This woman had made her point and it was time to move on.

"Now, look," Val declared, trying desperately not to scream at this woman. "I'm very sorry you were disturbed and if Jackson was anything less than polite, I apologize, but I've got other customers. If you don't want a complimentary pizza for your trouble, I need to return to work."

The woman turned and walked out without another word or backward glance.

"Good evening," Val said to the couple next in line, once again displaying her best customer service smile. "I'm sorry about that. Would you folks like a table or a booth?" She tossed a last look out the window as the disgruntled woman rounded the corner of the parking lot. Hopefully their paths would never cross again.

CHAPTER FOUR

It had been raining steadily all afternoon and evening, sending customers running across the parking lot to avoid being drenched. Joe rolled out extra carpet mats in the entry but a trail of wet footprints across the dining room became unavoidable and a cause for repeated mopping. It was a chilly rain. Val could feel the cool breeze when she passed the open door. It felt good. It had been a long day and she still had most of the dinner rush to go.

She delivered glasses of wine and a dessert to a couple celebrating their anniversary, then checked on her other tables. She refilled a man's coffee cup for the fourth time and picked up his empty dinner plate. He had finished his meal down to the last traces of pasta sauce, using the bread to mop the plate clean. He had been polite and congenial during the meal. She might even call him chatty.

"I understand you own the little building that's for rent on 410," he said as he poured creamer into the fresh cup of coffee.

"Yes," she said, retrieving his empty dessert plate.

"It isn't very big, is it?"

"Well, I doubt it could be a big box store," she joked.

"Can't be more than a couple of hundred square feet, tops." There was a judgmental tone to his declaration.

Val instantly knew where this was headed. He was prepping her to make a low-ball offer even though she hadn't officially listed the building yet. Or maybe a ridiculous offer to purchase it outright; to take it "off her hands," as Joe put it. It wasn't the first time she heard someone willing to "help out the little lady." She didn't appreciate it then and she didn't appreciate it now.

"Actually, it's four hundred and sixteen square feet," she said politely. "Good functional workspace."

"Probably even a little tight for selling coffee. Isn't that what it was? No wonder it went belly up."

"Yes, Heidi's Coffee Cabin." Val wanted to say the size of the building had nothing to do with the failure of the business.

He pulled a business card from his shirt pocket and set it on the table. "I think we can get you a very fair price for that little piece of property. Come on into the office and we can talk about it. There are a lot of technical details involved in commercial property. The longer a building sits empty, the less likely it is to move. That place has been vacant for months and you're running out of time, missy."

"It's been vacant only a few weeks." How long it had been empty was none of this man's business. And his condescending attitude was beginning to annoy her.

"Unfortunately, the commercial real estate market isn't in your favor right now. You'll need some help navigating the—"

Val cut him off. "The commercial real estate market is entirely in my favor, Mr. Moffet," she said, reading the name from his card without picking it up. "It's not a food truck. Unlike most small drive-thru buildings, my building has on-demand hot water, heat and air-conditioning; it has a bathroom as well as appliances. Plus, it's in a prime location. I'm not in the market to sell it. The only reason it isn't occupied is because I haven't had a chance to list it. But I will and soon. I don't need an agent to list it then take thirty percent of the rent."

"We don't take that much. Not nearly thirty percent. That's ridiculous," he scoffed.

She smiled as he frowned, seeming to realize his motives had been exposed.

"Will there be anything else?" she asked politely and placed his ticket on the table.

He stood and fished in his pocket for a money clip.

"Well, you give me a call, little lady. We'll see what we can do. Hopefully, it's not too late to find a buyer for that property. One way or another, we'll get you fixed up. By the way," he said, dropping some cash on the ticket. "You know the health department will have to inspect the building whenever there's a change of ownership or a new permit issued. From what I hear, it won't pass." He tossed a backward glance and headed out the door without waiting for her reply.

Val hated people patronizing her, especially men trying to make her feel incompetent. As frustrating as she sometimes felt with her renters, the building was hers. She didn't need help deciding what to do with it. It would be a cold day in hell before she asked Mr. Moffet for help. Not to her surprise, he'd left a dollar and seventy-three-cent tip for a nineteen-dollar dinner and four cups of coffee.

"What was that all about?" Audra asked, following Val into the kitchen.

"It was nothing. He's a real estate agent asking about my building."

"I heard that woman came in, bitching and griping about the pizza delivery Jackson tried to make. Is that true? Was she here creating a scene?"

"I don't know if I'd call it creating a scene. She was registering a complaint about how Jackson handled the delivery. She said he was rude and was using foul language."

"He said she was being a bitch about it. It was a simple mistake. She didn't have to treat him like that."

"Audra, we weren't there. And you know as well as I do, Jackson can be a little disrespectful at times. If she didn't place the order, he shouldn't have insisted she pay for it."

Val wasn't sure why she was defending the woman. After all, she had been brusque, arrogant and downright disagreeable.

"Was it one of our regulars?" Audra asked flippantly.

"I don't think so. I got the feeling we wouldn't see her again."

"Good." Audra walked away in a huff.

"Hey, Val? Don't let any real estate agent get their grubby paws on your building. If you want to sell it, you come talk to me," Joe said, overhearing their conversation.

"I'm not selling it. And I wouldn't let him anywhere near it, the creep."

"Here, take this to table three," he said, finishing the garnishes to two plates of pasta.

It wasn't her table but she delivered it anyway, relieved to have something to defuse her frustration with Moffet's pompous attitude. It was chauvinistic, pure and simple.

"No way in hell, Mr. Moffet," she muttered and headed into the dining room.

CHAPTER FIVE

It took over a week but after a follow-up cleaning, Val finally had a chance to list the little building for lease. She revamped her listing, updated the pictures, showing as much detail and benefits as she could, and carefully explained deposits and fees as well as when rent was expected to be paid and when late fees would be added. Heidi had finally opened her eyes to how she should handle renters. She'd lost money she could ill afford to lose. She wouldn't travel down that road again.

A few phone inquiries had already come in, but from no one ready to look inside. A call from No Caller ID suggested a professional property management company could solve the little lady's leasing issues. She stopped short of laughing at Mr. Moffet's persistence, realtor from hell. His misogynistic disrespect when he came in the restaurant to talk to her had been bad enough and she liked it even less a second time around.

With the building vacant and no rent coming in, Val happily accepted extra shifts at the restaurant although she was careful not to admit her reason to Joe. She didn't want another lecture on how she should sell it to him at a very fair price and wash her hands of it. So long as she could keep up the insurance, taxes and minimal utilities, she'd survive a few months of it sitting vacant. She hoped.

She was helping a customer carry a stack of pizza boxes to their car for a Halloween party when she overheard a voice that sounded familiar. It was the woman from the mistaken pizza deliveries. No doubt about that arrogant tone. Standing next to a pickup truck, she was talking to a man, several years younger, who seemed to demand she agree with him. It had something to do with the little boy, perhaps seven or eight, dressed in a Spider-Man costume, practicing Kung Fu poses.

"Come on, Susan," the man demanded. "What am I supposed to do with him? I can't take him with me."

"You've had two weeks to find a babysitter. Your oversight does not represent an emergency for me," she replied calmly, crossing her arms.

"You could climb down off your high horse and help out once in a while. Is that too much to ask?" His voice was condescending. "For God sake, you're part of this family whether you like it or not. Couldn't you show a little kindness once in a freaking while?"

Val turned and walked back inside to tend to her customers and not be noticed as an eavesdropper. But she was curious. What terrible transgressions had this woman done to warrant his anger? A few minutes later, Susan and the boy walked in and waited their turn to be seated.

Nardi's was busy. Not only was it Halloween, it was a Saturday evening. They didn't need to drum up business on the weekend but the ad in the newspaper offering free drinks with a dinner purchase for kids in costume seemed to have brought out plenty of witches, princesses, zombies, Ninja Warriors and caped crusaders. All the servers were in costume as well. Val wore a pink poodle skirt and saddle shoes with her hair in a ponytail tied with a pink scarf instead of the tight bun she normally wore at work. Audra was in a gypsy costume with a bright red head scarf and tassels hanging from a sash around her waist. And, of course, Joe was a pirate, his eye patch a perfect detail. After a few minutes wait Susan and Spider-Man were seated at a table in Val's section.

"Hello." Val set two glasses of water on the table and smiled respectfully. "Have you decided to forgive our delivery blunders and give us a try?"

The woman looked up at Val with a blank expression then narrowed her eyes as recognition kicked in. "Not by choice," she said flatly. "And hello again."

"I assume you're here for Halloween dinner, you and Spidey." She smiled at the boy. "What can I get you to start? Iced tea? Coke?"

Before Val could finish her list of suggestions tailored to the age of the customers, the woman interrupted. "I'll have water and he'll have milk."

The boy groaned. "Can't I have Dr. Pepper? Mom lets me have it."

"No. Milk. Unless you'd like water," she said, raising an eyebrow at him.

"Okay. I'll have milk," he sulked.

"Do you know what you'd like to eat or do you need a minute?" Val asked.

"Do you have a kid's menu?" the woman asked, flipping the pages of her menu.

Val pointed to the card attached to the table's condiment rack. "I'm sorry but we're out of chicken strips. They've been really popular this evening. But everything else is available."

The boy groaned again, louder.

"If you like pizza, we have a L'il Pal's Pizza. You can pick your favorite three toppings." Val showed him the picture and the list. "You can create your very own specialty pizza. If you're not a pizza man, you could have spaghetti and meatballs. It comes with a breadstick." Val was doing her best to speed things along.

The boy stared blankly into space.

"Connor, come on." Susan tapped her knuckles on the table. "What do you want? Pizza or spaghetti?"

Val suspected she'd need to offer assistance. After all, this was typical server duties when children floundered in too many choices.

"How about mac and cheese? Or how about number four?" Val suggested, pointing at the card. "Cheeseburger and fries. We make great cheeseburgers." She gave him an encouraging thumbs-up.

Susan watched, seeming relieved as Val explained the possibilities to Connor. Val wondered if Connor was Susan's grandson or nephew or some such relative. And she wondered how often she babysat, if ever.

"I want a cheeseburger and fries," he suddenly announced brightly.

"A number four and a side of milk for Spider-Man. Good choice." Val turned to Susan. "And what may I get you?"

"Nothing for me." She began drumming her fingers on the table.

Val suspected the woman's choice not to eat at Nardi's was a vindictive response to the mistaken delivery. Probably one of those who held a grudge. As she was ready to leave the woman stopped her.

"Do you have salad?" she asked, almost as an afterthought.

"Yes, we do. Chef salad with ham, Italian salami and three kinds of cheese. We also have a nice Greek salad with grilled chicken."

"A small side salad. No meat. No cheese. No dressing." She leaned back in the booth and dropped her hands in her lap.

"Maybe breadsticks with your salad?"

"Nope. One small simple side salad is all. Connor, quit picking your nose," she added without missing a beat.

Val nodded then impulsively asked, "Susan, is it? Do I need to apologize again for the problem the other day? It really wasn't our fault. Someone called in the order and we delivered to the address as we understood it. Please accept Nardi's sincere apology if we disturbed you. Trust me. It wasn't done on purpose."

"The Nardi name remains unblemished."

"We're very proud of our name."

"Are you a Nardi or merely an employee trained in what to say?" Susan tossed her a quick up and down look.

"I'm Val Nardi. It's a family business and we strive for customer satisfaction. I'll do my best to make your dining experience a pleasant one."

"By the way." Susan looked up at Val curiously. "How do you know my name?"

"I think it was on the delivery order."

"No, it wasn't. There was no name on it. Only an incorrect address."

"Oh, well, probably the cross reference for the address showed your name," Val stammered, not sure how to reply.

"Oh," she replied skeptically, handing Val their menus. "I assumed it was because you overheard my nephew in the parking lot." She looked up at Val, an accusatory arch to her brow, definitely judgmental.

Val headed to the kitchen to turn in their order. With the crush of rambunctious children in costume and the inevitability of spills, she relied on her work experience and put Connor's milk in a cup with a lid.

"May I please have a lemon wedge or two with my salad?" Susan asked, adjusting his cup back slightly. "On the side."

"Absolutely. Anything else?" Val asked with a bright smile, hoping to appease this woman's opinion of Nardi's. And her.

"No. That's all. Thank you."

The mob of customers meant Connor's cheeseburger along with other orders in the queue, got delayed. Val refilled drinks and offered apologies to those waiting for their dinner. She set the salad on the table, along with a dish of lemon wedges, but Susan pushed it back, presumably until Connor's dinner arrived.

"How are we doing?" Val said, striding into the kitchen, hoping to hurry things along. She had several tables growing impatient with the wait.

Cooks, servers, preps and dishwashers all looked like they were in fast forward mode. Dinners were being plated, pizza sliding in and out of the oven, garnishes added, trays filled and food going out as fast as could be done. She knew it was going to be a profitable night. People were ordering family-size pizza, dinner specials with extras and top of the menu items that not only meant big tickets but hopefully big tips, something she could certainly use.

"Here you go, Connor." Val set his plate in front of him and put a bottle of ketchup on the table. "Is there anything else I can get you two?"

"No. The delay was long enough. We don't have to attend the trick or treat function at the church." Susan squirted a puddle of ketchup on his plate. "Eat, Connor." She pushed his plate closer.

"I'm so sorry. We got hammered this evening. It's always a little crazy when the kids come in wearing their costumes." Val couldn't tell if Susan's remark was angry sarcasm or genuine relief at avoiding the kid's event. "I like your Spider-Man costume, Connor. There's a bowl of candy by the register. Help yourself on the way out."

He stuffed two fries in his mouth, wiped his fingers on his costume then slid out of the booth, ready to go claim some candy.

"Connor, on the way out. Sit." Susan pointed for him to sit down.

"Oh, man," he whined and flopped down in the seat.

Val chuckled softly then leaned down and said, "Connor, Nardi's says no Halloween candy unless you finish your dinner. I'm sorry but that's the rules."

"I am," he said with a mouth full of fries. "Can I have two pieces of candy?"

"You better hurry and eat or there won't be any left. Don't wait too long to finish," Val advised as if it were a secret then winked at Susan. She had no idea why she did it. It seemed like the right thing to do.

Twenty minutes passed, Susan paid the bill, and clearly her patience had run out. She waved Connor out of the booth and put the three fries in his hand back on the plate, used his napkin to wipe the ketchup from his face, then pointed to the front. Connor ran ahead, the candy bowl in his direct line of sight.

Three candies in his hand, he put one back then continued stirring the choices, not yet satisfied with his decision.

"You're good, Connor," Val said, nodding at him as she slid by on her way to the drink counter. "Three is okay this once."

Susan grimaced and shook her head. "Come on, Bud. Let's go." She pointed toward the door.

"By the way, this is for you." Val handed Susan a coupon good for fifty percent off a calzone. "From Nardi's, for the delivery confusion. Sometime when you don't want to cook, or need a takeout meal, call in your order and we'll have it ready when you get here. Our calzones are pretty good."

"Thank you." Susan took the coupon. "Hurry up, Connor."

Connor continued to examine his candy choices while Val delivered drinks to a table. When she returned to the beverage counter, Susan was in the lobby staring at a flyer taped to the window. She took out her phone and snapped a picture of the ad, then came back to where Val was filling drink orders.

"I presume this is someone you know?" she asked, showing her the picture.

"Yes, Nardi Tree Service is my brother. Vincent Nardi. Vinnie's been doing tree service for over twenty years."

"The ad says he has seasoned hardwood. Do you know if that's accurate?"

"I don't know exactly what kind of firewood he has right now. But if it says hardwood, I'm sure it is. He can tell what kind of tree it is by the bark. I'd trust him. I'm sure he'd sell you a bundle or two."

"I want more than a bundle or two. He delivers?"

"I think so." Val braced herself for some snide remark about past deliveries from Nardi's and Jackson's failed customer service. "I'm sure he can answer any questions you have about firewood." Val pointed to the second phone number on the ad. "That one is his personal cell phone."

"I might do that." Susan closed her phone and slipped it in her back pocket. "Come on, Connor. Trick-or-treat time is officially over. Put that handful back in the bowl."

She'd done her best, but Val wondered if this was the last time this woman would pass through their doors.

CHAPTER SIX

Susan finished the meeting at the hospital and headed home frustrated with the ridiculous questions and concerns, the same questions and concerns as in past meetings. This was the third meeting with the CEO, CFO, medical director and department heads as well as IT supervisors. And like previous meetings, there was a subtle butting of heads over who held the reins. Susan had sat at the corner of the long table, sipping coffee while the brass argued about cost effectiveness versus efficient transition of a new medical records system. She had explained the advantages and benefits of the new system, but medical functionality seemed directly opposed to fiscal restraints. She hadn't entered the arguments. Her responsibility was to present the information, answer specific concerns and let the chips fall where they may. The nitty-gritty details would be handled by the programmers on her team once a basic agreement could be reached. She remained objective. Or at least she tried to. She knew the advantages her proposal offered. Her company had been doing software development, including for the medical community, for twenty-five years. She was being paid handsomely for her time as well as the project package. But she had consumed enough coffee to float a battleship and the five-hour meeting had made her butt sore. She suspected she'd be doing this again in a week or two and hopefully by then an agreement could be reached.

Her usual forty-five-minute drive home, from the look of the rush hour traffic gridlock, would probably be at least twice that. And she was hungry. She didn't feel like fast food and she didn't feel like rummaging in the refrigerator for something to call dinner. Maybe sushi from Sapporo in Bonney Lake might be good. Another possibility crossed her mind. Nardi's Italian Ristorante and Pizzeria. The coupon Val Nardi gave her for calzone. She still didn't appreciate Jackson's rude attempt at a delivery but this had nothing to do with him. She could place the order. Pick it up. Take it home. From what she noticed when she was at the restaurant with Connor, the calzone looked large enough to offer leftovers. Traffic had ground to a complete halt on highway 167. She found the coupon where she left it in the center console and noticed a handwritten note on the back. *Please give us another chance.* Why not, she thought.

She pressed the button on the steering wheel and read off the phone number on the coupon.

"Nardi's," a young woman said, answering on the fourth ring. Voices in the background made it hard to hear.

"I'd like to place an order to pick up. Sausage, mushroom calzone, please."

"Calzone with sausage and what was it?"

"Sausage and mushroom."

"Spinach and what?" The woman sounded frazzled.

"Oh, good grief," Susan muttered to herself then repeated deliberately, "Sausage and mushroom. The name on the order is Castle. Susan Castle."

"Calzone, right?"

"Yes." Susan chuckled. "A calzone." She decided not to confuse the situation with the coupon.

The woman ended the call without a reply. Susan wondered if she would indeed get a sausage mushroom calzone or some obtuse variation. She settled back in the seat and headed for Bonney Lake, creeping along at fifteen miles an hour.

* * *

"Her name is Jennifer," Audra said as she followed Val into the kitchen. "I'm telling you, this woman is a catch. She has a good job." She grabbed Val's arm and whispered, "And I mean a *good* job."

"Audra, I don't need a date. I don't have time for a date. I don't want you fixing me up with one of your friends' daughter or sister or cousin or neighbor. Please." She tossed her a disapproving glance in emphasis. "No. Just No." Once again, she was having a conversation with her sister-in-law about a subject she'd rather not have. And if past was prologue, it wouldn't be the last time. Audra's track record in securing a date that Val found even remotely suitable was zero for eight. But she seemed undeterred.

"Val, sweetheart. You have to trust me on this one," she cajoled as she followed her into the dining room. "This woman makes the big bucks. She's a manager somewhere."

"No, Audra."

"She drives one of those big GMC trucks. A Denali something or other. And she owns a condo. Not rent, but owns." Audra nodded encouragingly, as if that should be the clincher.

"I don't care if she drives Santa's sleigh and lives in Shangri-La. The answer is still no." Val checked the coffee maker and started a fresh pot.

"And she's good-looking, too. What is it they call them? A soft butch?"

"You're like a dog with a bone." Val chuckled and shook her head. Audra wasn't going to stop until she persuaded Val to accept a date with this woman.

"What will it hurt to be pleasant? One date." Audra held up a finger. "One."

"How do you know I don't already have a date?" She raised her chin defensively.

Audra studied her a long moment then laughed out loud. "Yeah, right," she said and walked away, shaking her head. "That's funny."

"Well, I could," Val called after her. "I could," she muttered to herself. "If I wanted."

The restaurant became busy, enough so that Jennifer was largely forgotten. Many of the customers were parents of students participating in the regional debate tournament at the high school, and from the constant stream of middle-aged diners accompanied by teenagers, she guessed the tournament dinner break was from 5:00 to 6:30. Joe had supplied the high school event with discount coupons, something he frequently did for school functions, his way of supporting the community and reaping some of the benefits when an influx of families descended on Bonney Lake.

Most of the parents spent the meal telling their student how proud they were for their efforts. A few spent the time coaching, instructing and generally cheerleading their student into a better performance. There was one particularly aggressive father berating his daughter for poor posture, recurrent stuttering and an inability to control a coughing fit. The girl was probably fourteen or fifteen and clearly on the verge of tears as he continued to criticize, speaking loudly enough for tables in the area to hear his tirade. Val wanted to say something to him or at least compliment his daughter on her hair or clothes or something to bolster her self-confidence. But their table wasn't in her section. She didn't want to interfere and possibly affect their server's tip. Fortunately, karma helped deter his rant. When he came out of the restroom with his fly open Val couldn't help herself. She waited until he was in the middle of the restaurant, ready to take his seat and casually looked over at him.

"Excuse me, sir. Your barn door is open and the cow is about to escape." Val said it politely but loud enough for other customers in the area to hear.

He glared at her, obviously embarrassed, discreetly zipped his fly and stammered something incoherently. It was enough to bring a giggle and a smile to his daughter's face. Val winked at the girl as she passed their table. He said nothing else, concentrating on his dinner.

"I think she's here," Audra said in Val's direction, a suggestive arch to her brow as she nodded toward the parking lot. "I think that's her truck."

Val tossed a quick look out the front window. A woman climbed out of a large pickup truck, smoothed the legs of her jeans then checked her looks in the side mirror. She looked young enough to be Val's daughter.

Oh, good grief. I don't have time for this. Val shook her head and carried two glasses of wine and a mug of beer to a nearby table. When she returned the woman was standing in the outer lobby, trapped behind the congestion of waiting customers. Val hadn't noticed Susan standing at the register until that moment. She was tapping her credit card on the counter.

Audra burst through the kitchen door, carrying two coffeepots. She set one under the basket on the coffee machine and pushed the button to start. "You had a takeout order? What's the name on that?"

"Susan Castle. I ordered a sausage mushroom calzone."

"Be right back." Audra disappeared into the kitchen.

Jennifer waited in line to be seated, a mischievous little grin on her face as she scanned the restaurant. Val wasn't in the mood to go another round with one of Audra's hopeless fixups. Impulsively, she rushed up to Susan waiting at the counter for her order.

"Hello again," Val said. "Could you do me a favor?" She touched her arm and whispered frantically, "Please be my date."

"I beg your pardon." Susan leaned away and looked at her with a disapproving frown. "I don't think so, lady."

"See the woman in jeans and red jacket waiting for a table? My sister-in-law is trying to fix me up with her."

"Good for you but I'm here to pick up an order. Not be propositioned." She stepped closer to the register.

"I'm not propositioning you. I need you to let me tell Audra I've already got a date.

That's all. You'd be doing me a huge favor." Val stepped closer in spite of Susan's reluctance. "I really don't want to go out with her."

Susan turned to look at the woman in question.

"She's practically a child, for God's sake," Val whispered through her teeth and added a grimace.

"I'm not sure why you've chosen me for your charade but I'm not interested."

"If I knew anyone else in here this evening, I'd ask them but I don't."

"You don't know me either." Susan frowned.

"I know your name is Susan Castle and right now, that's enough."

"Why don't you tell your sister-in-law you don't want a blind date with a woman?"

"The woman part isn't the problem. It's that she's way too young, among other things."

"Well, I'm *way* too old for you," Susan said, scowling back at her.

"Age has nothing to do with it. I just need a warm body to run interference. You're the only woman in here whose name I know and who isn't a teenager or a resident of the senior living center. Please. Nod and go with it." Val raised her eyebrows wishfully and added a smile, hoping to sell the idea.

"Now look." Susan bristled but Val hurried away before Jennifer was seated.

"Here we are," Audra said, setting Susan's to-go box next to the register. She took Susan's credit card and swiped it through the card terminal.

Susan picked up the order then glanced over at Val who was filling glasses behind the drink counter. She walked over to her and said quietly, "I'm sorry if you're in an awkward situation but I'm not the resolution to your problem. I'm not sure why you thought I was in the first place." Her scowl grew deeper and more challenging.

"I'm sorry. My mistake." Val looked past her to the woman now speaking to Audra. She placed a stack of paper napkins on

Susan's to-go box. "Our calzone is drippy. You'll need several of these," she said quietly then patted Susan's arm. "I think eight or so."

"Eight?" Susan had a look of confusion.

"Yes. Eight will be perfect." She smiled and returned to work.

Susan gave Val a last look then walked out the door. Unaware. Her rebuttal to Val's request had taken long enough. Long enough for Audra to toss Val a disapproving look. And for Jennifer to walk out the door with an even more pronounced look of disappointment.

"You don't know that woman," Audra snipped. "Jennifer was pissed."

"I don't know Jennifer either."

"But you could have. And she's a lot closer to your age."

"I doubt it."

"You could have at least been cordial." Audra sniffed disgustedly. "It wouldn't have killed you."

"It also wouldn't kill you to ask before you arrange blind dates for me," Val said quietly. "I'm not a teenager who needs dating guidance. Audra, I know you mean well but I don't need help finding a date to the sock hop. Please stop."

"Jackson doesn't mind when I find him a date with a cute gal." Audra perched her hand on her hip. "I'm trying to help."

"I'm sure Jackson appreciates your efforts." Val knew he didn't. What teenage boy wants his mother fixing him up? His grumblings about it seemed to fall on deaf ears. So had Val's displeasure.

"I'm trying to introduce you to attractive, gainfully employed local women. What's the harm?"

"Who I spend my time with is my choice, thank you very much." She gave an emphatic nod and hoisted a tray over her shoulder, ready to deliver it to a waiting table.

"You know, people like that Susan Castle woman order takeout because they're too cheap to dine in and tip their servers."

Val ignored her, confident that she'd dodged a blind-date bullet. If Susan Castle was disgusted by her request, so be it. The woman was already frustrated with Nardi's. Their paths probably wouldn't cross again.

CHAPTER SEVEN

A week later, Susan was still arguing with herself over how she handled Val Nardi's situation. She realized it had been meant only as a diversion. She recognized that on the spur of the moment she had been abrupt, even rude. If she hadn't handled it maturely, today was the day to find out. She would return to Nardi's to offer an explanation and apologize. She needed to flush that guilt from her system and be done with it. Her OCD needed that. Whether Val was working this evening was the only variable and she was about to find out.

She parked her truck at the end of the spaces along the front of the restaurant and headed inside, trying to ignore the chilly rain that had begun to fall.

"Would you like a table or a booth?" Audra asked, taking a menu from the rack. Her smile was courteous, the kind meant to be polite, but it seemed disingenuous.

"A booth, please."

"Your server will be with you shortly." Audra placed the menu on the table.

"Excuse me but is Val Nardi working this evening?"

"Val? Yes, she's working but she's in the kitchen tonight."

"She's not a server?"

"No. Not tonight. You're the woman from the other night," Audra declared. It sounded more like an accusation than a question.

"Yes." Susan didn't plan on providing further information.

"We're really busy so I'm sure Val doesn't have time to come talk to you." There was a judgmental set to her jaw.

Susan glanced around the room, her gaze moving from one empty table to the next.

"Yes, I see you're really busy," she said, her eyes rolling up to meet Audra's.

"It's early. The dinner rush will start soon. Nadine will be with you shortly." She turned and walked away.

Susan sat with her hands in her lap, formulating how now to best apologize to Val. Hopefully she'd get a chance to do that. Her gaze had drifted out the window at the increasing rain when she heard a friendly voice.

"Hello. I thought I saw you sitting out here," Val said, striding up to the table as she wiped her hands on an apron speckled with pasta sauce and flour. "Audra should have told me you were here."

"She mentioned you were working in the kitchen."

"I'm helping out assembling pizza for a church fundraiser. Two dozen extra-large pizzas."

"Wow. That is big."

"And every one of them is different." Val rolled her eyes and chuckled. "The order sheet was two pages long and looks like chicken scratchings. We've had to call them twice already."

"Doesn't your online software handle that kind of thing?"

Val laughed out loud. "Nope. They don't trust online orders. They hand-delivered the order. And I better get back in there before Joe comes looking for me."

"Val, I want to apologize for the other day. I was rude and I'm sorry. I should have been more considerate in my refusal."

"Ah, yes, Jennifer. I'm the one who should be apologizing. I pushed you into an embarrassing situation. I was making assumptions I had no right to make. Even if it wasn't a real date, per se, it was presumptuous and I'm sorry."

"Presumptuous?"

"Asking you to be my date. Assuming you're gay and all," Val said quietly and apologetically touched Susan's shoulder. "I panicked and I caught you off guard. I'm very sorry for embarrassing you."

Susan looked down; her hands still folded in her lap. She released an apprehensive sigh then looked up and said, "Your presumption was more accurate than you realize. But I wasn't comfortable with your request."

"Val!" Joe called from the doorway to the kitchen. "Are you coming?"

"Be right there, Joe," she said but kept her eyes on Susan. "You have the strangest way of phrasing things, Ms. Castle. So, no, to being my date but yes, to being gay?"

Susan looked up at her, her expression speaking volumes.

"Okay, I can accept that. I won't embarrass you in the future. Enjoy your dinner."

"Thank you." Susan gave an appreciative nod.

Val hurried toward the kitchen but stopped at the dessert case, retrieved a piece of tiramisu and brought it back to Susan's table.

"Here. Enjoy this on me. My way of apologizing," she said, patted her arm then returned to work without waiting for a reply.

Susan studied the dessert, rotating the plate as she wondered if she should have been so forthcoming with her personal life. She didn't know this woman in spite of their paths repeatedly crossing. She hadn't come here intending to out herself. But she certainly couldn't take it back. And she did like the looks of the tiramisu. She took a small bite, testing its worthiness.

"Yes, I will accept your dessert, Val Nardi." She took another bigger bite. "Be your date? No. Eat this dessert? Absolutely." She leaned back, smiled and enjoyed the cake. "Truth is, I'm way too old for you," she muttered and took another bite as a small, satisfied smile settled over her face, a smile of contemplation.

CHAPTER EIGHT

Susan hadn't taken time out of her busy schedule in weeks to enjoy a bike ride. Even a short one. She considered them a reward. However much time she spent pedaling, twenty minutes, thirty minutes, an hour, it was an important destressing mechanism. It had taken her years to realize that she needed to put time and distance between her obsession for perfection and her peace of mind. At first, she thought it was the exercise she needed so she invested in an expensive exercycle for her office. She'd climb on and pedal away, watching the screen mounted on the handlebars displaying gorgeous scenery and rolling hillsides. She'd programmed videos of cycling through mountain roads or along coastal highways, hoping they would transport her to a mindless world free of stress and work. But the computer awaiting her attention a few feet away was an undeniable distraction. After only a few minutes of pedaling, hardly enough time to work up a sweat, she would climb off and go to her desk, determined to implement some unique idea she couldn't ignore. When a coworker teased that she should put the exercycle outside so she couldn't see her desk or anything that reminded her of software development, Susan took it one better. She decided to purchase what would indeed put her outside, away from her desk, home office, and any reminder she had lines of code to create. A thousand dollars later, she owned a Cannondale road bike with a lightweight alloy frame, bump-absorbing suspension, nine speeds and a "butt-friendly" saddle.

Today she rolled the bike out of the garage, checked the tire pressure, donned her cycling attire and helmet, filled a water bottle, put the bike in the truck and headed out. Sometimes she drove across town to a winding road with little traffic and nice scenery, and cycled the twelve-and-a-half-mile route then circled back to the truck for the drive home. Today she settled for a shorter, closer to home outing.

It was enough. When she returned, she felt invigorated. Refreshed. Her mind was clear, or as clear as it could be after she'd grinded through the gears on the steep uphill turn for home. She returned the bike to the garage and went inside to shower, her leg muscles cramping from fatigue. She told herself they wouldn't do that if she cycled more regularly and built up stamina but she'd take what she got and call it good.

After her shower, she took a look at the patio. According to the text from Miguel, her contractor, the stonework around the raised firepit had been completed, the mortar dry and ready to use. She had imagined a softly crackling fire, her feet propped up on the stone ledge and a cup of coffee or a glass of wine keeping her company as a gentle rain fell on the cedar roof of the new gazebo. Perhaps the faint strains of music in the background. Once she ordered a load of firewood and put a bottle of nice cabernet in the soon-to-be-installed mini-fridge, that image could finally come together. Unlike her office with its desk covered with keyboards and monitors, sitting by the firepit could be a relaxing though inspiring place to work and conduct Zoom meetings. That was the plan. The multiple electrical outlets installed around the patio guaranteed that scenario.

She had no sooner finished the package of sushi she brought home from her favorite Japanese takeout place when she heard the distinctive toot of a car horn, one she instantly recognized. Yep, the shave-and-a-haircut toot meant Jillian was in the driveway. Susan pulled on a smile and headed out the front door.

"Let me guess," she said to the tall blonde climbing out of the SUV. "You're here disturbing the peace because why?"

"Because you need someone disturbing your serenity once in a while." Jillian closed the car door and grinned warmly. "And I'm exactly the person for the job."

"But I like my serenity." Susan stepped back and waved her inside.

"You only think you do. Subconsciously you are dying for someone to turn your serenity upside down, Dr. Castle."

"Am not." She offered a small frown.

Jillian Ramsey was attractive with an upright posture and an amiable smile. She wore a slim-fitting navy-blue dress, heels, and had a red, white, and blue scarf tied around her thick blond ponytail. Fifty-one was the age Jillian was willing to admit to, and Susan had known her for nearly twenty years. Their friendship seemed self-sufficient. Weeks or months could pass without contact and without damaging the friendship. Jillian had once tried to boost the relationship to another level but Susan had made it clear she didn't need a friend with benefits, at least not from her. *You're married to your work*, Jillian had told Susan on more than one occasion.

"Hello, sweetheart," she said, ignoring Susan's resistance to her hug. "What's new in Castleland? How's the remodeling coming?"

"Almost finished, unless I find something else."

"As I said when you decided to move out here to BFE, why in the world did you buy a house that needed major repairs? You could have built a modern, efficient mansion for what you probably sold your house for in Seattle."

"It's not BFE. And it's not repairs. It's remodeling for efficiency and creature comfort."

"Your house in Seattle was perfect. Centrally located, nicely appointed and had great amenities. I loved that gourmet kitchen and the fireplace in the family room."

"It didn't have sufficient office space and as you well know, parking in downtown Seattle is a nightmare." Susan headed down the hall for the kitchen, Jillian following. "Red or white?" she asked, opening the refrigerator.

"Surprise me."

Susan examined several bottles and pulled one out. "Lombard Vineyards zinfandel," she read then held it up for Jillian's approval.

"Oh, Lombard's is good stuff. Are you sure you want to waste it on little ol' me?" She took the bottle and examined the label.

"If you promise to stop challenging my decision to move out of stressful downtown Seattle."

"I promise. At least not until I've had a glass or two."

"Here's to promises," Susan said, pouring two glasses and touching her glass to Jillian's.

"And here's to remodeling." Jillian sipped, and moaned. "That's good. What happened with the trip to Olympia?" she said, seemingly ready for a new topic. "Did they get on board with your proposal?"

"There are way too many witches stirring that pot. They need to decide on a hierarchy before we move forward."

"How out of date is their system?"

"Christopher Columbus was probably better scripted than this place. I have a feeling one of these days a big cargo ship is going to anchor offshore and they won't know what to do with it."

"Speaking of software development," Jillian said, raising a judgmental eyebrow. "I thought the whole idea of selling your company was to downsize and reduce stress. It doesn't sound like you've done much work reduction if you're still conducting meetings and arguing with a client about upgrades and revisions."

"I remained on board as a consultant. And you know I can't and won't discuss project details with you so don't ask."

"I'm worried about you. Can't a friend be concerned?"

"I'm fine, Jillian. Really. I'm doing considerably less than I used to do but I can't slam on the brakes and come to a complete stop. It's not happening. I'm not ready to be a has-been."

"Susie-Q, I know you. You're not a consultant. You're hands-on in charge. You'll never completely retire. It's not in your nature." Jillian smiled understandingly, then gave her another sideways hug. "You are in your element when you're doing software development. And you're one of the best."

Susan again stiffened at the hug and drew a deep gasping breath. She stood awkwardly until Jillian released her and stepped back.

"Yes, I know," Jillian said, studying Susan's rigid posture. "This makes you uncomfortable. You aren't a hugger but I am. So, deal with it." Jillian chuckled and stroked her face sympathetically. "One of these days you'll get past it. I hope. And yes, I'm a pushy bitch. But I'm your friend and you love me anyway." She cackled triumphantly. "Now give me the nickel tour. Show me what you've remodeled in Casa Castle."

"I'm not sure you deserve to see it," Susan teased and headed down the hall, carrying her glass of wine. Jillian followed after quickly refilling her glass.

"By the way, what is that coupon thing you have taped to the fridge? Where's Nardi's and who is Val? Are you hiding some nifty new restaurant from me?"

"What coupon? Oh, the one for a calzone. Mama Nardi's Pizzeria and Ristorante is exactly like it sounds. An Italian eatery. Pizza, pasta, normal fare."

"Who's this Val person? I noticed an apology note from her on the coupon. I have to ask. Anyone important or at least potentially important?" Jillian raised an eyebrow.

"She's the owner's sister. There was a misunderstanding about a delivery. The calzone and coupon was her attempt to mend fences."

"But how about the woman? Is she cute? Is she nice? Is she gay?" Jillian winked.

Susan gave her a dismissive glance as she stood outside the master bathroom, gesturing with her glass. "This was the first thing I had remodeled. I wanted a walk-in shower so I didn't bump my elbows on the wall."

"The showers you had in Seattle were more like a phone booth." Jillian stepped into the bathroom, admiring the features. "I like the whirlpool tub but why not have a tub big enough for two? The room is plenty large enough to accommodate one." She again winked.

"Why would I want to sit in someone else's filth while I try to wash off mine?"

"What is that?" Jillian looked up at the black screen mounted on the wall above the tub. "TV so you can binge-watch while soaking?"

"It's a voice-activated monitor," Susan replied dismissively.

"Oh, my God, Susan. You plan to conduct Zoom meetings while you're in the bathtub?" She laughed uproariously. "Naked and exposed for all to see?"

"*No*," Susan stammered defensively. "It's for work. It allows me to code remotely."

"You developed voice-activated programming software?" Jillian asked, staring up at the screen mounted on the wall.

"It's been around a couple years."

"That big project you were working on before the pandemic?" Jillian looked impressed.

"Yeah." She went down the hall and opened a door, waiting for Jillian to step inside. "What do you think of my new office?"

The large room was dominated by an L-shaped desk, several monitors, keyboards and docking stations. Two bookcases were filled to overflowing with technical manuals. A pair of twin stuffed armchairs sat in the corner. An ornate oriental rug was centered over hardwood floors. A mahogany credenza along the wall at the far end of the room held an expensive-looking coffee maker and a glass canister with three small bamboo plants, each with a single arched leaf. The closed blinds obscured the lush foliage outside the window and gave the room a sterile appearance.

"Okay. This is about what I expected but," Jillian said, scanning the room, "where is it? Where are you hiding it?"

"Where is what?" Susan leaned against the doorjamb, sipped her wine and watched innocently.

"Don't give me that. You're a software engineer, program developer and computer nerd of the first order. You couldn't exist without it. Now, where is it?" She looked behind the door.

Susan chuckled and went to the paneled door in the corner, opened it then stepped back and waved her inside.

"Ah-ha," Jillian announced. "I knew you'd have a server room bigger than your bedroom."

"Actually, this was the master bedroom once upon a time. I juggled rooms a little."

The room was filled with three rows of black metal racks holding dozens of computer servers and IT equipment, all with tiny blinking lights that resembled a test facility for Christmas lights. The room was a pleasant sixty-eight degrees according to a control panel on the wall indicating temperature and humidity. A web of wires snaked down the back of each rack, connected to the commercial quality outlets. There was a constant hum, and it brought a satisfied look to Susan's face as she scanned the equipment.

"How many more are you adding?" Jillian asked as she watched Susan's contentment, like a parent admiring a newborn through a nursery window.

Susan laughed. "What makes you think I plan to add more?"

"Because I know you. So, how many more?"

"Okay. I've got two units on backorder. But they're smaller ones. I think I've located a couple of server racks that could work. They aren't the brand I prefer but they're acceptable."

"Uh-huh." Jillian finished her glass of wine and chuckled as she passed Susan, patting her arm on the way out of the office. "And I'm assuming solar panels and fiber optics, right?"

"Yes, on the solar panels but the Tesla battery panels are on back order. And yes, fiber optics."

"Okay. Show me the patio."

"Don't you want a detailed tour of the kitchen?" Susan asked as they headed down the hall.

"I saw the kitchen. It's nice. Very upscale and efficient. It must have been pretty bad if you felt compelled to remodel it.

What did it have? A hand pump and an oak bucket to wash dishes?" Jillian teased. "You don't cook. You bring home takeout. Takeout calzone, for example. And no, microwaving frozen dinners is not cooking. Although that marsala chicken thing you recommended from Trader Joe's was good."

"I cook," Susan said defensively.

Jillian rolled her eyes at Susan and said nothing.

"Well, I do. I made an omelet this morning."

"Really? You scrambled eggs with veggies and meat and cheese?"

"Eggs, shredded cheese and a diced tomato."

"Okay, I'll give you a pass on the omelet." Jillian chuckled.

"The kitchen needed remodeling," Susan said. "The floor had some water damage and it seemed like doing it all at once was the most cost-effective."

"It looks nice. But it's like you driving a race car back and forth to McDonald's for a Chicken McNuggets happy meal. Way more horsepower than you'll ever use."

"You never know," Susan mused. "I may move my desk in here so I'm closer to the microwave."

"Now that, I'd believe." Jillian grabbed the wine bottle off the counter and headed out the back door. "Oh, Susan. I like this," she declared, stepping out onto the patio. "I love the brick pavers and the gazebo and especially the firepit." She stood under the cedar gazebo, grinning as she turned, taking it all in. "Did you do all this?"

"I planned it. This is more or less what I wanted in Seattle but there wasn't room in my yard."

"It definitely wouldn't have been this nice in the middle of a big city." Jillian sat down in one of the Adirondack chairs and propped her feet up on the circular stone firepit. "You did a superb job." She refilled her glass and set the bottle on the small cedar table between the chairs. "Here's to your expert plans."

Susan sat in the other chair. "Thank you. So, you approve of my remodeling?" She poured the last of the bottle into her glass and leaned back, propping her feet up on the rim of the firepit as well.

"Yes, you get the Ramsey stamp of approval. Okay, new topic." Jillian swirled her wine. "What's the rack thing in the back of your truck? I assume that's your Toyota in the driveway."

"Yes, it's a bike rack. I had it installed. I needed a way to transport my bike without it bouncing around the bed of the truck."

"You have a bicycle?" Jillian stared at her in disbelief.

"Yes, a Cannondale Topstone road bike. I decided I wanted to try road cycling. There's lots of trails and routes in this part of the state. Road cycling gives me a chance to recalibrate. It's about as far from my desk as I can get without getting on an airplane."

"Reduce mental fatigue and establish emotional balance." Jillian smiled at her. "Good for you, Dr. Castle. Anything you can find to reduce stress is great. I can't ride a bike to save my life but if you can, that's wonderful." She leaned over and grabbed Susan's arm. "But promise me, you'll be careful. Washington has a ton of idiot drivers out there. Be sure you wear a helmet and one of those reflective vests."

"You sound like my mom when I rode my bike to school in the fifth grade. I found out she waited until I left for school the first day then she followed me in the car."

Jillian laughed.

"It wasn't funny. She did it for an entire month. When I found out what she did I was embarrassed and told her so." Susan rolled her eyes and shook her head as she relived the memory.

"Did she stop following you to school?"

"Yes. But she got my aunt to do it for another week or two." Jillian laughed even louder.

"So no, I do *not* need you to follow me around Bonney Lake while I ride my bike," Susan said.

"Wouldn't dream of it. And now, my good friend, I am going home. I came. I saw. I drank the vino. I'm tired." Jillian rose to her feet, turned to Susan and smiled. "Brace yourself. Here comes another hug."

"Ugh," Susan groaned and stood stiffly while it was administered, knowing she didn't have a choice.

"Take care of yourself, sweetheart." She pinched Susan's cheek. "Call me when you need lunch with a buddy." She winked and headed for the front door.

Susan watched from the front porch as Jillian climbed in her car and offered a last wave before pulling away. Jillian's visits were uncomplicated. They weren't frequent and didn't last long but she was a friend and that put a smile on Susan's face.

CHAPTER NINE

"Oh, good grief," Val groaned as the marinara sauce ran down the leg of her pants. "That'll teach me to put too many plates on a tray."

It wasn't the first time she'd spilled. She'd rather slop on herself than on a customer but that, unfortunately, happened occasionally as well. Whichever server caused it, profuse apologies were extended and an offer to comp the meal. Most customers didn't take it personally. They understood accidents happen. Some even refused the free meal, laughing it off as a spill being not the worst thing in the world. Of course, there was always that one who screamed, cussed and demanded to speak to the manager, as if a free meal wasn't enough for an innocent splash of sauce or dribble of iced tea across a shoe. Joe often reminded his employees that customer service was important but they didn't have to put up with abusive behavior. He didn't allow it and they shouldn't either. So Val was glad the sauce was running down her pant leg and not over the lady in the pink dress at table six waiting for her spaghetti and meatballs with extra sauce.

"I need an original, Joe," she called.

"Again?" He chuckled.

"Oh, hush," she snipped. *Original* was code for I need an extra dish of marinara sauce, something added to a plate to remedy any sort of presentation deficiency. She delivered the other meals to the table, two at a time, giving Joe time to prepare the dish of sauce. She tidied up the wandering sauce on the lady's plate then delivered it, explaining the extra helping was in case she needed more.

"Doesn't that look good?" the lady said happily, turning the plate and examining the generous portion. "I don't know if I can eat all that. Glen, you may have to help me." She patted the hand of the man sitting next to her. The couple across the table from them had equally large portions. "I may need a to-go box."

"Not a problem," Val said happily. "Let me know how many you all need."

As she turned to walk away the lady dipped her finger to the dish of sauce and tasted it, dribbling a few drops across her lap.

"How did I know she'd do that," Val muttered and returned to the kitchen.

"Val," Audra said under her breath as she passed. "Table fourteen." She nodded in that direction as if passing some clandestine information.

"Who is it?" Val looked in that direction. She saw blond hair, the profile of a thin face and a black jacket. Best guess, a woman in her fifties she didn't recognize.

Audra also was looking at the woman across the restaurant. "I have no idea who it is but she specifically asked for you."

Val headed to the mystery woman's table.

"Hello." She offered her customary smile and good-natured greeting. "My name is Val and I'll be your server this evening. What can I get you to drink?"

"Could I have a strawberry daiquiri. No salt."

"I'm sorry, ma'am, but we only serve wine and beer."

"No booze, huh?" She smiled up at Val.

"Well, not hard liquor, no. Sorry. Is there something else you'd like?"

"How about prosecco?"

"Absolutely. Very good choice." Val often included a small comment on the customer's choice, as if offering information on their selection as well as sounding encouraging. Inexperienced wine drinkers simply ordered something red. Whoever this was, seemed to know what she preferred. "This evening's special is the Pick Two." Val pointed to the card clipped to the entrée page. "It comes with a salad and bread."

"I understand the calzone is good," she said, squinting at the list of calzone choices.

"That's what Dr. Castle said. She recommended it."

"Dr Castle?" Val inquired nonchalantly.

"Yes. I'm surprised she has time to eat out." The woman chuckled. "She's usually so busy she barely has time to breathe."

"Susan Castle?"

"Yes." She looked up at Val curiously. "If you're Val Nardi, I understand you know Susan. My name is Jillian Ramsey. I saw your name on a coupon Susan had taped to her fridge. She said she enjoyed dining here. I understand she came in with her great-nephew, Connor."

"Yes, on Halloween. He was dressed up like Spider-Man." Val smiled at the memory. "Cute little boy." She hesitated a moment, deciding how nosy she should be since she didn't know this woman. "I didn't know Susan was a doctor. What kind of doctor is she, if I may ask? General practitioner? Surgeon?"

"Susan isn't a medical doctor, although she is smart enough to be one. She has a PhD. Her doctorate's in mathematics. She's a software engineer and developer. It fits her personality perfectly."

"Wow. Mathematics and computers. I guess I shouldn't be surprised. She seems very literate."

"She's one of those people who have an insatiable thirst for technical knowledge. She can't get enough. She's a sweetheart when she's in her own element."

Susan, a sweetheart? The delivery mistake confrontation and her reaction to the request to be a surrogate blind date didn't conjure up images of hearts and flowers.

"How long have you known her?" Jillian asked.

"Not very long. Only the few times when she's stopped in here."

"Well, I've known Susan Castle for…oh, gosh. More years than I care to remember. One thing I have learned about her is some of her behavior has to be taken with a grain of salt." She rolled her eyes and shook her head. "A large grain of salt. But you've probably noticed that." She handed the menu to Val with a smile. "So, spinach calzone. Salad with Italian dressing on the side. And a takeout box. Susan said your calzone is huge and enough for leftovers. I'm all about leftovers. And probably a second glass of wine but I'll let you know."

"Any friend of Susan's, is a friend of Nardi's." Val touched her arm. "I hope you enjoy your meal."

She found herself curious. She wanted to know what kind of relationship Jillian had with Susan. And she wanted to know more about this Susan Castle person. Why she wanted to know anything about this difficult woman was a complete mystery.

She had a feeling that what Jackson said she spouted about the mistaken pizza delivery was an exaggeration. She had yet to hear Susan utter a single cuss word. Mathematics and computers—wow. Val felt a little intimidated. She also felt guilty for judging her on their limited interaction. She shouldn't have. There was obviously a lot more to this Dr. Susan Castle than what met the eye.

She formulated a few innocuous questions she planned to ask but Jillian quickly finished her meal, paid at the register, left a generous tip and disappeared before she had a chance to ask any of them.

CHAPTER TEN

Susan stepped out of the shower, towel-drying her hair. And like every other shower in the past month, as soon as she stepped onto the bath mat she wished she had remembered to replace it and was mad at herself for forgetting. She wasn't a procrastinator. It was more of a priorities issue that sculpted her to-do list. How important was a new bathmat when she had several clients and projects that needed her time? Amazon had bathmats. Tan. Beige. Khaki. Some neutral color but fluffy, large and absorbent. And nonslip. Definitely nonslip. She wiped her towel across the condensation on the mirror and kept her feet centered on the postage-stamp-sized mat as she went through her post-shower ritual, constructing a mental list of chores she needed to accomplish.

Like other mornings, she had a long list of work waiting. She'd tried to decrease her workload but it had consumed her for years, taken a toll on her health and mental balance but she found it hard to give it up completely. Cutting back, yes. At least she thought she was cutting back. Her friends joked she'd probably be late to her own funeral, hunched over a keyboard writing code and conducting online meetings. She did her best to streamline her daily life and lessen the stress. But it was a work in progress. One detail that kept rolling over in her mind was the ad she had photographed at Nardi's restaurant, that woman's brother's tree service. She wanted only seasoned, dry, aromatic firewood. Not the punky pine that did nothing but smoke and smell like rotten eggs.

Once dressed and ready for a busy day, she went into the kitchen and pressed the button on the coffee maker. While she waited for the first cup to dribble from the spigot, she looked at the photo on her phone of the ad.

Okay, she thought. I'll give Mr. Nardi three minutes to impress me with his firewood.

"It's Vinnie," was all the man said, picking up on the third ring. She could hear loud grinding and motor revving in the background.

"Hello, Mr. Nardi. This is Susan Castle. I saw your tree service ad posted in Nardi's restaurant. I understand you have firewood for sale. Seasoned firewood."

"Yeah. Lock that tailgate, Rick," he shouted. "No, you're going to have to cover the trailer. That crap will fly out as soon as you hit the highway." It was obvious Vinnie was conducting two separate conversations and the one with Susan wasn't commanding much of his attention. "I don't want another fucking ticket for littering."

"Excuse me?" Susan wasn't going to waste time being ignored and she didn't appreciate his language.

"Unroll the damn tarp and make sure it's pulled down tight. Sorry. What was it you wanted, ma'am?" he said, finally turning his attention to Susan.

"Firewood. Seasoned hardwood," she declared flatly. "Is that something you have?"

"Sure. You can drop by the yard and we can load you up. Most car trunks will hold two or three bundles."

"Mr. Nardi, your sister referred you to me. She was certain I could trust you to not sell me green wood that won't burn."

"Val is right. I stand behind what I sell. Our woodyard is open from seven to seven, six days a week. If I'm not here, someone usually is and can load you up. Tell me what time works for you and we'll have someone here."

"I don't want a carload. I want two full cords of seasoned hardwood. Cherry, to be specific. Cut, split, delivered *and* stacked."

"Two cords?" he repeated. "That's a lot of firewood, ma'am." He sounded judgmental and condescending and Susan didn't appreciate it.

"Yes. According to industry standards, a cord of firewood is one hundred and twenty-eight cubic feet when tightly stacked. Four feet by four feet by eight feet. So, two cords would be two hundred and fifty-six cubic feet when stacked. And yes, I agree. That is definitely a lot of firewood. I'll understand if you don't have that much seasoned cherry available for purchase right now. I can look elsewhere." If Vincent Nardi could be snarky and patronizing, so could she.

"I'm sorry, ma'am. I meant no disrespect. I don't get calls for two full cords of my premium seasoned firewood that often. It's usually a face cord or maybe two. Once in a while someone wants a full cord of mixed hardwood. You took me by surprise is all. My apologies. Yes, I absolutely have that much seasoned cherry. In fact, I have thirty or forty cords of nicely seasoned cherry. It's been cut and split for about twelve months." Susan heard a door close and the background noise vanish. "If you don't mind me asking, where do you plan to burn it? Inside, outside, woodstove, campfire?"

"Does it matter?"

"It's your purchase and you can do whatever you want with it but sometimes people's choice of firewood isn't the best for their intended use. Softwood like cedar, pine and spruce are lightweight woods that contain resins that burn easily. They're fine for campfires. They light easily and give off a nice flame, something a lot of people want. But most softwoods have a higher sap and moisture content. They smoke and give off sparks. Indoors in a fireplace might not be a good place to burn softwood. Some campgrounds don't allow burning softwood for this very reason. Hardwood like oak, maple, cherry, and hickory don't spark as much and have good coaling qualities."

"So, higher BTU?" she offered, growing appreciative of his insight.

"Exactly. And they smoke less."

"I plan to burn indoors in a fireplace and outdoors in a firepit. The last few times I've bought those plastic-wrapped bundles at the gas station the wood smoked and was a complete waste of money. Even the box of split wood I ordered from Amazon wasn't dry. I want burnable firewood, Mr. Nardi. Val assured me if I order seasoned hardwood from you, I can trust that's what I'll receive."

"Absolutely," he replied without hesitation. "Did Val tell you if you aren't happy with the product I deliver, I will refund your money. No questions asked. We come to an agreement on what you want and that's what I'll deliver."

"That sounds like a fair deal. I need it stacked into the row of racks behind my garage. The racks are covered. I don't want to worry about the rainy season making the wood unusable."

There would undoubtedly be a delivery fee, stacking fee, and premium wood fee. But she didn't care. She knew what she wanted and if Nardi's Tree Service could deliver on that, she'd pay for it.

"How much?" she asked. "I live off Lake Tapps Highway. Near Bartley Road."

"Okay, let's see. Two cords of cherry. Twenty-eight miles. Delivered and stacked." Susan assumed his hesitation was him calculating the price. "Thirteen hundred forty-six. No, wait. Thirteen hundred thirty-six dollars. I'm willing to call it thirteen hundred even. Delivered and stacked."

Something in his voice told Susan he expected her to gasp, groan and argue about the steep price. But she had already researched local firewood distributors online and this was about what she expected. Some were less but didn't offer stacking or couldn't guarantee it would be one hundred percent cherry, which meant she'd be lucky to get ten percent cherry.

"Okay. I want it delivered day after tomorrow. I'm going out of town and I want it delivered and stacked the same day. If it can't be stacked right away, I prefer not to purchase it. Rain is in the forecast for the next six days and I don't want it sitting on the ground soaking up moisture."

"I can have an invoice printed out and hand it to you if you'd like to come by the yard or we can meet somewhere. Whatever works for you." There was a hesitation, then he said, "I can offer a discount for a cash purchase. How's twelve hundred sound?"

"That's doable. How about meeting in the parking lot at Chase Bank in an hour or so. Does that work for you?"

"I need to run by Costco so that works great. Shall we say ten o'clock? I'll drop off a couple of bundles of pine kindling, too. It makes lighting hardwood a little easier."

"Thank you, Vinnie. I'll let Val know you were very helpful." Susan gave him details for the invoice and they agreed on exactly where they were meeting.

* * *

"Hello, Ms. Castle?" a man said, tapping on the driver's window of Susan's car. She had been busy formulating a line of code and hadn't noticed the truck parked directly behind her. He wore faded jeans and a blue and green plaid flannel shirt and was somewhere in his forties. He could have been almost anyone, but one look at his expressive brown eyes and gently arched eyebrows told her this was Val's brother. Yep, he was a Nardi. A Nardi who was late for his appointment with her.

"Vinnie?" she said, lowering her window. He extended his left hand to her through the window even before she could climb out. She took his hand and shook it. It was rough and dry, not surprising for a man who worked outdoors with his hands.

"I'm very sorry if I kept you waiting. I had an appointment at Costco to have two tires mounted and balanced but they got the time screwed up. And I found out cussing doesn't help move things along." He offered a chuckle. "I'm sorry." He pulled a folded paper from his shirt pocket and handed it to Susan.

She opened the paper and read the invoice. The order listed the details precisely as she had given them. When he took a piece of firewood from under his arm she noticed that the sleeve of his flannel shirt was cuffed back several turns, exposing a cast covering his forearm from his elbow to his fingers.

"I thought you'd like to see what you're getting," he said.

She sniffed the piece of reddish wood, knowing full well what it should smell like.

"Actually, it's wild cherry." He picked his nail across it as she held it. "Smell it again."

She did, pleased at the pleasant aroma. "I have to ask." She stared at his cast then up at him. "I notice you have a cast on your arm. That isn't going to interfere with getting this stacked, is it? As I explained on the phone, I'm going out of town and I need this stacked into the racks right away."

He nodded decisively. "It'll be stacked and off the ground by noon. You don't have to worry."

She signed the invoice and handed him the bank envelope containing the cash. He checked it, slowly ruffling his thumb over the stack of bills.

"What time did you plan to deliver the wood?"

"Around six. I've got you first on the schedule." He slipped the envelope in his back pocket, then offered Susan his left hand and a broad smile. "Have a great day, Ms. Castle, and thanks for your business. Anytime you need more or know someone who needs firewood, give me a call."

Susan drove home, satisfied that she had checked one thing off her to-do list. It might be considered work-related, she thought. If she planned to sit on the patio by a crackling fire while she worked on her laptop, it could be considered work-related. She laughed out loud as she considered the cost of firewood as a tax write-off.

CHAPTER ELEVEN

Vinnie was coming in the back door of Nardi's when Val entered the kitchen carrying a bin of dirty dishes. Vincent Nardi was a muscular man in his forties and the youngest of the Nardi siblings. He looked nothing like Joe other than his well-developed upper body. He had thick curly dark hair and like many men his age, occasionally sported a three-day old beard. This was one of those times. Val had always considered Vinnie a handsome man with his chiseled Italian features. Cute as a little brother, by the time he was in high school he had the athletic build and dazzling smile she knew would make him popular with the girls…and he was. Like Joe, Vinnie was generous and protective of Val, even when she wished they would allow her to make her own decisions. Whether it was selecting a car or the best steak, they regularly intervened. They'd early on accepted she was gay but had voiced an opinion about every woman she dated. Often an objectionable, sexist opinion. But when times were tough, the Nardis banded together. It had always been that way. And Val took comfort in that.

"Hey, Vinnie. How's the arm?" she asked, patting his shoulder as she slipped past.

"It fucking hurts like hell." He gave a deep groan. "The doctor said I may need an x-ray next week. There might be a problem with the cast. The idiots probably put it on wrong."

"No," Audra interjected, overhearing his comment. "What the doctor said was you've been doing things you shouldn't. It's broken, Vinnie. Broken! You can't keep using it like it isn't." She glared at him. "You don't listen and you're going to end up needing surgery to fix that arm." She wagged a finger at him.

"I won't need no fucking surgery," he replied vehemently.

"Vinnie!" Val scowled at his language, although she wondered why she bothered. Joe and Vinnie both spewed foul language whenever the situation warranted. Or for the fun of it to aggravate her.

"Order up, Val," one of the cooks announced, setting two plates of spaghetti on the counter.

"Val, when you get back, I need to talk to you," Vinnie said, eating a slice of pizza from the reject rack.

"Be back shortly, Vinnie," she said and carried the order into the dining room.

She delivered the meals and took a couple's order before returning to the kitchen. Vinnie was waiting with a nervous fret to his brow.

"What did you need?" she asked as she assembled a tray of desserts for the family celebrating a birthday.

"I had a phone call from one of your friends. They ordered some firewood.

That Castle woman. Susan Castle. She said you recommended me."

"I did. So, what's the problem?"

"She wants two cords of cherry, all of it dry and seasoned."

"That's a lot of firewood. Do you have what she wants?"

"Sure. I've got it. Plenty of it. Nice and dry and seasoned. She wants a year's supply for a firepit and fireplace. But that's the problem." Vinnie looked over at Val. "She wants it stacked."

"And?" Val shrugged, not sure how this represented a problem.

Vinnie held up his cast-covered arm. "I can't stack it with one hand."

"Then have one of your guys do it. Isn't that what you pay them to do?"

"My entire crew and all of our equipment are going up to Yelm on a job tomorrow. I need everyone on-site for this one, especially since I can't climb or operate a chainsaw. I'll be ground crew. She doesn't want it if our delivery doesn't include immediate stacking. I'll lose the sale, Val. Things have been slow. I need this order. I've got doctor bills to pay."

"Ask Uncle Arnie to do it. Pay him to stack it. Didn't he do that last year?"

"He and Aunt June are in Portland with her family. They're driving down the coast to San Francisco in their camper."

"Well, I certainly hope you aren't asking me to do it. I have a job." Val let her gaze drift around the kitchen.

"There isn't anyone else. She's your friend. This is your doing. You recommended me. You could help this one time."

"Will you stop saying I recommended you. She saw your ad and asked if I knew who you were is all."

"Come on, sis. Please. I really need this order. It won't take any time at all. Half hour, tops."

"Two cords would take me hours. I can't do it. You'll have to tell her you can't deliver it right now. Sorry."

"She's already paid for it. Cash. Two cords, seasoned prime firewood, delivered and stacked. It's over a grand, Val." His eyes flashed.

"So, give it back."

"I can't. I already spent it."

"Vincent!"

"I had to. I had to make a payment to the hospital and I needed some stuff for this job we're going on. A new limp saw and chains for the big saw. And chain oil is hard to come by these days so I stocked up. When I can buy a case at a time, I will."

"You spent money you received for goods and services you hadn't yet delivered?"

"Look. I'm not shafting her. I'm delivering two full cords of seasoned cherry, my best stuff. This is primo firewood, Val. And all I'm asking you is help me out and stack it." He pulled an envelope with Val's name on it from the thigh pocket of his cargo pants. "I'll pay you a hundred bucks." He smiled confidently and flipped the envelope back and forth, as if that revelation made it a done deal. "I need this done, Val. The Yelm job with the Forest Service is too important to pass up. It'll put Nardi Tree Service back on the map. It could lead to bigger job offers from the state."

He had changed from asking to pleading. This was important to him and she understood why. The Covid restrictions that closed down her cleaning business were the same ones that curtailed Vinnie's revenue. He was struggling like the rest of the Nardis to keep their businesses afloat in stressful times. He'd lost two members of his crew to Covid and two more quit for fear of catching it. This was a rebuilding time for him like it was for Joe's restaurant.

"Please, Val," he asked with quiet desperation. "I'll drop the wood in the driveway tomorrow morning. All you have to do is stack it in the wood racks behind the garage."

"Oh, Vinnie." She sighed deeply as she considered it. "You're asking me to give up an entire day of work to do this, aren't you?"

"I already asked. Joe said whenever I can deliver the wood, you can have off. So, you'll do it?" He brightened, and she knew he'd be ignoring any further argument she offered. He thrust the envelope at her. "The address and instructions are in there. It's off Lake Tapps Highway."

"How early?"

"Six." There was fresh enthusiasm in his voice. "I told her someone would be there around seven or so to start stacking. I've got to go. Tomorrow morning. Early," he said, kissing her cheek. He started for the back door but came back to her and handed her a pair of leather work gloves from his back pocket.

"You'll probably need these. Thanks, sis. I love you." He hurried out the door.

"You're welcome, I think."

She opened the envelope and took out a slip of paper with an address scribbled on it. She also pulled out a Walmart gift card.

"What's this?" She looked toward the door but Vinnie was gone. "I don't want a Walmart gift card. I want cash. I can't pay my bills with this." She heaved a disgruntled sigh and stomped her foot. "Vincent Nardi," she sneered, resigned to this being her payment.

Val could hear Joe chuckling. "Sucker," he said, shaking his head.

"Shut up, Joseph." Val went back to work, resigned yet again to helping a family member.

CHAPTER TWELVE

According to the instructions in the envelope this was Susan Castle's driveway. It was long and gently curving with trees on one side and lush rhododendron bushes on the other. From the length, width and gentle curve, it seemed more like a meandering country lane. The house was a popular house color in this upscale area, pale grayish-blue, shingle-sided with a matching though detached four-car garage. Both the house and the garage were partially obscured by overgrown trees and greenery. The driveway circled a large madrone tree centered between the garage and the front of the house. Its branches arched out in all directions, a few low ones nearly dragging the ground. A brick walk led from the driveway to an alcove she assumed was the front porch and door.

Vinnie had indeed delivered the firewood and lots of it. She had known it would be but this was more than she had envisioned. *Far more.* The pile was tall enough that she could barely see over it. It looked like two trailer loads had been dumped and drawn out in a pile twice as long as her car. The wood was reddish-brown and as soon as she parked and stepped out of the car, she could smell the rich aroma of cherry wafting through the air.

"Oh, Vinnie. What have you talked me into here?" She heaved a sigh, slowly scanning down the pile. "This is *so* much more than a hundred bucks worth of sisterly help."

Before she began she wanted to see exactly where it was to be stacked. She followed the narrow, well-worn path down the side of the garage and around the corner. Sure enough, at least this was as described. The entire back side of the garage was lined with wooden raised racks about a foot off the ground with slanted wooden roofs, presumably to discourage rain and keep the wood dry.

"Dang, that's a lot of wood racks." She grabbed one of the posts and gave it a shake to test stability. "I guess it's too late to say no." She went back to the pile, tossed her jacket in the back seat of her car, pulled on the gloves Vinnie gave her and went to work. It was going to be hard enough without adding extra steps. She also knew by the end of the job she would be tired, mad, blistered and ready to strangle her brother. So, she decided to start on the far end of the racks, working her way toward the end nearest the driveway. She was certain the shorter the last few trips, the better. The individual sticks of wood were small enough in diameter she could lift them with one hand but she wished she had a wheelbarrow or a dolly to haul them.

She had made three trips, occasionally singing silly songs to entertain herself, when she felt her cell phone vibrate in her back pocket.

"Hello, Vinnie. And the first words out of your mouth better be thank you, oh wonderful sister," she advised.

Vinnie laughed then said, "Thank you, oh wonderful, sister. I assume you're there and stacking, right?"

"Yes, I'm here and yes, I'm stacking. And yes, you are going to owe me *big time*."

"I know. I texted Susan a photo of the delivery so she knows it's there."

"So, she knows I'm here?" Val glanced over at the house but she didn't see any lights on, other than the front porch light and a row of path lighting.

"I have no idea. I got a thumbs-up reply."

"Um, Vinnie. I have a little question for you," she started then cleared her throat tactfully. "I know when you guys have to go, you just do it in the woods but that isn't exactly an option for me."

"So, piss behind a tree," he chuckled.

"Vincent!"

"Then knock on her door and ask to use the bathroom. I gotta go, sis. Let me know when you're done." He hung up without waiting for her reply.

"I'll let you know, all right," she mumbled and went back to gathering another load. "I may keep the last stick of wood and shove it right where the sun doesn't shine, Vincent." She scraped her arm with a splintered piece of wood. "Ouch," she gasped, sucking wind. "Maybe the last *two* sticks of wood," she grumbled.

It was a nice house. A very nice house, she mused as she worked. Knowing property prices in the Bonney Lake area, Susan could probably well have afforded the seventy-eight dollars for the pizza delivery. After all, she'd purchased over a grand's worth of Vinnie's best firewood. Val had a feeling Jackson's smug opinion of the woman had had everything to do with the size of her house and presumed worth. If that was the case, Jackson had indeed been disrespectful. Val stretched her back, heaved a replenishing breath and went back to work, muttering to herself how much was left to do.

"Hey, who's out there?" a voice shouted, startling her, nearly causing her to drop the wood.

"Oh crap. Who's that?" Val demanded, clutching a piece of wood to her chest as if it could protect her.

"The property owner," the voice said, the sound crackling from the speaker. "And what are you doing?"

"Stacking firewood." Val held up a stick of wood as if the voice could see it. "Are you Susan Castle?"

"Yes. And you are Val Nardi?"

"Yes. Did Vinnie tell you I'd be stacking your firewood?"

"He didn't mention exactly who would be doing it but I recognized you, Ms. Nardi."

"You can see me?" Val gasped.

"That's what security cameras are for. Visual property surveillance."

"You can see and hear me? Oh, good grief," she groaned. "Shouldn't you let people know they are being surveilled? It seems like an invasion of privacy."

"On my property?"

"Well, it would be nice to know I was being watched." Val scanned the roof line for a camera.

"Back corner of the garage, black box under the eave. Right over your head," Susan said, as if she was watching Val's search. "There's one at each corner of the garage. Also the front door, back door, side door, patio, driveway entrance, and there's a couple inside the garage."

"Sounds kind of paranoid." Val stared up at the one under the garage eave that seemed to be following her as she moved.

"They provide protection and discourage potential criminal behavior."

"Are you sitting in your house watching me stack your firewood?"

"Surveillance is available remotely through my phone or laptop. I receive alerts when there is movement or voices picked up on any of the locations around my property."

"Then you aren't home?" Val's bathroom urgency was growing.

"No. Did you need something?"

"Umm. Perhaps." She cleared her throat, wondering if this request was going to be unappreciated.

"Are you needing access to a restroom?"

"Yes. As a matter of fact, I am."

"I can let you in from here. There's a powder room down the hall to the left, second door."

"Thank you, Ms. Castle. I really appreciate this." Val dropped the piece of wood and hurried over to the front door. After a moment, a series of beeps then a click and the door released. "Thank you."

Val rushed down the hall, desperately maintaining a measure of decorum in spite of her urgency. The bathroom was small but tastefully decorated and clean with bamboo flooring, white and gray tiled walls and a freestanding sink. A basket of hand towels and one of soap dispensers and hand lotion were on the side of the sink. The hand towels were thick and luscious.

When she was finished, she refolded the towel and headed to the front door and beckoning pile of wood. Resisting the urge to snoop, she glanced down the hall toward what she assumed was the living room, dining room and the like. On her way out, she picked up bits of bark she had tracked in on the carpet. Knowing someone was watching her from every corner of the property, whether she was singing, talking to herself or scratching an itch, seemed creepy. And invasive. But, surprisingly, Susan Castle doing it wasn't actually all that terrible. Making her self-conscious, yes. But it wasn't tragic.

She went back to work, tackling the ominous pile of wood. It was like eating an elephant, she told herself. One bite at a time. As slow and methodical as it was, she had a feeling Susan was watching every bite she took.

After nearly three hours, with a couple of short timeouts to catch her breath and stretch, Val could see the end in sight. Maybe five more trips around the garage and the job would be finished. She texted Vinnie twice with progress. The wood racks were nearly full, requiring juggling and struggling to get the last few pieces shoved into a vacant spot. She hadn't needed to use the restroom again, thankfully.

"There!" she declared triumphantly, tapping the last piece into place. "All stacked and finished." She placed her hands on her hips, smiled down at the long row of racks filled with firewood and heaved a satisfied sigh. She pulled out her phone, took a picture and sent it to Vinnie. She included a proud smiley face. She retrieved the broom from the back of her car and swept the bark and debris into the grass. Susan deserved top shelf service and Val considered cleaning up after the job part of that service. She set the bundles of kindling and an armload of small pieces at the end of the racks, assuming they'd be used first. As she opened the car door, ready to head home for a shower and clean clothes, she heard Susan over the speaker.

"Nice job, Ms. Nardi. Very thorough. Thank you."

"You're welcome. I hope you enjoy the firewood. It smells nice."

"Yes, I'm sure it does. From the dimensions of the wood racks and how full they are, I'm guessing your brother delivered more than two cords. I'm happy to pay for the extra."

"I don't think he expects you to do that. I strongly suspect he loaded the trailers with a backhoe instead of precisely stacked piles. He probably rounded up, so to speak."

"I appreciate it but I don't expect to receive more than I contracted and paid for."

"That's between you and my brother. I'm merely the stacker." Val smiled at the camera.

"Have a nice day, Ms. Nardi."

"You may call me Val."

"Then have a nice day, Val."

Val offered a small salute then climbed in her car and pulled away. She was exhausted and sore. This Susan Castle person—she was curious about her. Strangely curious and she had no earthly idea why.

CHAPTER THIRTEEN

It had been a week since Val stacked Susan's firewood and her shoulders and arms were still a little sore. She was a little surprised Susan had stopped by the restaurant for dinner, alone and dressed like she had been in a business meeting, slacks, a stylish shirt and jacket. She'd ordered water, salad with lemon on the side and the special. Vegetarian lasagna. But Val noticed Susan watching her. They were discreet, quick glances, but she was definitely watching her. Even after she brought her dinner to her table, she continued to watch, catching fleeting glimpses.

Val considered herself an efficient server. Polite, courteous and knowledgeable, or at least she tried to be, and a few customers always tested that capacity. She took pride in her work ethic. She hadn't always been good at it. As a teenager working summer and weekends at whatever job she could find, some below minimum wage, she quickly learned the truth of that tenet passed onto to her at an early age by Grandma Nardi, that honey attracted more flies than vinegar.

"Take pride in your work, whatever you do," she had told Val after she'd been fired from the local donut shop for being repeatedly late for work. It didn't matter that Val's mother was often late getting home and Val wasn't allowed to leave her little brother unsupervised. Val was inconsolable after being lectured by the shop owner. She knew her excuses were flimsy at best but she walked home in tears, feeling defeated and ashamed. She vowed to never let that happen again. She couldn't control unforeseen bumps in the road, like the devastation the pandemic had caused. But whatever the job, whatever was asked of her, she was determined to do her very best. Working for Joe was another bump in the road, one she was taking in stride with a smile on her face. But something about the curious arch to Susan Castle's brow as the woman watched her made her think she had somehow failed to measure up.

"Can I get you something for dessert?" she asked, finding a moment to refill her water glass. She noticed Susan had finished barely half of her dinner. "Is the lasagna all right? Is there a problem with it?"

"No, no problem." Susan swallowed visibly, as if she wanted to admit something but hesitated to do so.

"You look like there's a problem."

"Why would you think there's a problem?" Susan looked down at her plate then up at her. "And if I wasn't enjoying my meal, I wouldn't feel compelled to eat it. Trust me."

"Call it my sixth sense. Call it the fact you didn't finish your dinner. Call it me being nosy. Take your choice." Val pulled an impish smile.

"I don't have a problem but…" Susan scanned the room. "I see you're busy so perhaps another time."

"Give me three minutes. I'll be right back," she said and hurried away before Susan could object. She delivered two orders, refilled a couple's coffee cups and cleared a table before telling Audra she needed a break. After all, she hadn't had one since she clocked in before noon.

She slid into the booth across from Susan, folded her hands on the table and offered a reassuring smile. "Okay. You have five minutes of my undivided time."

Susan returned her smile. "With that kind of a timeline, I should probably reduce the chitchat and get right to the point."

"I'm listening."

"I would like to hire you." Susan leaned back in the booth and watched for Val's reaction.

"Please don't say you ordered two more cords of firewood and want me to stack it."

Susan's smile widened. "No. I have a sufficient stockpile to last at least through to spring. I need someone to receive a delivery at my house. I've been waiting two months for this shipment. It's been on backorder. Unfortunately, I'll be out of town the entire week of the prospective delivery window. I'll pay you to be at my house and sign for the shipment. I can't risk weather damage or porch pirates. I understand you work most days but since Nardi's isn't open for breakfast, I was hoping you'd be available for a morning delivery."

"Why me?" Val asked curiously, crossing her arms on the table. "What about your nephew? The one who met you in the parking lot with Connor."

"That isn't an option," Susan said and didn't elaborate.

"Even so, why me?"

"You did a very professional job while you were at my house and I appreciate it. Vinnie called to ask if I was satisfied with the delivery. He mentioned he paid for your time and service."

"He did." Val wasn't sure this was any of Susan's business, but replied courteously.

"It was a big job. A time-consuming, big job, never mind the physicality of it. You swept off the debris instead of leaving a mess of bark and chips on the driveway. So, yes, he should have paid you, brother or not."

Val shrugged. She didn't consider that anything more than completion of the job.

"And, although you probably don't want me to bring this up, I noticed you showed great restraint and respect inside my house."

"From the limited part I saw, it's a lovely home. Very neat and clean."

"Thank you. I'll be sure and tell Mrs. Palmer you approve. She'll be pleased you picked up the bark you tracked in as well."

Val cocked her head at Susan's remark. "Mrs. Palmer is your cleaning lady?"

"Yes."

"Salt-and-pepper short hair. About sixty. Five foot three. Wears white sneakers with pink shoelaces?"

"You know her?"

"Amberly Palmer. Yes." Val smiled reflectively. "Lovely woman. Very efficient, for the most part."

Susan stared curiously, as if seeking clarification.

"She worked for us," Val finally said.

"As a server or a cook?"

"Neither. She worked for our cleaning service several years ago. Maids For You."

"You worked for a commercial cleaning service?" Susan seemed surprised.

"Sort of. I owned it. Well, co-owned it. Amberly was one of our long-term employees."

"You owned a cleaning service?" Susan leaned back and stared over at her, as if evaluating the news.

"Yes. Kate Morrison and I owned it jointly." Val heaved a thoughtful sigh, a reflective smile settled over her as Kate's image crystalized in her mind.

"May I ask what happened to your business?"

"Covid." She pulled her hands into her lap in a gesture of finality to the matter.

"Ah. Government restrictions and customer paranoia."

"You got it. We couldn't survive with only ten percent of our clientele requiring our services. And…" Val swallowed at the memory of all that grief, and looked away. "So, what is it you wanted to discuss with me?" She needed a new topic of conversation.

"Accept a delivery and put it inside my house, if you have the time."

"When?"

"Thursday morning, between eight to ten in the morning."

"I don't clock in until noon on Thursday so that could work."

"Good." Susan pulled an envelope from her jacket pocket and set it squarely in front of Val. "There's a copy of the invoice and a printout of the delivery schedule, in case you need it. The access code for the house is in there as well. I'm expecting three boxes. One of them is large but more awkward than heavy."

"Where would you like me to put them?" Val picked up the envelope but didn't open it.

"If you wouldn't mind, in my office. Second door on the right. But anywhere inside is fine."

"Val," Audra called as she seated a couple at a nearby table, nodding in that direction.

"Coming," she said, sliding out of the booth. She reached down and rested her hand on Susan's arm reassuringly. "I'll take care of it. Thursday morning. Between eight to ten." She slipped the envelope in her apron pocket, patting it protectively. "Don't worry. Finish your dinner and I'll check on you shortly."

"Thank you, Ms. Nardi."

"Thank you for trusting me." Val started to walk away. But something else was gnawing at her. She came back to the table and asked, "Why haven't you corrected me when I call you Ms. Castle?"

"I beg your pardon."

"Why didn't you tell me you are actually Dr. Castle? A friend of yours was in and mentioned you have a PhD in mathematics. You're a doctor. I certainly didn't mean to be disrespectful by not calling you by your rightful name."

"I don't advertise it since as soon as people hear I have that moniker they immediately assume I can either diagnose their skin condition or write them a prescription for narcotics. When I explain it's a PhD in mathematics I usually get smirks and remarks about the relationship of diameter to circumference. It's easier to avoid the subject. And again, I apologize, Ms. Nardi. I don't consider you disrespectful in the least. I'm going to assume the woman who told you this was Jillian Ramsey? Blond. Tall. Attractive."

"Yes. Very pleasant woman."

"She is indeed. A bit of a Chatty Cathy and occasionally intrusive but a long-time friend."

"Val, are you coming?" Audra called, nodding toward the table where she had seated a family of five.

"On my way," she replied then looked down at Susan with a smile. "Enjoy your dinner, Dr. Castle."

Val headed back to work but couldn't help wondering if Susan was romantically involved with Jillian Ramsey. She could see it happening. Both were attractive and seemingly intelligent women. And Jillian appeared to have drawn a bead on Dr. Susan Castle's inner workings. Her knowledge of Susan's personality held a strange allure for Val. Knowledge she surprisingly wished she had.

CHAPTER FOURTEEN

Val had dropped the envelope in her purse and headed home, exhausted from her shift and ready for a long soaking bath. She considered adding a glass of wine to her soak but she had a feeling it would only make her more tired and she'd be snoring in the tub.

She finished her bath, pulled on her long T-shirt with panda bears rolling across the front, remembered the envelope and went to retrieve it from her purse. She crawled into bed, snapped on the bedside lamp and opened it. As Susan said, it contained an invoice listing highly technical-sounding computer parts, an expensive office chair and an assortment of cables and connectors. It also had a printout of the delivery schedule with the driver's name and the address for delivery. And a Walmart gift card. Like the one Vinnie had given her. It didn't state an amount and seemed like a strange payment for services rendered.

"Swell," she muttered sarcastically, set the card on the bedside table, turned out the light and went to sleep.

* * *

She'd decided to allow a little extra time, in case the driver was early. It turned out that it was a good thing she did. A delivery truck was pulling away. The middle-aged man smiled and waved, then continued down the driveway toward the road. Even before she climbed out of the car she could see a stack of boxes that blocked the front door. She took a picture of the boxes with a 7:28 a.m. time stamp on her phone to verify delivery but she strongly suspected Susan already knew about the delivery if she was watching her cameras.

It took some doing but she pushed the boxes aside, entered the code and opened the front door. She carried the smallest box down the hall and set it in Susan's office. She couldn't help taking a quick look around the room. After all, she had been invited in and she wanted to see what a software engineer's office looked like. Impressively large, with a vast array of computer-related equipment, overstuffed bookcases, and top of the line office furniture including an L-shaped desk. She went back for the second box, deciding she'd save the largest one for last. As Susan had said, it wasn't heavy but it was cumbersome. She scooted it toward the open front door, deciding she'd have to push it down the hall.

"This must be one whopping big office chair," she said with a groan as she tried wedging it through the opening.

"Yes, probably so," a voice called.

"Are you watching me from afar?" Val asked, scanning the entry for the camera.

"From Portland, yes," Susan said.

"Well, I hope it fits through the door or you may have to move your office outside."

"You probably can't hurt it if you need to turn the box on the side to get it inside."

Val tried that but only succeeded in jamming it in the doorway. She bumped it with her butt, then knelt down and pushed her shoulder against it.

"Any other suggestions, Dr. Castle?" She sat back on her heels and looked up at the camera on the porch.

"This may be above the job description but we may have to go with plan B.

Open the box, remove the chair and all parts. Carry said chair and parts to office minus the box."

"No wonder you're a computer geek. Good idea. Where might I find a box cutter?"

"Knives are in the kitchen. The undercabinet fold down near the stove."

Val went into the kitchen. "Wow," she said, looking around at the large room and its high-end features. Commercial grade stove and oven, granite countertops, sink in the island as well as by the window, expensive-looking stand mixer, automated coffee maker, side-by-side stainless-steel refrigerator, and gorgeous walnut cabinetry. She wondered if Susan was a gourmet cook as well as a mathematician.

"Behind you," Susan said. "Second cabinet from the end. It folds down toward you."

"Oh, okay," Val said, quickly retrieving a knife from the rack. "Nice kitchen, by the way."

Val went to work opening the box, pulling out chair parts and paperwork, carried them into the office and lined them up along the wall. It took four trips to get everything inside. Once she had it all delivered to the office, she returned to the front door and the still stuck box.

"With your permission, I'll cut up the box, unless you want it for something."

"Nope, don't need it. You're welcome to cut it up to get it out of the way. I'll put it in the recycling. I'm sorry it became such a nuisance."

Val began slicing up the box. She pulled the pieces inside and added them to the items in the office. She returned the knife to the kitchen, turned out the lights and closed the front door.

"All done," she said, smiling up at the camera.

"Nicely done, Ms. Nardi. Nicely done. I need to add to your payment. You went above and beyond, especially considering they delivered earlier than scheduled."

"No, you don't." Val stood on the front porch, staring up at the camera. "I don't need anything more. In fact, I didn't need anything to begin with. I was available and I'm happy to help."

"Did you see the card in the envelope?"

"The Walmart gift card, yes. Thank you." She had no idea how much was on it but she appreciated it anyway.

"Vinnie said that's how he paid you for stacking the firewood. I assume you use gift cards for groceries and the like."

That explained it. Vinnie had said he paid with a gift card, as if that was her preference. Whatever was on the gift card she appreciated.

"I'm glad we got your equipment successfully delivered and inside. I need to get going. Audra needs me to clock in a little early today. I think someone called off."

"Then I won't keep you. Thanks again, Ms. Nardi."

"Anytime," Val shouted, hoping the surveillance equipment could still hear her as she climbed into her car. She had turned onto the road and headed home as her phone rang. It was Audra.

"Yes, Audra, I'm coming in. I'll be there by eleven," she said before Audra could say anything.

"We need you to stop and pick up four number ten size cans of crushed tomatoes. Six number tens of tomato puree. And two gallons of half and half. Will you be going to Walmart?" Audra asked, sounding like she was poised to add something else.

"Probably. It's on the way."

"Could you see if they have one of those chocolate swirl cheesecakes? The big one with ten slices. I love Walmart's chocolate cheesecake. Thanks, hon. Bring me the receipt and I'll reimburse you. Gotta go. Produce delivery is here." Audra hung up without another word.

Val headed to Walmart, hoping to get her purchases complete and out of there before Audra called back to add multiple produce items the delivery failed to provide. She hurried through the store like a woman possessed, adding a quick trip down the toiletries aisle, before moving through the checkout line. She'd use the Walmart gift card Susan had given her and pay the rest in cash.

Val loaded her sacks in the cart, retrieved the receipt and headed for the door, surprised nothing else was due in payment on the order. She was halfway across the front of the store when she noticed the card balance on the bottom of the receipt.

"*What?*" she shrieked, jerking the cart to a stop. She stared at the balance in disbelief. Susan had given her $250 to open her house, slide some packages inside and close the door. She must have meant the card to be for $25, not $250. This had to be a mistake. She could have easily done it without compensation at all and hadn't really expected any. And she certainly couldn't take advantage of her like that.

"She's going to want this back," Val muttered, folding the receipt around the card and slipping it back in her pocket.

CHAPTER FIFTEEN

Val carried the groceries in the back door and set them plus the cheesecake on the counter.

"Last cheesecake," Val whispered as Audra came to investigate. As she washed her hands and tied on an apron, ready to start her shift, she heard Audra lecturing Joe about *her* cheesecake and he was *not* to touch it or he'd be sleeping on the couch.

"Can you take table twenty-one?" Audra asked a few minutes later, a grimace clearly indicating something was wrong. It wasn't in Val's usual section and it was the furthest from her tables but she was willing to cover it. "The woman's been in here before and Marcy refuses to wait on her," Audra added.

Val carried a tray of drinks to a table of waiting customers. Whatever the problem was at table twenty-one, she'd deal with it in due time. Marcy was relatively new and young and hadn't developed a thick skin against difficult customers.

"Hello," Val said to the middle-aged woman. She had a butchy edge to her looks. No problem, she thought. "My name is Val and I'll be your server this evening. What can I start you with to drink?"

"Water." She looked up at Val then smiled and began a slow deliberate scan down and back up, her eyes lingering at Val's bustline and crotch.

Oh, good grief, not one of those…

"Do you know what you'd like? Our special is chicken alfredo or linguine with asparagus tips."

"How about a small pepperoni pizza, extra cheese. Thin crust," the woman said with an unmistakably lusty innuendo.

"We can do that. Small thin crust pepperoni with extra cheese." Val nodded her approval.

The woman handed the menu to Val, her hand lingering on it while her eyes did another deliberate up and down inspection. She smiled coyly and added, "Thanks."

The more Val pulled at the menu to reclaim it, the tighter the woman held it and the wider her smile grew. Val recognized her behavior and didn't want to play. She released the menu. The woman sat holding it then, after a moment, dropped it to the floor.

"Oops." She looked down at the menu then up at Val mischievously.

Val groaned, knowing this woman expected her to bend over and pick it up. She either wanted a look down Val's red blouse or at her rear. Did her tip depend on it? Probably. Was it worth it? Definitely not. This wasn't the first rude customer to cross her path and it wouldn't be the last. She wasn't going to submit to such offensive and dehumanizing behavior. No wonder Marcy refused to wait on her.

"I'm guessing you want me to bend over and pick that up. That's why you dropped it, right?" Val said without expression.

The woman chuckled and said, "You never know." She offered a wink.

Val chuckled back at her then leaned down and said quietly, "You really shouldn't disrespect the people who handle your food."

Val returned to the kitchen with the woman's order. The menu remained on the floor. She served the woman her pizza and put the receipt on the table. The fewer trips she needed to make to her table, the better. That didn't keep the woman from ogling her at every opportunity. The menu remained on the floor until the woman finished, paid and left.

"A menu dropper?" Audra asked with a chuckle, noticing Val finally pick it up after the woman pulled out of the parking lot.

"You got it," Val said as she cleaned it with an antiseptic wipe and returned it to the rack. "And I bet she didn't leave a tip on her card."

"Actually, she did." Audra held up the credit card receipt. "A dollar sixty-nine." She grinned wickedly.

Val rolled her eyes and went to retrieve the rack of clean wineglasses from the kitchen.

"Val!" someone called from the kitchen. "Where is she?"

"I'm out here, Owen," she said to the cook, squatting behind the service line as she unloaded the wineglasses into the lower shelf.

"Your car." He pointed out the window. "Someone ran into it in the parking lot."

"*What?*" she shrieked and tossed the glass rack on the counter. She bolted for the door.

Audra had overheard their conversation and rushed out as well. Sure enough, Val's Subaru had been struck in the front on the driver's side. The tire was flat. The wheel and front fender were crumpled and bent, suggesting the axle was damaged as well.

"No, no, no," she screamed, rubbing her hand across the damage. "Who did this?" She scanned the parking lot as if searching for the perpetrator.

"I'm calling 911," Audra announced, already holding her phone to her ear.

"How can someone do that and drive away?" Val demanded.

"What the hell happened?" Joe said, coming to see what the commotion was all about.

"Whoever did this has a red car," Val said, picking at the flecks of red paint on the damaged fender.

Joe and Val scanned the parking lot for any red vehicle, his brow arched menacingly.

"Don't do anything stupid, Joseph," Audra warned. "Cops are on the way."

"They hit you and took off." Joe sneered disgustedly and spat as he continued to scan the lot. "Assholes."

"What are the cops going to do if we don't know who hit my car?" Val asked, although she already knew. Her insurance would have to cover the damage.

Audra took pictures as Joe squatted next to the car, peering under the fender and behind the wheel.

"You'll probably need an entire wheel and axle assembly plus the quarter panel."

"How long do you think it'll take to fix it? We're talking special order parts, right?" Val asked, remembering Joe dealt with something similar several years ago.

He shrugged, continuing to examine the damage.

"If your car was newer, they might have the parts in stock. Finding OEM parts might be a problem."

"What's OEM?"

"Original equipment manufactured parts. You might have to settle for aftermarket parts."

"Is that bad?" Val squatted next to her brother, hoping to understand what he was talking about.

"It means replacement parts that aren't made by the original manufacturer. They're okay." He didn't sound convincing. "It might mean a reduction in what your insurance will cover in the future."

"You mean my insurance company won't offer top shelf coverage on second shelf parts?" she suggested.

He nodded, then went back to scrutinizing the damage. "It's not terrible, Val. Shouldn't take very long, assuming they can get the parts."

As Val suspected, the police could do little other than take a report and pictures of the damage. The restaurant's security camera unfortunately didn't get a clear image of the culprit's car or the license plate. They offered sympathy for Val's situation but left after a few minutes. They assured her she wasn't the only victim to such crimes, as if that would magically appease her anger.

"Take all the time you need," Joe said, rubbing Val's shoulder. "Do you want Audra to take you home?"

"Thanks, Joe. I don't need to go home." She gave a last look at her car and followed him inside. "I'll call the dealership in the morning. I want to talk with my insurance agent first."

"Good idea. Don't let him scrimp on the coverage. You paid for insurance. They have to fix it."

Val appreciated her brother's protective nature but she knew how insurance companies worked. It was hard not to worry about the repairs and how much she would have to pay, considering she had a hefty deductible. She needed to work and with no renter as yet for her building, now more than ever. She needed her income and tips.

"Give me lots of customers," she said to Audra as she passed on her way to the dining room.

CHAPTER SIXTEEN

Val climbed out of Jackson's car, thanking him for the ride to work, although it was clear he wasn't pleased about it. It was his day off and he had plans. A noon five-mile ride didn't seem excessively demanding when he had borrowed her car twice in the past two weeks. But she understood being asked to give up even part of a day off.

"Thanks, honey," she said and slipped a five-dollar bill in his visor then patted his arm. "Drive carefully."

"What did you find out about your car?" Joe asked. He was standing at the prep counter, opening cans of tomatoes. "Insurance going to cover repairs?"

"Sort of." She deposited her tote and jacket in the office and tied on an apron before coming back to talk with him. "I have collision and comprehensive coverage, fortunately. But no rental car coverage and a thousand-dollar deductible. Plus they'll only pay for aftermarket parts."

"They're cheaper."

"Exactly," she said with a snort. "The good news is, aftermarket parts are easier to find so it could be a week, maybe a bit more. And the prices are about the same so I think I'd rather go with the Subaru dealership. Their warranty is better. And if I have them do the work, they'll come tow the car for free."

"That'll save you a couple hundred."

"Probably. They can't start on it until next week." She heaved a disgusted sigh. "But they'll come get it today. They said by two."

"Don't leave anything in your car you don't want stolen." He was doing the protective brother thing again.

"I won't." She patted his shoulder and headed into the dining room to begin her shift.

The lunch crowd was low-key and light. The unusually bright sunshiny day was keeping people outdoors, enjoying the first pleasant day Bonney Lake had had in a week. Rain brought people indoors. Sunshine didn't. The Subaru dealership sent a tow truck and hauled away her car, raising her hopes it would be repaired and back in her hands soon.

"Save table four, it's about finished," Audra said as Val carried a pizza to a table.

The people at table four soon left, and Val bussed the table, occasionally watching the door for whoever might be the special guest for this good table, near the front with a nice view out the window but not too close to the lobby congestion. There were always a few customers who demanded to be seated at one of the "best tables in the house." If a customer asked for a specific table and it was available, no problem.

"Audra," Val whispered, returning menus to the podium. "Who is this mystery person who has to have table four? Elected official? Health department inspector?"

Audra looked out the window, then nodded in that direction. Val squinted at the woman climbing out of a blue car on the passenger side.

"Grandma Nardi? Nana? Why didn't you tell me she was coming?" Val exclaimed gleefully. She rushed out the door. "Hello, sweetheart," she said, hugging her.

Irene Nardi had shrunk with age. "Someday they'll bury me a shoebox," she'd said whimsically. Barely five feet tall with salt-and-pepper hair cut short and with what looked like pin curls around her forehead, she had a weathered face, deeply wrinkled but with a perpetually pleasant expression. She frowned at her family's insistence that she use a cane, but today she was using a red metal one with floral detailing.

"It's so good to see you," Val cooed and kissed her grandmother's cheek. She ran a reassuring hand up and down her arm as she walked her to the door. "Come inside and let's get you comfortable. Hi, Megan," she added over her shoulder to her soon-to-be sister-in-law and smiled.

"Val, you were so sweet to drop off the new sweater." Nana squeezed Val's hand. "I love it. Next time you come by, you wake me up, you hear me? I can nap anytime but I only get to see my favorite granddaughter once in a while." She pointed a finger at Val as if scolding a child.

"Did it fit? I can exchange it if you don't like it." Val held the door for her and waited while she entered, her steps short and cautious.

"It's perfect. Pumpkin is such a fun color to wear. I wore it to bingo the other day and got lots of compliments."

"She insisted I bring her in today." Megan followed them through the door, carrying Grandma's purse. She heaved an exasperated sigh as if waiting for the slow-moving woman was an imposition. "She couldn't wait until tomorrow. I've got an appointment I can't miss. I need to leave for an hour or so. Is that okay?"

In her late thirties, round-faced, with an ample figure and a few inches shorter than Val, Megan had blond hair, blue eyes and wore jeans and a fuzzy sweater. She was usually kind, friendly and habitually happy but today she seemed stressed.

"I'm so glad you brought her in and sure, we can handle things. Take as long as you need." Val hooked an arm through her grandmother's and escorted her to table four. "We've got your favorite table waiting for you."

Megan waited for Grandma Nardi to get settled, set her purse in the booth next to her then excused herself and left.

Val was thrilled to have her grandmother in-house so they could pamper and feed her. She didn't come in very often, the effort to dress and cross town sometimes more that she wanted to tackle. Val appreciated it when she did. She and her grandmother were best buddies. Most of the employees knew Grandma Nardi and loved her. She was kind and never spoke ill of anyone. It wasn't in her nature. She had been an elementary school teacher for over thirty years and had been good at her job, schooling children to be polite, respectful and to value their education. She had been a source of great comfort when Val's grief over Kate seemed too much to bear.

"What would you like to drink, sweetheart? Tea?" Other customers could wait. Nana was first on her list while she was there. "How about a little glass of *vino rosso*?" Val leaned down and winked.

"Yes," she whispered then giggled. "Vino rosso."

Grandma Nardi was in no hurry. She sat sipping her wine, nonchalantly looking over the menu, something she enjoyed doing. She knew what was on it. After all, she had made some suggestions and offered recipes. She had absolutely refused to allow Joe to call the restaurant Grandma Nardi's. It had to be Mama Nardi's or he couldn't use the name at all. So Mama Nardi's Italian Pizzeria and Ristorante was born with her blessing. She now lived in an assisted living facility where she had her own apartment with a small kitchen but she ate most of her meals in the common dining room. And once a month or so she ventured out to enjoy a little family time.

She settled on the daily special, chicken parmesan, fully expecting to take at least half of it home for tomorrow. Val knew how she liked it and brought a little extra sauce with pepper flakes on the side.

"Hey, Mama Nardi," Joe said, coming to her table with a wide grin and a piece of lemon bundt cake. He leaned down and kissed her cheek. "How did you like your dinner?" He set the dessert plate on the table.

"Hello, sweet Joseph." She smiled up at him. "It was good. A touch more garlic in the sauce, Joe. But it was good." She held up her thumb and index finger to show how much he needed to add.

He chuckled and nodded. She usually had some tiny detail to share with him and he didn't mind. It meant she was paying attention and carefully considering his creations.

"Okay, Mama Nardi. I'll remember that."

"Come down here," she demanded.

He was a big man but she was not intimidated by his size. She grabbed his shirt and pulled him down, smiling adoringly. She reached up and stroked his face below his eye patch as if her loving touch could magically heal his eye. It was a ritual she often performed and one he allowed.

"Enjoy your dessert and have a little more wine. I've got to get back in there." He kissed the top of her head then returned to the kitchen.

Like Val, Joe had a special bond with Grandma Nardi. Vinnie too developed one over the years but he'd had a wilder youth and she didn't approve of some of his high school friends. They still occasionally butted heads. She wasn't above scolding Vinnie, most recently for wearing a ripped shirt to a family celebratory dinner at the restaurant. "You can afford better, Vincent," she had said with an angry scowl.

She and Audra didn't always see eye to eye. They were cordial for the most part but Audra preferred to be hands-on when it came to most family decisions. Grandma Nardi considered her pushy and wasn't afraid to say so. Joe and Val rolled their eyes and exchanged coy smiles when little tiffs bubbled to the surface between the two women. It was all Italian family affection. They could disagree and argue, blustering their displeasure. But if someone outside the family tried it, woe be unto them.

Megan called and announced she was running late and would be back in thirty minutes. Neither Val nor Grandma Nardi minded. It meant more time to visit with family and a few locals she recognized and another glass of wine.

"We're sending you home with a couple of meals for later in the week," Val said, setting a plastic sack with four to-go containers on the chair next to her. "Is there anything special you'd like? Extra meatballs?"

"What's in here?" she asked, peeking in the sack with a girlish grin.

"Angel hair pomodoro, four-cheese lasagna, and grilled chicken dinner," Val announced. "And some breadsticks."

"Val?" Audra called as she seated a family of four.

"You go on, honey," she said, giving Val an encouraging wink. "I'll sit here and wait for Megan. It's time I go home. I'm tired." She patted Val's hand.

Val knew what would come next. There would be an argument at the register with Grandma insisting she pay for her meal and Audra absolutely refusing. Joe would come out of the kitchen to defuse the situation, refusing to allow her back through his doors if she didn't put her money away and forget it. Like other traditions, she offered to pay, he refused to take it, she acquiesced and everyone was happy. The tip she left on the table for Val would mysteriously find its way back into Grandma's purse the next time Val visited her at the senior facility.

"Bye-bye, sweetheart," Val said, holding the car door and helping her get situated. "Come back and see us real soon. I think Joe is trying a new lasagna recipe next week." Val leaned in and kissed her cheek.

"I'm sure it will be wonderful. Thank you, honey," she said, patting the sack of dinners on her lap.

"Thanks for bringing Nana in for dinner, Megan. We love having her stop by for a visit. It was sweet of you but I wish you had stayed to eat with us, too."

Megan didn't look like she felt well. And if rumors around the restaurant were to be believed, a little Nardi might be in the works. But Val wasn't going to mention it. It wasn't her place to make that announcement. That would be up to Megan and Vinnie. And she certainly didn't want to open the floodgates for Nana's insistence they have nuptials before they had a baby. She was an open-minded and supportive woman for the most part and Val's sexual orientation had never been an issue but some things rubbed her the wrong way.

She reached over and squeezed Megan's hand, offered a reassuring smile, then backed out and closed the door.

CHAPTER SEVENTEEN

"Val, table seven," Audra said, sticking her head in the kitchen where Val was eating a sliced tomato. "I think you know her."

"Who is it?" she said after swallowing the bite.

"That woman," was all she said and went back into the dining room.

"That really narrows it down," Val muttered and headed for table seven. "Oh, hello, Dr. Castle," she said. "Nice to see you."

"Hello. I'm meeting a friend for dinner. Or rather late lunch." Susan scanned the restaurant. "Jillian. I think you've met her. I didn't see her car in the parking lot."

"Would you like something to drink while you wait? Iced tea? Coffee?"

"Water, please. And speaking of cars in the parking lot, I didn't see your car out there."

"That's because mine is in the shop. Front-wheel, front fender, brakes and CV axle. Somebody hit me in the parking lot, then drove off without a backward glance. And without leaving their insurance information." Val scrunched her face disgustedly.

"Hit and run?" Susan offered a pained expression.

"Yep. Got away cleaner than a whistle. I can't believe they didn't own up to what they did. I would have."

"You would have because you are honest and respectful of other people's property. They obviously are not. My best guess is they didn't have liability insurance or had past offenses which will raise their premium. I assume you have insurance, right?" Susan asked cautiously. "I'm sorry. That's none of my business."

"That's okay. You may ask and yes, I do, thank goodness." She should have insisted on rental car coverage and a lower deductible but she didn't need to share the shortcomings of her policy with this intelligent and obviously successful woman. "Repairs shouldn't take too long, hopefully." She forced a smile.

"Hopefully? You've got your family to help out, right?"

"There's always Uber."

Before Susan could reply, Jillian came through the door, spotted them and made a beeline for the table.

"I'm so sorry I'm late, Susan," she said breathlessly. "There was a three-vehicle accident on 167 and it has traffic down to one lane. I thought I'd never get here. Hi, Val. Nice to see you again."

"Hello, Jillian. Late or not, it's great to have you both back at Nardi's."

She slid into her seat and smiled up at Val. "Now what are you two talking about? And where is my glass of wine?" She mock-glared over at Susan. "If you were a good friend, you would have already ordered me a glass of something sparkly and alcoholic."

"A glass of wine for the impatient one, please," Susan said with a chuckle.

"Shall I bring two glasses so she doesn't have to drink alone?"

"Yes. The stuffy computer geek needs to loosen up and I'm feeling like white wine," Jillian said.

"Sauvignon blanc?" Val suggested.

"Fine," Susan said. "Sauvignon blanc for two."

When Val returned to their table with glasses of water, wine, and silverware, Susan was rifling through her pockets with a concerned look on her face.

"I need to run out to the truck," Susan said and slid out of the booth. "I'll be back in a minute."

Val stepped aside as she headed for the door with long strides. Jillian chuckled and shook her head, watching Susan trot across the parking lot.

"Yes, Dr. Castle is absentminded and occasionally forgetful. She's smart in other areas so it's forgivable."

"Um, Jillian," Val said hesitantly, wondering how she should word this and if it was any of her business anyway. "May I ask you something? Something about Susan." She slid into the booth across from Jillian.

"Sure. What did you want to know?"

"It's probably nothing, but I occasionally get the feeling she'd prefer I'd keep my distance. Sometimes I put my hand on her shoulder when I'm refilling her glass. I do it so the customer knows I'm there and we don't collide. Or I do it to be friendly. I want them to know I'm approachable if they have a problem. But she…"

"Stiffens and holds her breath?" Jillian suggested.

"Yes. Does she do that to you?"

Jillian looked back out the window as if checking Susan's progress then back at Val and said, "Susan is a real sweetheart but she can really go against the grain with some of her attitudes. Physical contact being one of them." Jillian used air quotes as she said in mockery of Susan, "All that platonic and indiscriminate hugging that goes on all the time is just plain silly and meaningless." She smiled reflectively. "Of course, I ignore that and plop my hugs on her anyway."

"I'm sorry if I'm being nosy." Val didn't want to embarrass herself or Jillian.

"You aren't. You're a friend and you're curious. I understand. If you're asking what I think you're asking, yes. Susan is completely neurotypical." She smiled reassuringly. "Smarter and more insightful than most but completely normal. She's standoffish but that's her defense mechanism. I don't think she even knows she's doing it."

Jillian glanced out the window. Drew a deep breath. "She checked you out. Don't take offense. She does that to everyone.

She said she wants to avoid surprises. Be yourself, Val. She'll accept you." She laughed. "It took her a little time but she finally got used to me and my flamboyant crap."

"May I ask? Did you and Susan date?" Val assumed they had. After all, Jillian seemed to know a lot about her.

"Susan and I? No." She chuckled dismissively. "She dated my sister years ago. Unfortunately, Dallas wasn't a good fit for Susan."

"It didn't work out?" Val asked hesitantly.

"Susan needed someone a bit more patient." Jillian rolled her eyes. "I can't speak from experience, but I know my friend Susan Castle." She reached over and squeezed Val's hand. "She's a smidge different. She's so consumed with work she doesn't have time or interest in matters of the heart."

Susan seemed to have found whatever she was looking for and was heading back. Val slid out of the booth.

"Do you know what you'd like to order?" she asked when Susan settled herself. "Or do you need a few minutes?"

"Here," Susan said, holding up a gift card. "I thought I put it in my wallet but nope, stuck it in the glove box. This is yours." When Val didn't take it, she wobbled it back and forth.

"No, it isn't. Let me go get the other card you gave me." Val started for the kitchen.

"No," Susan demanded.

Val came back to the table and leaned down, whispering so only Susan could hear.

"The card you gave me was for two hundred and fifty dollars. Like I said in the phone message, you must have made a mistake when you purchased it. Didn't you look at your receipt?"

"Of course, I looked at it. The job turned out to be more of a problem than I expected. It's only reasonable." She tried again to get Val to take the card.

Val heard Jillian chuckle softly.

"I'm not taking that gift card." Val snatched the card out of her hand, stuffed it down in Susan's shirt pocket and patted it. It wasn't intentional but she could definitely feel Susan's breast, surprisingly firm for a woman her age, whatever it was. And that momentary touch provided a rush of emotion she didn't expect.

It also brought a blush to Susan's face. "Now, you two decide what you want for dinner and hush about gift cards. I'll be back in a minute to take your order."

Jillian chuckled even louder.

"What are you laughing at?" Val heard Susan say as she walked away, bringing on even more laughing from Jillian.

Val took their order, spinach prosciutto stromboli and bucatini carbonara, dishes they planned to share. It sounded like Jillian was on a culinary adventure and had convinced Susan to accompany her although she had misgivings.

"Both good choices," Val said. "I think you'll like them."

"I bet you can cook anything on the menu, right, Val?" Jillian speculated.

"Probably. But Joe and his assistant cooks are excellent at their job," she quickly inserted.

"She occasionally works in the kitchen so yes, I'm sure she can cook about anything on the menu," Susan offered.

"Really? A chef as well as a server. I'm doubly impressed. I can't do either. My feet wouldn't allow it. I need a sit-down job," Jillian said and shuddered. "Of course, Susan can't cook either." She winked at her. "You should see her kitchen."

"I have. And yes, it's very nice. The warming tray is a bonus feature in the stove. And the microwave looked like it's also a convection oven."

"Ask Susan how many meals she's cooked in her new kitchen and I do *not* mean the frozen dinners she microwaves or the leftovers she brings home and reheats," Jillian teased.

"I told you I'm going to learn how to use that stuff." Susan glared over at Jillian.

"You really don't cook?" Val asked, somewhat surprised. "You've added high-tech all over your house but you don't cook?"

"I cook," Susan said defensively, seemingly flustered by the accusations.

"Honey, I've known you for twenty years and I have seen you cook exactly four meals. One was hamburgers on the grill. The rest of us brought potluck so all you did was apply a patty to the bun."

"It's handy to have cooking skills but it's not mandatory," Val said with a smile and a pat, coming to Susan's defense. Susan stiffened from the pat. "Now, let me get your order turned in." Val had no more time to visit. By the time she checked on them they had finished and were leaving, waving goodbye on their way out the door. Much to Val's dismay, Susan had left the extra gift card on the table as a tip.

"I told you no, Dr. Castle," Val muttered as she slipped the card in her pocket and cleared the table. "That woman does *not* listen to me."

CHAPTER EIGHTEEN

Val noticed two women, probably late twenties, talking with Audra at the podium. Tables were available but they weren't being seated so she assumed they were in to pick up an order or place one to go. But when Audra pointed at Val, that didn't seem likely. The taller woman gave Val a scrutinizing glance then headed toward her, the other woman following.

"Are you Val Nardi?" the woman said with a critical arch to her brow. At Val's nod she asked, "Are you the one in charge of renting the building on Highway 410? The one with the drive-thru window? We're interested in renting it," she added, looking at the other woman as if seeking agreement. "Is it still available?"

"Why don't we step over here?" Val said, escorting the two toward a table in the corner, away from prying eyes and ears. She took a seat across from them. "Yes. It's still vacant. What kind of business did you plan on opening?" She needed to know how serious they were before she wasted time discussing it. She also wanted assurance they didn't plan on opening a brothel or anything illegal.

"Power Protein Products. They sell smoothies and health food items."

"I haven't heard of that company but I'm not really into smoothies." Val smiled approval, wondering how healthy a protein smoothie really was. But if these women trusted the brand, who was she to argue.

"I know the building used to be a coffee place. So, it has a refrigerator and a sink, right?"

"Yes, also air-conditioning, stainless-steel countertops and workstations, hot water, and plenty of cabinet storage. It also has a bathroom."

"I'm Marsha and this is Tess," the woman said, pointing at her cohort. "I saw in your ad you require a deposit and two months' rent in advance."

"That's right. It's a cleaning deposit. I have insurance on the building but I do not cover your contents. I encourage my tenants to purchase their own insurance to cover equipment and liability. Rent is due on the first of the month and considered late on fifth, incurring an additional late fee for every day after the fifth. Two months' worth of late payments is grounds for eviction and loss of the deposit. Sorry about all this up-front warning, but I've had some renters try to take advantage of me. If you'd like a tour inside, I can arrange to meet you there. What time works for you?"

"Tomorrow morning?" the taller woman said.

"I can do that. Say, nine-thirty?" Val offered cheerfully, hopeful she finally had a renter to take Heidi's place. "I think you'll like the workspace. It's been cleaned and sanitized. Everything is in working order."

"Yeah, I'm sure it's great." Marsha hesitated, looked at Tess, then cleared her throat. "Um, Val, we have a small concern though. The rent. We would like to negotiate that. Perhaps postpone the deposit and first two months' rent until we establish a clientele. You know, repeat customers we can count on. We'd be willing to offer you a percentage of our revenue for the first three months. It's possible the revenue could actually be more than the deposit and rent. It could be way more." Marsha said this as if she were offering a winning lottery ticket. "We're very confident the long-term benefit for you could be really huge."

With a sinking feeling, Val knew where this was going. It had been tried before and she wasn't agreeing to anything other than cash in full and in hand.

"You want to rent my building to sell smoothies. Pay no deposit or rent for the first two months. Or three. Use my facility, and probably my utilities, with the outside chance you'll be profitable? And you are offering me this *tremendous* opportunity with a straight face?" Val stared at them.

"Well, yes. We're offering you a chance to get in on the ground floor," Marsha encouraged, as if she believed what she was saying.

It was all Val could do not to laugh in her face. "Marsha, Tess," she said, then stood and looked down at them. "No, I'm not interested in your offer. I won't rent to you."

"Why?" Marsha seemed dumbfounded.

"Honey, I think the term you are trying desperately to avoid here is MLM. Multi-level marketing. I have to pay taxes, insurance and utilities on my building and letting you occupy it for free won't help me do that."

"But that place has been vacant for weeks. Don't you want a business in there that can make you money?"

"I'll make money when you pay rent and deposit. I have no desire to let you take advantage of me, or be part of your pyramid scheme. Now, if you'll excuse me, I need to get back to work."

"What was that all about?" Audra asked as Val headed to the kitchen to check on orders and defuse her anger. "They were interested in renting your building, right?"

"Yeah, but they changed their mind."

The women's brash proposal wasn't the most outlandish proposition she had ever heard but today wasn't a good day for it. She had been respectful, for the most part, and hadn't raised her voice but she needed a few minutes to calm herself. Marsha and Tess weren't worth the headache that threatened to consume her.

"Val?" Audra said, sticking her head through the door to the kitchen. "That woman is back again."

"Who?" Val asked then chugged the last of her reheated coffee.

"Susan." Audra shrugged.

"Why do you refer to her as 'that woman'? She's a very pleasant person." Val wanted to add that she was still getting to know Susan Castle and understand her idiosyncrasies but that was none of Audra's business.

"Isn't she the woman who refused to pay Jackson for the pizza order?"

"No. She's the woman Jackson tried to coerce into paying for a pizza order she didn't make. And from what I understand, he wasn't very polite about it." Val hurried into the dining room.

Susan was sitting in a booth, on her phone. "Did you test the code?" she said, scowling slightly. "No. The new one. Well, when you complete that, then give me a call. I think you'll find the problem yourself."

Val approached the table when she ended her call. "Hello, again." She smiled down at her but instantly noticed a strange, almost worrisome look on Susan's face. "How are you this evening? Everything okay?"

"Why would you think there's anything wrong?" Susan asked as the wrinkles on her forehead deepened.

"No reason," Val said hurriedly. "Can I get you something to drink while you look over the menu? Ice water with lemon? How about a glass of that sauvignon blanc you had last night?" she offered, hoping to soften whatever had furrowed Susan's brow.

"I have a proposal for you," Susan said and folded her hands on the table.

"You want me to be your date to avoid a blind date?" Val asked with a crooked grin.

"Okay, I probably had that coming. Can we please get past that fiasco?"

"Sure. What did you need?"

"I want to trade services, so to speak."

"Trade what services?"

"You are without a vehicle, correct? At least temporarily."

"Yes, but I'm hopeful it won't take too long."

"I have a spare I'd like to offer until repairs are completed on your car. I know I can trust you. I've checked, and you have an excellent driving record. It seems like a win-win situation."

"How is it a win-win situation? How is it a win situation for you?"

"I was getting to that." Susan cleared her throat as if preparing how to proceed. "While you have use of a vehicle and won't require hiring an Uber, I was hoping I could ask a favor, a trade for services, as it were." She seemed nervous, as if what she was about to ask was presumptuous, something she might regret asking.

"Okay?" Val said cautiously.

"As Jillian so succinctly put it, my kitchen is far beyond my abilities. I was wondering if you'd consider teaching me how to cook. Perhaps an Italian pasta dinner. I'm having a dinner meeting at my house for several friends in a few weeks. I'd like to cook an authentic Italian dinner for them. I don't want to open a box of spaghetti and dump sauce over it. I know that's the normal thing to do and my friends probably wouldn't know the difference but I would. To be honest, I am not domesticated. At all. In any way. Cooking is *not* part of my skill set." Susan turned a worried look on Val. "It doesn't have to be a complicated menu. I know the easy thing to do would be to have the meal catered, which I have done before. Or buy a stack of takeout meals from Nardi's. But I want to do this myself. That's if you think I can master it in one or two lessons. I'll buy whatever groceries we'd need." The more Susan explained what she wanted, the more deeply furrowed her brow became.

Val couldn't help herself and chuckled at how serious Susan seemed with the idea.

"So you want me to teach you how to cook a spaghetti dinner to impress your friends and in exchange I can use your car?"

"Yes. Actually, it's a truck. But I don't need to impress my friends. I doubt a bunch of my colleagues are going to be impressed by spaghetti and sauce, I don't care who makes it or how good it is. They'll all be stuffing food in their face with one hand while tapping on their phones and iPads with the other and asking whose interface they're using. And you may use my truck whether you have the time and inclination to teach me or not."

"Learning how to cook pasta isn't hard. Timing is the big thing." Val smiled and added, "You're a smart woman. I'm sure one lesson will be sufficient. I'll write out a recipe so you'll have it for reference. Take it one step at a time and you'll be preparing pasta like an expert in no time." Val patted her arm. "Trust me. It will be *bellissimo*," she said, pinching the air. "*Eccellente.*"

"I trust you. It's me in a kitchen I don't trust. In case you haven't guessed, I'm intimidated by the complexity of meal preparation. I have an automatic coffee maker and it's smarter than I am. I dump in the beans, set a cup under the spigot and press the button. Granola is simply poured in a bowl with milk so my breakfast requires little skill."

"Can you follow a simple recipe?"

"I'd like to think I could follow a linear sequence, assuming the algorithm is presented with adequate data," Susan replied thoughtfully.

"Algorithm? What the holy heck is an algorithm?"

"A recipe. Well, almost. An algorithm requires things be done in a specific sequence. Most recipes are lists of ingredients without being order specific. Add, stir, and hope for the best, right?"

"No. Not always. Well, sometimes, maybe. But if you're worried, I'll be as specific as I can."

"I'll do my best not to disappoint." Susan seemed dead serious.

"I'm sure you couldn't. Start with small batches. When you feel comfortable, repeat the process, increasing until you have the amount you need."

"Iteration. The process of repeating the steps in an algorithm," Susan said matter-of-factly.

"I never knew making a batch of tagliatelle had anything to do with computer data." Val studied her for a long moment. "Would you be happier if I showed you how to get started?"

"Yes. I would."

"No problem."

"I'll pick you up after work and you can give me a ride home. The truck is yours to use until your car is repaired. How's that? I'll need to know what to order for the cooking instructions."

"You won't need to order anything. You supply the kitchen. I'll take care of the groceries. You have pots and pans I assume. And we'll probably need to schedule this on a Tuesday."

"We'll pick a Tuesday that works for you. Maybe you should give me a list of what you'll need and I'll have it on hand. It's the least I could do since you'll be giving up your time to teach me how to do this."

"Susan, if you have even the basic kitchen utensils, it'll be fine. Relax. I don't need anything special. By the way, I want you to know you don't have to lend me your truck. I'd show you how to make pasta anyway. We'll consider that you already paid for the cooking lessons with that gift card you left on the table last night." Val scowled at her. "I wish you hadn't done that. But thank you."

"I have no idea what you're talking about," Susan said with a cheeky grin.

"You better behave yourself, Dr. Castle, or you'll be feeding your friends ragu over Great Value penne pasta." She wagged a finger at her.

"And they'd probably enjoy it." They both chuckled. "My friends are as culinarily challenged as I am."

"We're going to fix that." Val winked. "What can I bring you to eat? Calzone? Salad? Something adventuresome?"

"I've already eaten but what was that cake thing you gave me the other day? It had layers and chocolate dusted on top."

"Tiramisu?"

"Yes. I think that's what it was."

"Great dessert choice. One tiramisu coming up."

Val went to get it. She delivered a large piece with two strawberries on the side.

"That looks good," Susan said, smiling down at the generous serving.

"Enjoy," Val said, leaving to serve newly seated customers. She stopped and came back to the table. Placed her hand on Susan's arm and said quietly, "Thank you." She swallowed the emotion in her voice over an act that seemed so healing to her heart. Tears pillowed in her eyes over Susan's generosity. "I'm not sure how to express how much I appreciate your offer. I didn't look forward to Ubering to work for a week or two. I hope it won't be that long but they couldn't promise how long it would take to get the parts for older cars."

"You're welcome," Susan said, looking down at Val's hand on her arm. "I'm glad I can help."

Val hesitated then leaned down and kissed Susan on the cheek, whispered another thank-you through a quiver in her voice, then headed across the dining room. She knew Susan probably preferred she hadn't done it, but she couldn't help herself.

The restaurant became busy for over an hour as was normal for a Friday evening. Val had been on the clock for nine hours and she was ready to go home. It was nearly eight. She had no idea if Susan was punctual or not so she planned to work until she appeared or at least texted that she was on her way.

"Val?" Audra called from the podium where she was reviewing the schedule. "Can you work a little later this evening?"

"How late?"

"Probably until close. Owen's sick and left early. Joe might need your help in the kitchen."

"Can't, Audra." Val noticed pickup truck headlights pulling into the parking lot. It was precisely eight o'clock, on the dot.

"Why not? What have you got planned?"

"I've been here nine hours and there's my ride." She pointed toward the white truck parking near the door. "And before you ask, Susan Castle is my ride. She's offered to lend me her extra vehicle while my car is being repaired. And since Jackson refused to offer me a ride this evening, I took her up on it."

"Couldn't you have her come back in a couple of hours?" Audra frowned.

"She needed to do this transfer at eight o'clock and I'm not keeping her waiting." Val took off her apron, collected her tote bag and a to-go box.

"Early shift tomorrow," Audra called to her, as if getting in the last word.

"Yep," Val agreed and headed out the door.

Susan reached over and opened the passenger door for her.

"Sorry I kept you waiting," Val said, climbing in.

"I've only been here two minutes."

Susan's truck was immaculate. The dashboard, upholstery and floorboards looked pristine and showroom fresh, but for three charging cables leading from the console. Val assumed that it was, indeed, brand new.

"How was your evening?" Susan asked, pulling out of the parking lot.

"Busy. Yours?"

"I'm sure not as hectic as yours. I understand food service workers are occasionally subjected to customers expecting all sorts of preferential treatment. I imagine that makes your work even harder."

Val chuckled. "After a while you develop thick skin and learn to ignore it. Some people can't be pleased, no matter what you do for them."

"I think that's true in most service industries." Susan leaned back in the seat and steered with two fingers. "You seem to handle yourself well in most situations."

"I try. There's always a few who try to push my buttons."

"What does it take to push your buttons? For future reference, of course? Nontippers?"

"That's one of them but I usually don't know they stiffed me until after they leave. It's the ones who walk the check that really bug me. That's out-and-out theft. People who dine and dash usually order expensive items and several drinks." Val chuckled. "If Joe catches them, they always claim they forgot then get all huffy and say they're never coming back. He has a sign on the wall by the front door that says we reserve the right to refuse service to anyone. And he means it. He won't let the servers follow them into the parking lot. We're not allowed to confront them."

"Protective big brother?"

"That and it's something to do with being sued."

"I don't think you should confront them either. Some desperate jerk is liable to take out his frustrations on you." Susan gave her a cautionary glance.

"Like this?" Val revealed a small scar on the back of her hand.

Susan gasped. "A customer did that?"

"Yeah, but she was drunk."

"She?"

"Yep. She didn't understand why she wasn't allowed to walk out with a glass of wine. She threw it at me, glass and all. She's now on our do not serve list."

"I'd think so." Susan frowned.

Susan turned in to her drive, pulled up to the house and climbed out. Val followed.

"You'll need these." She took a keyring from the cupholder and handed it to Val. "I just assumed you can drive a pickup?"

"It's not much different from a SUV." Val looked back across the driveway toward the garage. "Where is said truck I'll be driving?"

"You're standing next to it," Susan said, lifting her briefcase out of the back seat. She left the driver's door open and motioned for Val to climb in.

"*This?*" Val exclaimed with wide eyes.

"I said you'd be driving a truck. This is a truck." She couldn't hide a chuckle.

"Yes, I know. But this is…" Val hesitated, not sure what to say as she scanned the vehicle. This was not what she expected.

"It's a Toyota Tacoma four-passenger. Normally there's a bike rack in the bed but I removed it. I didn't think you needed it. The tank is full. It uses regular unleaded. There's only three hundred miles on the oil change so you're good to go. If you have any problems, let me know."

"Susan, you're letting me use your new pickup truck?" Val stared at her in disbelief.

"It isn't new, per se."

"Darn close." She looked it up and down.

"Your coach awaits, m'lady." Susan waved her in with a smile.

"Here, this is for you." Val handed Susan the to-go box as she continued to survey the truck. "It's not much but I thought you could microwave it for your dinner sometime. You can pop it in the freezer for later if you prefer."

"What is it?"

"Fettucine bolognese. It's wide noodles with a special meat sauce. Sprinkle parmesan cheese on top after you reheat it."

"Thank you." Susan sniffed the box. "It smells fantastic."

Susan showed Val the automatic adjustment levers and mirror controls, how to connect her phone and use the CarPlay and Bluetooth, accessories Val's older Subaru didn't have. Val enjoyed her help, enjoyed her occasionally leaning over her to demonstrate. Susan was so consumed with explaining the tech features of her truck she didn't realize her hand was touching Val's knee or thigh. Susan was in her element clarifying every detail.

It wasn't until Val was halfway home that she wondered what Susan was going to drive if this was a spare vehicle. The entire drive home was a mix of glee over how generous this was and guilt over using her truck. She had to admit, the glee was winning out.

CHAPTER NINETEEN

Val drove the truck to work and parked it in a secure corner spot. She carefully locked it, rechecked the door handle and wiped her hand over a smudge on the fender before heading inside to clock in. As she expected, Joe had heard the news and came to the back door to see what she was given to drive.

"Nice wheels," he said, grinning at the shiny white truck.

"And very generous of Susan to allow me to use it."

"Have you heard how long you'll need it?"

"The service manager says he's still waiting on parts."

"Val, can you work a double today?" Audra asked, standing next to her and squeezing her arm. "Did you hear? Jolene may have Covid."

"No, I didn't hear. Is she sick?" Val offered a worried frown. She couldn't stop the sudden rush of anguish that washed over her. It was moments like this that she was powerless to avoid.

"Evidently. She called in and was coughing like crazy."

"She already had it once; didn't she?"

"Yeah, early on. So, can you cover her shift?"

Val heaved a resolute sigh. "I can cover her late shift but I'll need an hour or so around two. I've got an errand I have to run."

"What errand?" Audra asked, as if it was any of her business.

"I need to stop by my insurance agent's office to drop off the police report and sign something. Then I promised to deliver a few groceries to Nana. I told her I'd be there today."

"Could you do that tomorrow morning?"

"The car repairs will be held in limbo until I sign this. And I promised her I'd come by. She's counting on me so I'm doing it today. It's either two o'clock for an hour or so or I'll do it after my shift at five and not work a double." Val raised her eyebrows, waiting for Audra's reply.

"Okay. Two o'clock but try not to be gone too long."

Val worked continuously from eleven until nearly two. It had started to rain when she trotted out to the truck, wishing she had brought an umbrella so she wouldn't drip on the upholstery. She made a quick stop at her insurance agent's office then headed for the assisted living facility. She had just turned in to the parking lot when her phone rang on the CarPlay. She could see it was Susan calling but it took a few rings before she figured out how to answer.

"Well, hello there. Is this the Castle Rental Service?" she said happily, hoping she'd done it correctly and didn't delete the caller.

"It depends. What kind of service are you and your chariot requiring? Problems?" Susan queried.

"I don't have a darn thing to complain about. I'm a happy camper. Although I'm sorry to report your pretty white truck is getting rained on."

"It's happened before, believe me. And it'll dry." Susan offered a little chuckle.

"I promise I'll wash it before I return it to you."

"Why? That's not necessary. I can deal with a dirty truck."

"I'll return it clean and with a full tank of gas, exactly like I got it," Val said sternly.

Susan chuckled even more loudly. "Don't worry about it, Val. Really. I only have a few minutes before I'm due on a video call but I wanted to thank you for the fettucine bolognese. It was very nice."

"You're welcome. I thought you might like it."

"I assume you aren't at the restaurant."

"Actually, I'm pulling into the parking lot to deliver groceries to my grandmother."

"Your grandmother lives in Bonney Lake?"

"In the Prairie Ridge Assisted Living Facility. Did you need something? I promised Audra I'd be back within an hour."

"Then just a quick question. Could fettuccine bolognese be the pasta dish I serve my colleagues at the dinner meeting?"

"Sure. It's a little more time consuming than simple marinara but it's doable. I'll create a readable algorithm. Isn't that what you called a recipe?"

"Absolutely. Algorithm. Very good, Ms. Nardi."

"Did you have another question?"

"Possibly. We may need to change the projected timetable for the dinner meeting and food preparation."

"I didn't know we settled on a specific date other than probably a Tuesday," Val said with a smile.

"Val, can I call you back? My video chat is incoming and I need to take it."

"Sure."

Susan ended the call, the sound of voices in the background.

The few minutes she had been on the phone were enough for the light rain to increase to a full-fledged downpour. Val gathered the three plastic sacks of groceries and rushed inside, hunching her shoulders as she scurried into the lobby. She could smell the remnants of lunch lingering in the air. Fish sticks usually announced their presence on the menu. Not as much as sauerkraut but still noticeable.

"Hello, Nana Nardi," she said, tapping her knuckles on the open door. "Why is your door open?" She came in to give her grandmother a kiss on the cheek.

"Because I spilled pickle juice on the floor and it stinks. Hello, sweetheart." She reached up and took Val's face in her hands, smiling lovingly at her.

Val saw several paper towels soaking up a wet spot on the floor by the sink. She set the groceries on the small kitchen counter and squatted to finish mopping up the spill.

"There, all clean." She washed the remnants of the pickle juice from her hands.

"Thank you, honey. I was going to finish that but I needed to catch my breath first."

"No problem. I got you some of that sourdough bread you like. Nice and fresh."

Val helped her grandmother unpack the groceries and put them away, surprising her with a few goodies she knew she enjoyed. "Can I fix you some tea and a slice of this sourdough?" she offered. Her grandmother seemed a little tired and did occasionally skip lunch in the dining room in favor of a nap.

"You know, I would like that." She patted Val's arm then sat down in her chair to wait. It only took a few minutes but Val was satisfied Grandma Nardi had had a little nosh and some of her favorite cinnamon spice tea to get her through the afternoon.

"Are you feeling okay, sweetheart?" Val squatted in front of her and placed her hands on Grandma's knees. "You look tired. Are you sleeping okay?"

"Yes, I'm fine. Sometimes I think I sleep too much. I have things to do and don't seem to find time for them. I promised Rachel Pelletier I'd finish crocheting that baby blanket for the nurse in physical therapy and I need to get back to that. They want beige with tan trim. They said it's the new unisex colors. Who knew?" she chuckled. "What happened to green or yellow?"

"Times are changing." Val smiled reflectively. "I still have the one you made for me in my bottom drawer. Pale yellow cable knit."

"I remember you used to stick your chubby little fingers through the holes then suck them."

"No wonder some of the holes are so stretched out." Val laughed.

"And so you know, there's a sage green one all finished and folded in a box in the closet for Vinnie and Megan's little addition. Yes, I'm not blind. I know she's expecting. But you know my preference on that," she said with a stern look.

"I know and so do they. You want things to happen in the proper order."

"Am I being old-fashioned when I say that?" Nana asked warily.

"Nope. Not at all." Val knew Vinnie and Megan would do things in their own sweet time regardless of Grandma's preference or suggestion. So what if they married on their child's graduation or twentieth birthday. It was their choice. Val saw no need to tell her that. "I'm sure they'll love the baby blanket, especially coming from you."

"Val, are you eating enough? You look thinner," she said, her gaze concerned.

"Sure. And no, I'm not thinner." She laughed. "I wish. I'm still the same." She wasn't sure what her weight was but her clothes fit the same. She was and had been size twelve for years, although gravity was playing cruel tricks on her figure. Saying she looked thinner was probably her grandmother's way of showing love and care.

"Have a little more pasta, honey." She pinched the air. "Put cheese on it and enjoy."

"I will," she said, standing up and smiling at her. "But now I need to get back to work. Audra will be looking for me."

"Don't let that woman run your life, Val," she said with a tiny scowl. "Don't let her."

"She doesn't." She swept a stray lock of hair across Grandma's forehead. "They're a little short-handed today and I promised to help out. I think I'll be cooking the pasta this evening." She grinned, knowing Grandma Nardi would approve.

"Good for you. You are a good cook. You've always been the best pasta cook in the family. Joseph is good but you're better. He's always in a hurry. Doing a lot of things halfway isn't the same as doing a few things well." She patted Val's cheek. "Remember, al dente. It means 'to the tooth' you know."

"Yes. I remember you telling me." She kissed Nana's hand and clutched it against her face lovingly. "I'll see you in a few days. Are you coming in for the fundraiser? It won't be a turkey dinner for Thanksgiving but Joe says it will be good."

"I don't know, sweetheart. I'll see how I feel. I'm sure it will be crowded."

"It usually is, yes. We've got dozens of reservations. But we'd love to have you there. So will your friends." Val tried to sound encouraging but she wouldn't force the issue. When Joe changed from a family Thanksgiving dinner at the restaurant to a fundraiser to benefit the Wounded Warriors charity was when Grandma Nardi had withdrawn enthusiastic attendance. She loved her family, enjoyed the holidays with them, but the event became too chaotic and she wasn't above saying so. "If you need a ride and want to come join us, give me a call. But it's completely up to you, sweetheart."

Grandma tossed her a kiss then waved. Val headed back to work, knowing the ninety minutes she had been gone would raise a barrage of comments from Audra. It wouldn't be a day at Nardi's without her complaints about something. Today Val would be on the receiving end of her rant but it wouldn't last long and within a few minutes everything would be hunky-dory again. Audra was like a teakettle. Every now and then she needed to let off a little steam to keep from exploding. She meant well. That's what Val told herself yet again.

CHAPTER TWENTY

"Hey, there, Val," Jackson said, standing at the counter dipping a breadstick in a little dish of pasta sauce.

"Hi, Jackson. I like the haircut."

"Mom said I look stupid." He groaned, took a bite then dipped again.

"What do they call that? A mohawk?"

"Mohawk fade," he said proudly.

"Well, it looks nice and neat on the sides. But I'll keep my ponytail," she joked.

He stepped closer, and looked around to see who was watching. "Say, Val?" He popped the last bite in his mouth and wiped his hands on his jeans.

"Yeah?" She continued to assemble the tray of plates, referring to the ticket for order details.

"So you're driving that white Toyota Tacoma in the parking lot?"

"Yes. They're having trouble locating parts for my car. If I had a newer model I'd probably have it back already," she grumbled disgustedly.

"Too bad no one saw the creep who hit you."

"No kidding. Hand me that shaker of pepper flakes, please?" She pointed over his shoulder.

He handed it to her then took another step closer. "Nice-looking truck." He was after something and Val had a good idea what. "Automatic? Dad's isn't, you know."

"Yes." She adjusted the plates on the tray so she didn't have to make two trips. She was an old hand at being efficient and conserving steps.

"Are you working through dinner tonight?" He followed her down the line as she prepared to hoist the tray over her shoulder.

"Yes, Jackson. I'm working until nine and no, you can't." She lifted the tray, tossed him a don't-bother-to-ask glare and headed to the dining room.

"What? I didn't say anything."

When she returned, he was waiting, a twenty-dollar bill in hand. "I'll pay you," he quickly offered, holding out the money. "One trip. Please?"

"No, Jackson. You may not drive Susan Castle's truck. You drive your own car."

"Oh, come on, Val. What's the harm? I'll be careful. She'll never know." Jackson had launched into whiny mode, something he had perfected at an early age and one she found childish and annoying.

"No." She returned the tray to the counter, ready to carry three personal pan pizzas to the men having a coach's meeting. "And in case you forgot, you were rude and disrespectful to her. I'm sure she'd say you're absolutely not allowed to drive her truck after how you treated her."

"I wasn't rude," he argued.

"You not only wanted her to pay for something she didn't order, you insisted on a tip. I would have slammed the door in your face." Val turned to face him, a hand on her hip. "And you owe her an apology, Jackson. You're an adult. You can't go around acting like that. It's immature and it's unprofessional."

"Hey, I didn't drive all the freaking way out there for nothing. She could have at least given me a few bucks for gas."

"She didn't owe you squat. Nardi's mistake wasn't her responsibility. It's one of those things you accept in business and move on. You don't try to find someone to blame. Now, why don't you go deliver pizza and try to be polite about it." Ignoring his angry stare, she went back to work.

"What was that all about?" Joe asked her as he transferred a large pizza from the oven to a serving tray.

"The usual Jackson being Jackson."

"That's nothing new." Joe laughed. He adjusted his eye patch and the strap around the back of his head.

"Val, how about running an errand?" Audra said. She was reading down what looked like a grocery list.

"Walmart or Costo?" she asked, checking what was next to be served.

"Neither. Seattle. Pike Place Market." She said it as if it was no big deal. She ignored Val's wide-eyed stare.

"You're kidding? Again?" The last shopping trip to Pike Place Market Audra had sent her on took over an hour each way. By the end of the day she was lugging two heavy canvas tote bags full of tediously specific grocery items. She didn't mind helping out occasionally but Audra's idea of a running an errand to downtown Seattle was often more of a punishment than a reward.

"We'll pay you plus gas, lunch and parking. I don't have time to do this myself."

"Not to mention you hate going to Pike Place Market," Val said, rubbing Audra's arm teasingly.

"Well, there is that," Audra muttered. "So, we can discuss it?" she called after Val as she headed to the dining room with the order.

When Val returned to the kitchen, she told Audra apologetically, "I'm not sure I can do it. I don't have my car back yet. Can you wait a week or so?"

"No, I need it done tomorrow," she said, adding a couple of items to her list. "And you've got that woman's truck while you wait for your car."

"I'm not sure she'd want me driving it all over downtown

Seattle. I have no intention of taking advantage of her generosity. Did you want me to take your car?" Val knew the answer to that even before it came out of her mouth. Audra didn't give up her car easily. It was her baby. Her escape when stress overwhelmed her. It didn't happen often but occasionally she found an excuse to get away, even for a few minutes. Knowing the trials and tribulations of restaurant ownership, parenting, and being married to a very demanding ex-military officer, Val understood that Audra's anxiety level dictated her mood. Joe seemed to understand it as well. If Audra grabbed her keys, shot a fire-breathing dragon stare across the kitchen and stormed out the back door, it was best to say nothing and wait her out. She'd be back in twenty minutes or so, usually with a Starbucks coffee cup in hand and a smile on her face, ready to resume her duties.

"Call her," Audra insisted. "Ask if it's okay to go grocery shopping with her truck. I'm sure she'll say it's perfectly fine. Ask her."

Val gave Audra a stern look, deciding how to respond. She could use a day off, even if it was a day off in Seattle shopping. Would Susan mind? Maybe. Maybe not. She was certainly going to ask first and not assume.

"I'll check with Susan but if she says no, please don't argue, okay? I don't suppose you could ask Jackson to do this?"

"Yeah, right, Val," Audra scoffed and rolled her eyes. "Ask her. It'll be fine. Why would she care if you buy groceries at Walmart in Bonney Lake or DeLaurenti in Seattle? Want me to call her?"

"Absolutely not. I'll ask and you will accept her answer." Val carried the family-size pizza to the dining room, glad to have a diversion. It also offered a chance to decide how to best word her conversation with Susan so she didn't sound presumptuous or juvenile. She stepped out the back door for a breath of fresh air and a moment of privacy to call her.

"Hello," Susan said happily, picking up on the fourth ring. "How's the truck person?"

"She's well. At least as well as she can be after spilling a dish of pasta sauce on the floor then stepping in it."

"Sounds bad."

"Fortunately, my shoes are washable. I'm not bothering you, am I? Are you in a meeting or something important?"

"No. No meeting. I was rewriting a line of code for the fifth time. And it may require a couple more versions." Susan released a groan. "Good place for a break. What did you need?"

"Audra asked me to run an errand for the restaurant and it has everything to do with you and your truck."

"I'm listening."

"Some specialty items we can't get from our supplier— they're in Seattle at the Pike Place Market. She's asked me to go up there and it would mean me driving your truck into downtown Seattle. Traffic can be a little hectic and there's always road construction."

"Seattle traffic isn't my favorite place to drive either but I'm happy for you to do whatever errands you need to do. Any trouble, there's a copy of my insurance in the glove box in the black folder. When are you planning this little sojourn?"

"Tomorrow."

Val walked across the parking lot, putting more space between her and the back door to the kitchen as she felt a lump rise in her throat. "I hate having to ask."

"Why?"

"I hate not having my own car and being in charge." she said, her voice cracking. "I'm used to doing for myself. I don't want to take advantage of anyone and especially you. You've been so sweet. I hate having to ask this. This Covid thing has taken away so much." *You have no idea how much for me.* "I know, I know, restrictions are easing but it's not the same. At least not yet. And I hate it."

"Val, I understand," Susan said in a reassuring tone. "I do. I know what you're saying. It's been a rough time for everyone. You don't need to apologize. I'm very glad I'm the one to offer assistance. You are *not* taking advantage of me. It's a truck. A lump of metal and plastic used to transport people and possessions from point A to point B. I told you I have an extra vehicle. Drive to Seattle or Portland or Timbuktu. You have my permission."

Val took a replenishing breath, hoping the insecurity in her voice had faded. Susan Castle was a new friend at best but somehow Val trusted her with these fragile feelings. She may regret it later but for now, she was relieved to admit it to someone.

"I'll do my best to return your pretty white truck unscathed and unscratched."

"Tomorrow, huh?" Susan said reflectively. "I'm still waiting to hear but I may be in the area myself. I have a meeting with a client about a new app. Or rather revisions to an existing app that has been updated so many times it's barely recognizable from the original. But I have every reason to think he'll cancel again. Reliability isn't his forte."

"I plan to be at the market by ten. Earlier if traffic allows. The earlier I get there, the earlier I get out of there. I love shopping the market but when I'm on a mission it isn't as much fun."

"I hope you enjoy your outing and I'll be available if you need to call." Her voice took on a teasing note. "After all, I need to protect my interests. You're my cooking instructor. I don't want anything to happen to you."

"Oh, right." Val laughed. "And I planned on picking up a few things for the bolognese."

Audra opened the door and waved Val back inside, impatience on her face.

"I need to pay you for anything you're getting for my dinner meeting," Susan insisted.

"It's not that big a deal. It's a few spices I routinely keep on hand anyway. Have you decided when you'd like to schedule our cooking seminar?"

"Not yet. I'll let you know. Soon, hopefully. I need to finalize who all is coming to the dinner meeting. Getting a firm commitment is like herding squirrels. Too many people with too many irons in the fire. They keep insisting we do this meeting but when I try to pin them down they scatter like cockroaches when the lights come on."

"Susan, I need to get back to work but thanks again. I really appreciate your understanding."

"No problem. I'm glad Castle Car Service can be of assistance."

Val heaved a relieved sigh, happy with Susan's help and generosity and looking forward to a day at Pike Place Market.

CHAPTER TWENTY-ONE

Val pulled into the multilevel parking garage behind Pike Place Market in downtown Seattle. It wasn't her favorite place to park. It was crowded, expensive and the tight parking spaces made her nervous. More than once on previous visits she had noticed a small scrape on her car door or a tiny dent where someone obviously whacked their door into hers. And maneuvering Susan's pickup truck added an extra layer of stress. Life in the big city, she told herself. But she couldn't deny that she enjoyed an occasional trip to the market even if it was more of a chore than pure pleasure. And with Audra's offer to pay all expenses, how could she say no? But when her tote bags weighed down both shoulders, she'd probably be rethinking that assumption.

She rode the elevator up to the market level, ready to fight the crowd of tourists and fill the canvas bags. The list Audra handed her included specialty herbs and spices and a gallon of Joe's favorite truffle oil.

But first she decided to look around. She loved to smell the floral bouquets, drool over the goodies in the bakery windows, soak in the charm of the market before she loaded herself down with purchases. Maybe a little lunch from her favorite seafood stall was a possibility.

As she guessed from the crowded parking garage and the clogged elevator to street level, Pike Place Market was teeming with customers, many of them obviously tourists taking pictures of the market and the ferry boats crossing Puget Sound. Families with children in tow, wide-eyed seniors wearing hats, and foreign speaking couples thoughtlessly stopped in the middle of the walkway to point, stare and take a selfie. More than once Val barely caught herself before bumping into someone when they stopped right in front of her.

An older, tiny Japanese woman with a weathered complexion, her dark hair pulled back into a bun, stood behind a table. She wore a floral smock and green yoga pants. She was wrapping green tissue paper around a luscious bundle of dahlias and mums, one of many such bouquets along the table standing in metal buckets. When she saw Val she waved and broadcast a big smile.

"Hello, Val," she said with bubbling enthusiasm.

"Hi, Hanna." Val had to wait for the crowd to thin so she could dart across to her. "How are you, hon? How is your husband? Has he recovered from surgery?"

"Yes, he is much better. He should be back to work in a week or two." She nodded as if she appreciated Val had asked.

"Oh, my. Aren't those gorgeous?" Val declared, leaning down to smell the blooms.

"For you, Ms. Val." Hanna held them out to Val and smiled warmly. "Special colors for my friend."

Val took another long, deep whiff, closing her eyes as she enjoyed the sweet aroma.

"Thank you, Hanna. That is sweet of you but I can't." Val patted the large empty tote bags slung over her shoulder. "Shopping trip. I'd hate for them to get squashed. But they are beautiful, as always."

Hanna frowned dramatically and continued to wrap the paper tightly around the stems, knowing that Val wasn't being rude by refusing the flowers. By the end of her shopping trip there would be no room for an arrangement of flowers, regardless of how sturdy the blooms were. But Hanna always offered.

She pulled one small purple bloom from the bouquet and handed it to Val, smiling warmly. "One for my friend."

"Oh, Hanna. Thank you," Val declared and bowed. "I love it." She sniffed it then affixed it to the tote bag. "You're a sweetie."

"Take care of yourself, Ms. Val."

"You, too. And your husband."

Val meandered up the arcade of stalls, booths and tables, window shopping as she called it. She stopped to examine a vendor's selection of handmade jewelry. She didn't need any more jewelry but she liked to look. Her taste was simple. Plain gold loop earrings or perhaps silver studs with her birthstone, anything with an amethyst. But it was fun to imagine a pair of dangly French hooks with feathers and beads hanging from her ears and tickling her neck. She was admiring a pair of earrings with spiral copper wires suspended from a tiny piece of driftwood when she thought she heard her name. She looked back up the sidewalk.

"Val Nardi?" the voice called. A hand rose above the crowd. "Val?"

Susan stood near the entrance to the market, her tall figure statuesque in charcoal gray slacks, a black leather jacket and black ankle boots. Business professional was the first description that popped into Val's mind.

"Hey!" Val called and waved. It was like swimming upstream to cross to where she stood. "Can I assume you had your meeting?"

"Yes. Just finished."

"First of all, how can you have a business meeting without a briefcase, backpack or something large and cumbersome?" She hooked an arm through Susan's and led her out of the stream of traffic.

Susan immediately pulled a small zipper pouch from her pocket. "This. It's my brief, briefcase," she declared with a coy smile. "Everything I needed is on a couple of flash drives."

"Very clever. I wish I could get everything I need in one of those. By the way, how in the world did you see me through this sea of humanity?"

"Actually—" Susan started but quickly stepped aside as a delivery man wheeled a hand-truck piled high with boxes toward them. "I saw you get out of the elevator from the parking garage. I almost caught up with you at the flower lady but I was cut off by a kamikaze salmon."

Val laughed and said, "Yeah, you have to watch out for the flying fish. They're harder to catch than you think. One of the guys let me try it once."

"Did you catch it?"

"What do you think?" Val mused, again hooking her arm through Susan's as another delivery man hurried past.

"You don't look like you've done much shopping. Were they out of what you needed?"

"I haven't started shopping yet. I wanted to look around first before I get weighted down with stuff." She unzipped her jacket and adjusted the empty bags up over her shoulder, knowing full well they would be pulling at her soon enough. She noticed the top of her blouse was being pulled open slightly, straining against the top buttons.

"I like your shirt," Susan said, seemingly struggling with where to allow her eyes to go.

"It looks nice with your tan slacks."

"Thank you. A Christmas gift from my grandmother. She loves blue, any shade. She thought it was whimsical." She noticed Susan had finally allowed her gaze to hesitate at the top of her blouse. There was nothing lewd or invasive about it. More appreciative and respectful.

A commotion from the sidewalk across the street came from equipment being unpacked from the back of a van by two men in their twenties and one in his fifties, all of them in faded jeans and matching black T-shirts with red dragons on the front. They were setting up musical instruments, small amplifiers and a microphone. A cowboy hat to receive tips was strategically placed upside down in plain sight with a card that read THANKS.

"Oh, look. A street band," Val declared with delight. "Let's watch for a minute. What do you say?" She waved Susan to follow as she stepped off the curb to dart between the traffic.

"Wait!" Susan shouted and yanked her back just in time as a delivery truck backed out of a parking spot.

"I didn't see him."

"Look next time," Susan demanded and scowled. "It's fine that we listen to the music so long as you don't walk out in front of trucks."

The band started playing something with a Latin flavor and the crowd thickened. Even more people pushed their way onto the sidewalk when the song changed to a rhythmic vintage rock and roll song. A man with a child perched on his shoulders moved forward, bumping Val to the side. Another gawker bumped her from the other side. Off balance, she immediately felt hands on her shoulders, steadying her.

"I didn't know watching street performers was a contact sport," Val joked, and reached up and patted Susan's hand on her shoulder.

Susan kept her hands on Val's shoulders as the crowd continued to grow and push forward. Susan held her ground, her hands firmly in place to discourage being bumped apart. Val occasionally felt Susan's leg muscles against the back of her own, pulsing in time with the music and her fingers rippling on Val's shoulder.

Susan stood close enough and was tall enough Val was sure she could see over her shoulders. And down her shirt. If those top two buttons should pop open, Susan had an unobstructed view down her cleavage. The feel of Susan's warm breath on her cheek told her that she'd availed herself of that view. Val smiled and didn't move. In spite of the growing crowd, they remained until a dark cloud drifted overhead and began to drizzle.

"Are you going to stand in the rain to listen?" Susan asked, releasing her hold on Val's shoulders as the crowd began to disperse. She dropped a couple of bills in the cowboy hat and nodded her approval to the band.

"I think I'm good to go," Val said. "Come on. I'll buy us a shrimp cocktail from my favorite fish stall. It's one of my must-do things when I'm here."

They headed down the sidewalk, dodging the crowd of shoppers. Val ducked into a walkway and stepped up to a counter.

"They have great fish and chips but it's the shrimp cocktail I come for."

"I'm game," Susan said, quickly pulling out a money clip before Val could pay.

"Hey." Val frowned deeply. "This is my treat."

"Next time." Susan grinned dismissively.

They ate their shrimp standing up since the row of a dozen stools were all occupied.

Susan stabbed a bite of shrimp and swirled it around the puddle of sauce. "May I ask a personal question? How long have you worked for your brother? You mentioned he hired you when restrictions forced you to close your commercial cleaning company."

It was such a beautiful, joyful day—and she chose not to cloud it by telling Susan about the loss of Kate. "He had to suspend in-house dining, and home deliveries were his only option if he wanted Nardi's to survive. Jackson was barely old enough to drive so I stepped in to help." Val heaved a soulful sigh. This was a painful subject in so many ways and one that still raised a lump in her throat. "I owe him a great deal. It was touch-and-go for nearly two years. We worked long hours with little pay and minimal profits but Nardi's survived."

"Sounds like a testament to perseverance."

"Absolutely. Joe knew what he wanted and we supported him. I'm very proud to be a Nardi's employee."

"Val Nardi, the survivor." Susan smiled proudly. "And speaking of names—"

"We were?" Val chuckled, digging the last tiny shrimp from her cup.

"Yes. Since you know my name and my honorific, may I ask your name? Is your given name actually Val or is that short for Valerie?"

"Well, my honorific is Ms. and my name is Valentine. Valentine Rose Nardi to be exact."

"Valentine? May I assume your birthday has a great deal to do with your given name?"

"You may." Val offered a smile. "My mother went into labor on the thirteenth but she said I held out for a holiday to make my grand entrance." She laughed. "I understand she wasn't happy about it. Being in labor for almost twenty hours must have been gruesome."

Susan laughed as well. "Wow. I can't imagine being in labor at all but twenty hours, yes, gruesome. I hope you apologized profusely. Valentine Rose, huh?"

"Speaking of names, what's your middle name? Dr. Susan what Castle?"

"Ann."

"Dr. Susan Ann Castle."

"It was my mother's name. It's not as lyrical as Valentine Rose but I seldom have to correct the spelling."

"I like it." Val looked her up and down. "You look like a Susan Ann. Modest with strength of character. Unimposing yet confident. Yes, I definitely like it."

"It's a name, Val. It's not a proclamation."

"I know. But I like to analyze names and see if they fit the person." Val dropped her cup in the trash barrel. "Did you like the shrimp cocktail? And thank you, by the way."

"Yes. I enjoyed that. Good suggestion."

"Ready to do some serious shopping or are you heading home?" Val adjusted the bags on her shoulder.

"How serious are we talking?"

"Spices. And fresh herbs to start with. Then tea and some other goodies. I go home loaded down but I enjoy the outing."

Val looked both ways then darted across the street, waving at Susan to keep up as she threaded her way down the covered sidewalk. She was following a few feet behind, repeatedly bumped by those milling down the walkway.

"I don't remember the market being this crowded the last time I was here," she complained.

"You're kidding. It's always like this." Val waited for her to catch up. She suspected Susan had problems with crowds. Lots of people did. Audra preferred Val make these occasional shopping runs to Seattle for this very reason.

They walked along together, occasionally stopping to admire the bouquets of flowers, fresh fruit and handmade crafts. The simple act of strolling the market, enjoying a shrimp cocktail and listening to a street band put a smile on Val's face. Susan might not feel entirely comfortable with the crowds but she hadn't exercised an escape plan. At least not yet.

Val methodically shopped and checked items off her list, filling both tote bags. Susan took one of the bags from her, hoisting it over her shoulder. Val hadn't expected her to offer but it was a kind gesture and she appreciated it. When a group of seniors clogged the aisle, coming between them, Val stopped, waited for them to pass then reached back for Susan's hand.

"How you doing back there?" She pulled her up next to her, Susan only offering slight resistance. "I don't want to lose you in the crowd."

"It's like running with the bulls at Pamplona."

Susan's wrist iPhone jingled insistently.

"Excuse me, Val. I need to take this," she said but held tight to the tote strap when Val reached for it. "Hello, Rick. What did you decide?" she said, holding the watch to her ear so she could hear above the noise in the market. "I can do that. No, I'm still in the area. Give me twenty minutes and I'll be there." She ended the call. "Sorry, Val. But our shopping extravaganza must come to an end. If I don't go back and talk with him now I'll have to drive back up here tomorrow. Are you heading home now?"

"Yes. I don't know about you but I'm exhausted." She reached for the bag again but Susan kept her hand on it.

"Come on. I'll walk you to the truck. This is heavy and I don't mind. Rick needs a few minutes to argue with himself and his team about details before I get there."

Val hooked her arm through Susan's as they walked toward the elevator to the parking garage.

"I have to thank you again for allowing me to use your truck for my shopping adventure. And I want to thank you for your help."

"It was fun. Plus, I learned a few things."

"Let me guess. You're an in and out shopper? Not a browser?"

"I have a list. I secure said items on the list. I pay. I leave."

She held the driver's door while Val climbed in. "Drive carefully. By the way, I enjoyed myself today. It was nice of you to include me in your shopping trip."

"I had fun, too." Val took the flower Hanna had given her from the strap of the bag. It was still aromatic and full. She dropped it in Susan's sack of purchases and smiled. "Bye-bye, Dr. Susan Ann Castle."

"Bye-bye, Valentine Rose Nardi."

CHAPTER TWENTY-TWO

Susan came through the door to the restaurant several days later, dressed smartly in a charcoal gray pinstripe pantsuit. Like always, she was neat and well-groomed and had a confident though reserved look about her. And like always, Val felt underdressed in her presence. "Well, hello, Dr. Castle," Val said brightly. "If you keep showing up randomly, Nardi's is going to think you like Italian food."

"Good evening. And yes, I enjoy Italian cuisine."

Before Val could seat her, Susan pulled her buzzing phone from her pocket and read a text. Then scanned the restaurant. She gave a small resigned sigh.

"Val, I'll be right back." She headed across the room to a far corner where a couple was seated. Val remembered the man as Ryan, Susan's nephew and Connor's dad. She hadn't paid much attention to them since they weren't seated in her section. But it was definitely Ryan. They were drinking large glasses of iced tea and had a plate of fried appetizers between them and a large supreme pizza balanced on a metal pizza rack.

Both people in the booth were in their forties, Ryan in athletic apparel, the woman in a dress at least one size too small, pulled tightly over her ample bosom. Both were large people, the woman more so. His hair was thick and dark. He had a three-day-old beard. His eyes were brown like Susan's but judgmental and accusatory.

"Hello," Susan said, standing at the end of the booth.

"Have a seat," he said, motioning for Susan to sit next to the woman across from him.

"What did you want, Ryan?" She remained standing. "Where's Connor?"

"At a friend's house," the woman said dismissively, then popped a fried bite in her mouth.

"Go ahead, sit down," Ryan insisted. "I need to talk with you a minute."

"About?" She crossed her arms and stared down at him.

"Did you see Uncle Theo finally retired?"

"Yes. Three months ago. His blood pressure was getting to be an issue."

"I thought he was going to keep the business open another year or two. I guess he wimped out," Ryan added bitterly. "He told me he'd find a place for me. I was going to be his assistant. He promised me a job." He pointed to a place next to the woman. "Sit down, Susan. Take a load off. We need to talk."

"What do we need to talk about? And no, I don't want to sit down."

"Can't we be civil? Damn, Susan. I'm trying to get along here."

"I'm guessing whatever you want to talk about has something to do with my funding your financial deficiencies. How much, Ryan?" She said it loudly enough that her voice carried and that seemed to embarrass him.

"Susan," he said, lowering his voice and scowling up at her. "Sit down and let's talk like adults."

Susan reached into her pants pocket and pulled out a money clip. She dropped two hundred-dollar bills on the table and walked away.

"Table or booth?" Val said when Susan came back to the podium. She pulled a menu from the rack, ready to seat her and not wait for Audra.

"Val, I need to talk with you if you have a minute," Susan said, following her to a table. "And yes, that was Connor's parents. Don't ask," she added.

"How about a glass of something refreshing while I get a couple of orders delivered." She nodded to a nearby table of rowdy teenagers and their parents.

"Take all the time you need. I'll sit here and defuse."

Val served two tables of customers and refilled drinks before returning to Susan, carrying a glass of water with fresh lemon wedges.

"Sorry that took so long. Family birthday celebration. And a wedding rehearsal dinner. What can I help you with? Have we got a date for our cooking lesson?"

"Oh, no. It's not about that. I'm still trying to get a firm response on that dinner meeting." Susan reached into her pants pocket and pulled out a key ring. She placed it on the table and leaned back as if the keys were explanation enough.

Here it comes, Val thought. She wants her truck back. And rightfully so.

"I'm here to conduct a trade. I need my truck to haul a pair of server racks from Olympia to Bonney Lake. They won't fit in my car's trunk unless I disassemble them. We're talking hundreds of screws and brackets and that's something I'd rather not do. So, with your permission, I'll leave you my car and I'll take the truck." She raised an eyebrow. "Does this meet with your approval?"

"Sure. Server racks sound like something I might use to carry large pizza orders to a table. May I ask what you do with them?"

"I'm a software engineer. I use the racks to organize network components. That's why I prefer rack-mount equipment. By increasing density, I can conserve space in my server room."

"Uh-huh," Val said although she had no idea what she was talking about. "But what is it you actually do with your increased density?" She hoped she didn't sound ignorant.

"I design and develop mission critical applications, operating systems, network control systems, robots. Roughly anything that uses computer technology."

"Wow. Even not understanding all that I'm impressed. Algorithms, huh?"

"Yes, algorithms." Susan chuckled softly.

"Val?" Audra called. "Order up."

"Let me get this then I'll bring the truck keys."

"Take your time. And maybe a spinach mushroom calzone to go?"

"Absolutely. I'll get that order turned in right away." Val hurried into the kitchen, muttering, "Oh, thank you, thank you, thank you" to herself the whole way.

Susan's continued generosity was a godsend. More than she could ever acknowledge. Simply teaching Susan how to cook pasta couldn't possibly equal how much Val valued her help. She turned in Susan's calzone order then grabbed the truck keys from her tote and dropped them in her apron pocket.

"No ticket on that one," she called in Joe's direction.

"Okay." He tossed her a quick look but didn't question it. She didn't make this request very often and never for a large extravagant order. Whatever her reason to comp the order, it was important and justified.

"Hey, Jackson?" Val called as he came in the back door with an empty insulated pizza carrier.

"Yeah?" He tossed the carrier on the counter and looked at the pan of available pizza slices. "What?" He folded a slice and took a big bite.

"You have a job and I want you to do it without complaint." She tossed him a critical stare. "You hear me?"

"What?" His petulant tone told her he wasn't going to cooperate, regardless of the task.

Val stopped what she was doing and turned to face him. "Susan Castle is sitting at table three and I want you to go out there and apologize to her. No arguments. No excuses. No cussing. Go out there and apologize for your attitude that night you tried to deliver pizza. You were wrong and you know it.

Now go out there and fix it," she said in a quiet but demanding tone, pointing toward the dining room.

He opened his mouth, presumably to argue, but she continued to point and glare at him. They had attracted attention from Joe and several of the kitchen staff, everyone frozen in place, staring at them. He glanced around the room then lowered his eyes and gave a small nod.

"And I mean a real apology, Jackson."

"Okay," he grumbled obediently and headed in that direction.

"Smile and be polite," she called after him. "I'm not asking you to donate a kidney."

Val followed, carrying orders to nearby tables. Jackson was in no hurry, ambling to Susan's table, his hands in his jeans pockets and a disgruntled expression on his face.

"Hello, Jackson." Susan looked him up and down curiously.

"Hi." He swallowed nervously.

"Sit down. Can I help you with something?" she asked, her voice calm and self-assured.

He moved his hands from his jeans pockets to the pockets of his hoodie and took a seat across from her with trepidation.

"Okay," he finally said, pulling his hands from his pockets and folding them on the table. "I'm sorry about trying to make you pay for pizza you didn't order. And I shouldn't have been an ass about giving me a tip. You didn't place the order and I didn't deserve one. I'm sorry."

"You're right. I didn't place that order. I saw no legitimate reason to pay for it. And with your offensive insistence I do so, I saw no reason to offer you a tip. If you had been polite and apologetic about the mistake, I probably would have compensated you for the drive. Your repeated banging on my door was intrusive and disturbing. I was in the middle of an international business meeting and I guarantee my time was far more valuable than a ten or twenty-dollar tip you seemed positive I owed you."

"You were going to tip me?" He seemed surprised.

"If you had been a mature, respectful adult about the mistake, yes, probably."

"Damn," he muttered.

"You made your choices on how you wanted to handle the situation. I made mine." She leaned back and stared solemnly at him.

"Son of a bitch," he moaned, shaking his head as if at himself. "You'd have given me twenty bucks if I had been polite?"

"Why does that seem so foreign to you, Jackson? Have you ever watched your Aunt Val while she's serving her customers? She's always polite and engaging. She doesn't swear or argue. She knows her attitude and how she treats people has everything to do with her income."

"It's hard when people treat delivery drivers like crap. They don't want to pay for shit," he said, his gaze lowered submissively.

"Do you like your job?"

"Somebody has to do it." He shrugged indifferently.

"What would you rather be doing?" She folded her hands, aligning them directly across from his.

"Playing video games," he said with a chuckle. "Actually, anything with computers."

"As a job?"

"Yeah, but I don't have a college degree."

"Some tech industry jobs don't require a college degree."

"Like what?" He laughed, as if he didn't believe her.

"Introduction to computer programming. Introduction to algorithms. Small platform game apps. Lots of possibilities with online classes to get you started."

"Yeah, right. And that's not free. My grades weren't that good. I couldn't get into college or qualify for scholarships."

"There are dozens of online courses you can take for free. You don't need a college degree to move your career down a new path."

He looked skeptical of her suggestion, as if she was mocking him.

"Anyway, I want to apologize for being an ass. I shouldn't have done that. You didn't order the pizza and I should have accepted that."

"I accept your apology. And, Jackson, in case you're interested in opening some new doors, you could continue working while you do online studies. Something to think about."

"Yeah, sure."

Val passed him as he returned to the kitchen, muttering to himself.

"Your order will be ready in a few minutes," she said, refilling Susan's water glass.

"Thanks, Val. For Jackson." Susan gave her a small appreciative smile. "I assume you were behind that apology."

"He needed to do that. It was long overdue."

"He's a nice young man. He ate a healthy helping of crow and didn't choke on it. You should be proud of him."

"He has his moments." Val smiled. "By the way, when are we doing this trade thing?" Val pulled the truck keys from her apron pocket as Susan's phone rang.

She held up a finger then pointed at the phone, as if signaling she needed to take the call. The conversation immediately became deeply technical and protracted. Val nodded toward the kitchen and returned to serving other customers. When Susan ended the call and finished scribbling notes on a pad, Val approached.

"How are we doing here, Dr. Castle? Are all your meals this bogged down with work?"

"You don't want to know." Releasing a groan, Susan slipped the pad and pen into her jacket pocket, then looked up at Val. "That was one of my dinner guests. It looks like we have a date for the meeting. Eight nerds coming to my house for pasta bolognese. However, there's a snag in the plans."

"What kind of snag, dare I ask?"

"Next Tuesday is the proposed date," Susan announced cautiously.

"Tuesday is good. I'm not on the schedule."

"But the dinner is for *next* Tuesday. That doesn't give us time for me to learn how to make it."

"Oh," was all Val said, trying to figure out how they were going to handle this. "I guess I could come over early Tuesday and give you a crash course on Italian cooking."

"Or, you come over midday and I pay you to cook the meal for the meeting. How long would it take to prepare bolognese with fresh pasta for a bunch of culinarily challenged computer geeks? I'll pay whatever you think is fair. Labor and time. And of course, I'll cover the cost of all ingredients. My kitchen is completely at your disposal. And to tell the truth, I was a little apprehensive about preparing a big meal for a dinner meeting. I didn't want to poison anyone." She looked genuinely worried. "If you'd rather, I can order takeout dinners from Nardi's and have Jackson deliver them. He'd probably like the idea of me actually paying him."

Val slid into the booth and stared squarely at her.

"Now, here's what we're going to do, Dr. Castle." She tapped her index finger on the table in emphasis of her words. "I'm coming to your house on Tuesday. I'm going to prepare tagliatelle ragu alla bolognese with Italian bread and a wonderful tossed salad. For dessert, I'll bring pistachio cannoli. You will provide a couple bottles of cabernet sauvignon or pinot grigio. Both go well with bolognese. You choose the brand of wine to serve to your friends. I'll cook the fresh pasta and you serve it to your guests. You can even take credit for it, if you'd like. And before you ask, no, you don't need to get, buy, borrow, order or procure anything. I'll bring what I need for the meal. I'll handle it. You just provide the wine. That's all there is to it. Done deal. You will not argue or insist on paying me. You know you can't win. Understand?"

"I'm sure it will be fantastic," Susan finally said and leaned back with a relieved, satisfied smile on her face. "Thank you, Valentine Rose."

"You're welcome, Susan Ann." They shared a smile. "Now, if you'll give me five minutes to take care of a couple of things and package your calzone, you can show me what car I'll be driving."

CHAPTER TWENTY-THREE

Susan was sitting on the bench in the lobby of the restaurant replying to an email on her phone when Val pulled on her jacket and headed in her direction.

"Ready?" Val said. "The truck is around the side of the building. I wish you'd told me you were coming to trade vehicles. I would have washed it and filled the gas tank. I think it's only about half."

"That's fine. Don't worry about it. Like I said, I should have given you the car from the get-go. I use the truck more because I can haul stuff in it."

"If it has doors, tires and a steering wheel, I'm a happy camper."

Val unlocked the truck and took out her umbrella, canvas tote bag, water bottle and what she called her female emergency kit, a ziplock baggie with the essentials for any surprise visit from her monthly "friend." She snatched it up from the floorboard and discreetly stuffed it in the bag.

"I think that's everything," she said, checking the console between the seats for trash. She held out the keys to Susan. "I'll give you these and I repeat, thank you so much for allowing me to use your lovely truck."

"No problem." Susan took Val's hand and slipped a keyring on her finger. It had a silver Pi medallion dangling from it.

"Which car is it, Dr. Castle?" Val scanned the parking lot. "Is it the blue Honda Civic? They're very energy efficient."

"Val, you're standing behind it." Susan said, waiting next to a white sedan with tinted windows.

"You're kidding. This one?" She stared at the sleek Mercedes sedan. It looked new. It screamed expensive.

"Press the remote to unlock it," Susan advised.

"Susan, this is a Mercedes Benz," Val muttered, pressing the button on the remote. The car beeped, the interior lights flashed and the doors unlocked.

Susan opened the driver's door and stepped back, waiting for Val to look inside. "It has CarPlay and plug-ins like the truck. I'll give you the quick tutorial so you don't curse my name when you try to drive it for the first time."

"Susan, you have got to be kidding me. You're letting me drive your new Mercedes?" Val knew she was gawking. This was extravagant and lavish. Susan deserved free meals for an entire year for allowing her to use this car. She also thought about liability for her using it. This car undoubtedly cost more than her annual salary.

"It's not new. I've had it almost a year. It doesn't have that many miles on it." Susan waved her inside. "It's a car, Val. I like some of the new tech advances. And I like the creature comforts. But it's still just a car. A safe, dependable and efficient car. It'll probably get three hundred thousand miles on it before I need to replace it. My last one had two hundred sixty on it when I traded it in on this one. Climb in." Susan again waved her inside.

Val slid into the driver's seat, the comfy leather seat cradling her tush like a warm glove.

"It has seat heaters," Susan offered and pointed to the controls as Val ran her hand over the passenger seat upholstery. "Press the lever and bring the seat forward. Your legs are shorter than mine."

Much like when she showed her how to use the truck, Susan leaned in, immersing herself in the details of the car, seemingly unaware her face was sometimes mere inches from Val's. Val found it hard to concentrate on what she was saying, the lyrical sound of her voice and the fragrant aroma of her cologne a distraction too pleasing to ignore.

If you don't stop bringing your face so close to mine, you're going to get more than a hug. One more time and I'm liable to kiss your cheek. Who could blame me? One kiss. One teeny tiny itty-bitty kiss, right there on your cheek. Or maybe on your lips. Yes, on your lips. Your delectably soft-looking lips...

"Would that be all right with you?" Susan asked, breaking the spell as she looked down at her, her hand poised to adjust something.

"What?"

"Never mind," Susan said with a chuckle. "We'll leave this off for now."

"I'm sorry. Brain freeze." Something about this woman had her thinking like a teenager. An infatuated love-starved giddy teenager. And she wished it would stop.

"If you have any questions, you have options," Susan continued. "Ask Siri. Or text if you're in desperate need of rescuing. Or the owner's manual in the glove box."

"What about insurance coverage while I drive this?" Val asked, looking up apprehensively.

"My auto coverage covers anyone I allow to drive my vehicles. Insurance and registration are in the folder in the glove box. Anywhere you need to go is fine with me." Susan looked down at her reassuringly.

"My only plans are back and forth to work, the grocery store and to your house on Tuesday for bolognese. Nothing more."

"Hey, Val," Audra said from the front door, waving her back inside. "We're getting backed up in here. Can you hurry?"

"I guess I better get back to work." Val climbed out and pressed the remote to lock the doors.

"It'll lock automatically if you have the remote on your person." Susan twirled the truck keys around her index finger. "Have a good evening, Ms. Nardi."

"Thank you, Dr. Castle. You are a sweet woman. I hope you know that." Val leaned up and kissed Susan's cheek. Susan froze, a surprised look on her face. When she didn't move, Val offered a coy smile and kissed her again, this time briefly on the lips. She patted Susan's arm then hurried inside. If Susan wasn't happy with the kiss, Val didn't want to see it.

"What was that all about?" Joe asked as she came into the kitchen, ready to drown herself in work. "Audra said that woman with the truck was here."

"First of all, and for the fifth time, her name is Susan. She needed to use her truck so she came by to trade for her car. She needs to haul computer racks or something."

Val wasn't going to explain Dr. Susan Castle to him. It was none of his business what she did or what she drove. She went to wait on customers, hoping he would drop the subject but as soon as she walked back into the kitchen Joe grinned over at her. "A goddamn Mercedes Benz E450?" he declared loudly.

Val groaned and rolled her eyes. Audra no doubt had seen her in the parking lot with Susan.

"Yes, Joe. A Mercedes."

"Shit!" He chuckled, shaking his head in disbelief. He looked over at her and grinned wickedly. "What is she expecting in return?"

"If you really want to know, she's having a dinner meeting at her house for a few business associates and I offered to cook an authentic Italian meal for them. Tagliatelle bolognese. Nothing else."

"Tagliatelle, eh?"

"Yes. Now can we get back to work and forget it?"

"Sure," he said, but continued to chuckle.

Val released a disgusted sigh. Joe was being nosy and suggestive and she didn't appreciate it. But there was the kiss. That, unto itself, was reason enough to put a smile on her face. She wondered if she'd find the courage to do it again. Yep. She would. She knew she would. And for no reason other than she wanted to experience Susan's soft lips again.

CHAPTER TWENTY-FOUR

Val stepped out of the car and smiled up at the camera on the corner of the house.

"You've got company," she announced, then popped the trunk. "So either open the front door or tell me the new security code."

The front door opened to Susan's smiling face. She was dressed in her signature gray slacks and a burgundy cable knit sweater, both nice accents to her dark hair, especially the few sprigs of gray at the temples. Val instantly wished she had worn something dressier, and whether her denim capri pants and pink blouse were appropriate for this event. But still, she was the cook. Not one of the guests. She'd have everything prepared and be gone before anyone noticed she wasn't dressed for a professional meeting. Her apron would prevent pasta sauce spattering down her front.

"Any issues with the car?" Susan said, coming to help.

"Nope. It drives like a dream."

Susan looked in the trunk at the four boxes of ingredients, accessories, utensils and refrigerator dishes of food, all lined up neatly. "All this?"

"Everything your cook will need to prepare a satisfying Italian feast fit for a room full of computer professionals."

"I thought you didn't need anything special." Shaking her head, Susan lifted out one of the boxes.

They each made two trips, lugging the boxes into the kitchen whose counters, floors and appliances all looked freshly scrubbed and clean. It veritably sparkled.

"What can I do?" Susan stood in the middle of the room, rubbing her hands together, poised to spring into action.

"Okay, first," Val said, removing her jacket and hanging it on the back of a chair, "you stand over here." She moved Susan to the end of the counter closest to the door that led out onto the patio. "You wait here and let me know if we're being invaded by aliens." She patted her hand. "I'll take care of the food thing."

Susan crossed her arms. "You know, I can actually help, assuming you give clear and concise instructions." She watched Val unload one of the boxes.

"If I need your help, I'll let you know. How's that?" Val grinned at her.

"You came prepared," Susan said as Val pulled an apron from one of the boxes, gave it a shake then tied it around her waist.

"Rule number one. When cooking pasta, wear an apron. Write that down." She pointed at her, then smoothed her hands down the front. "If it's possible to make a mess, I'll find a way." She turned back to the boxes, sorting and removing items. She assembled what she needed on one of the counters and immediately became embroiled in meal prep. She used a large pot for the bolognese sauce with every intention of having leftovers. Susan's friends may or may not be big eaters but since the sauce was time-consuming to make she could justify making extra. If Susan didn't like it or didn't want it, Val would take it home, perhaps sharing it with her grandmother. She knew some people didn't care for leftovers. Susan could be one of those.

"Oh, by the way," Susan said. "Make yourself at home. There are three other bathrooms as well as the little one."

"I wonder if I'll need a map," she said softly.

Susan seemed to overhear. "There's one in the master bedroom. It's the largest. One in the guest bedroom and one in the hall next to my office. All at your disposal." She smiled. "I think I made a pun."

Val laughed and said, "I won't hold it against you."

"Sometimes I surprise myself. According to Jillian and most of my family, I'm a stick in the mud with no sense of humor."

"Where does Jillian fit into the picture? She seemed like a very nice person."

"Jillian Ramsey is an old friend. I developed a program for her business several years ago. And yes, she is a nice person."

"Jillian mentioned that you dated her sister. I think she said her name was Dallas."

Susan frowned but said nothing.

"I'm sorry, Susan. I'm being nosy. You need to tell me to shut up." Apparently she had resurrected a subject Susan would rather not revisit. Memories of a failed relationship could be so raw and painful that they were better left in the past. Val could well identify with those kinds of memories.

Val stirred ingredients into the pot, constantly checking the burner setting. She then prepared the cutting board for pasta production as she considered her next question.

"Would I be nosy if I asked what you said to Jackson? Whatever it was sure had him talking to himself."

"I asked him if he liked his job. I asked him what he'd rather be doing. When he said computers, I explained there were online free technical courses that could get him a leg up in technical skills necessary to change professions. That seems to be the point where he thought I was talking down to him."

"He wasn't a very good student his senior year, hanging out with his friends instead of going to class or doing assignments. He's smart but he was easily distracted. I have to be careful not to say anything. I have to let Joe and Audra parent him as they see fit."

"But you're the one who sent him out to apologize to me."

"I suggested he was wrong and he knew it so he needed to correct it. That particular situation affected me so I felt like I was justified in calling him out on it."

"Affected you how?"

Val stared at Susan. She didn't want to explain how their relationship had grown. She shouldn't have to. If Susan didn't know that, she wasn't going to tell her. Maybe Susan was simply a polite, kind and generous woman who saw their connection as nothing more than casual friends.

"Jackson knows where I am if he wants to discuss it further," Susan added before Val could formulate a reply.

"I'll tell him." Val returned to the one of the boxes. "What wine did you get for the dinner?" she asked.

"Three bottles each of the ones you suggested."

"Six bottles of wine for eight guests?" Val laughed. "Isn't that overkill?"

"It was cheaper to buy a case. And if it's the appropriate choice for Italian food, why not stock up?"

Susan's cell phone rang again. "Excuse me. I need to take this." She meandered out onto the patio, leaving the door open.

It was clear from Susan's side of the conversation that the call had something to do with another software project in progress. She finished one quick conversation and had two more. She disappeared into her office as she was explaining something about converting code to another language. Val had finished adding spices to the sauce when Susan returned to the kitchen, her laptop open and balanced on one hand while she held her phone to her ear with the other. She walked straight through the kitchen and out onto the patio, continuing her conversation. Motion-activated lights mounted on the beams of the gazebo came on as she settled into one of the wooden Adirondack chairs, propped her feet up on the rim of the firepit and balanced the laptop on her knees as she read something on her screen to the caller. Something about AI, unexpected creativity and sophisticated algorithms. Val had heard AI referred to artificial intelligence but she didn't understand what it meant. She wondered where and when she'd lost contact with the modern technical era. If Susan understood such complexities, good for her. And yes, Val was intimidated by her.

"Well, I can make fresh pasta even if I don't do it with algorithms," Val muttered to herself with a cocky grin.

She checked the simmering pot then went to the doorway to the patio and pointed toward the hall. Susan offered a thumbs-up and continued with her conversation. Val meandered down the hallway, peeking in doorways as she passed. She passed two bedrooms, neither with ensuite bathrooms. A large bedroom with a king-size bed and two dressers appeared to be the master bedroom with a bathroom. The bedspread was a silver-gray and white paisley print with several plump pillows lined up along the paneled headboard, pleasantly complimenting the carpeting. It looked inviting. Curiosity kept her walking. After all, Susan had offered carte blanche so why not look. This was an impressive home.

The door next to the office where she delivered the Amazon chair led to a bathroom with a double sink vanity, walk-in shower and a separate toilet room. The lusciously thick towels were various shades of sage green, all coordinating with the walls and tile. The last door was a bedroom with a queen-size bed with a multicolored antique-looking quilt. An oval navy and burgundy braided rug on the dark wood floor was centered under the bed. The room had a colonial feel. A bouquet of lavender and white flowers in a crystal vase sat on the antique dresser. Val crossed to the dresser and drew a long deep whiff from the blooms. They reminded her of Hanna and her bouquets at Pike Place Market. And of the afternoon she spent with Susan, roaming and shopping the stalls and stores.

"Lovely," she muttered and took another smell.

"I like flowers," Susan said from the hallway, surprising Val into a gasp. She was leaning against the doorjamb, one hand in her pocket. "They always soften even an austere setting."

"Yes, they certainly do that. I hope it's okay that I found what looks like the guest room." She pointed to the door in the corner she assumed was the bathroom.

"Sure. But why not use the big one in my master bedroom?"

"I took the opportunity to see all three." Val grinned, hoping she hadn't done something wrong.

"I'm glad you did. Make yourself at home."

"I like this room. It's very homey and quaint." Val ran her hand down the quilt.

"The bedspread was my grandmother's. She made it years ago."

"Really?" Val studied it, tracing her fingertip along the tiny stitches. "It's lovely. Is this her room when she comes to visit?"

"No. She's been gone many years." Susan heaved a small reminiscent sigh. "She gave me the quilt when I graduated from high school."

"Grandmothers are special people. Now, if you'll excuse the chef, I'm going to do what I came snooping to do." She grinned and nodded toward the bathroom.

"By all means," Susan agreed and headed back up the hallway.

When Val returned to the kitchen, rubbing lotion into her hands, Susan was back on the patio, studying something on her laptop.

"Sorry but I couldn't help myself. I used some of the hand lotion in the bathroom. It smells wonderful. I'll have to look for that brand."

"I have no idea where it came from," Susan said without looking up. "Probably an Amazon order."

Soon, heavenly smells of culinary delight were emanating from the kitchen, occasionally drawing Susan's gaze. When it appeared that Susan was between calls, Val came out onto the patio and handed her a glass of wine, then leaned down and rested her arms on the back of her chair. Val placed her hands on Susan's shoulders and massaged gently.

"Thank you." Susan took a sip then set the glass on the arm of the chair.

"Is that the cherry firewood from Vinnie?" Val asked, noticing the pleasant ambiance and fragrance.

"Yes. Smells nice, huh?" She quickly typed something, studied it then added something else.

Val leaned closer and squinted at the screen. "Wow, you sure use a lot of punctuation and some of that isn't even real words. You carry on typing gobbledygook and gibberish and I'll go check on the sauce." She patted Susan's shoulder and went back into the kitchen. "And drink your wine."

"It's called coding and are you trying to get me drunk?" Susan took another sip, then continued to type.

"I'm trying to get you to mellow out. You've got friends coming over for dinner and you're so deep in work you'll need a ladder to climb out. Time to come up for air."

"Something sure smells good. And it's not the firewood. What all is in the sauce or is it a secret?"

"Lots of goodies. Ground beef, ground pork, ground prosciutto, tomato puree, carrots, celery, shallots, spices, a pinch of sugar and of course, vino rosso. Later I'll add a little cream and some pasta water. If you'd attended the Nardi bolognese cooking class you'd have learned that detail. Part of the algorithm."

"Yes. Algorithm." Susan set the laptop aside and came into the kitchen, rotating her neck as if it hurt.

"Too much screen time?"

"Occasionally. Comes with the job," Susan chuckled, making light of it.

Val gave another quick check of the sauce then removed her ring, ready to turn her attention to the pasta making.

"That's amethyst for February, right?" Susan asked, trying on the ring.

"Yes. What's your birthstone, if I may ask?" Val had begun adding eggs to the pile of flour on the pastry board.

"Garnet." Susan admired the ring then set it back on the counter.

"January," she declared as she worked the eggs into the flour, creating a lump of dough. She continued kneading, pushing and pulling, until she was happy with the feel of it. She floured the pastry cloth then rolled the dough out flat, working it into a delicately thin rectangular layer. She applied a thin dusting of flour then carefully rolled the dough into a tight tube.

"Tagliatelle," Val said, noticing Susan's intense stare. "Approximately a quarter of an inch wide. The perfect size to hold the sauce." She cut the tube of dough into quarter-inch slices, all without measuring. She had done this a thousand times and could all but do it in her sleep.

"You really do know what you're doing," Susan said, admiring her work.

Val gently lifted the pasta strips, loosening and releasing them into a pile of noodles. "I'll let these rest and cook it right before you sit down to dinner."

Susan's phone rang, presumably another work-related call. "Sorry. I do need to take this. One of the dinner guests. He probably forgot the address." She again headed out onto the patio to answer the call.

Val had seen a sparkle in her eyes and a contentment in her smile. Yes, Susan was grateful for her efforts for her dinner guests. But it was hard not to read something else into her satisfied smile. She had to admit that it pleased her and on several levels.

CHAPTER TWENTY-FIVE

"Hey, Joel. How's it going?" Susan settled into the chair and propped her feet up on the firepit. "And before you ask, yes, I got some of that Rainier Beer you like so you don't have to complain you're being persecuted. It's in the mini-fridge, nice and cold."

"That's great, Susan. Thank you. But about that. I don't think I can make it for dinner this evening." He said it matter-of-factly, no regret or apology in his tone.

"Oh?"

"Yeah. Amber, Bill, and Megan won't be there either," he added after an awkward pause.

She gripped her cell phone hard and said evenly, "May I ask why? I thought we'd all committed to this date. And in case it matters, I'm not doing the cooking. I hired someone who actually knows what they're doing."

"That's good to know." He laughed. "We all know you can't boil water even with a recipe and guidance, Susan." He continued to laugh but it sounded artificial.

She didn't reply. Her culinary skills weren't the point of the conversation. He had something to admit and his laughter was his attempt at delaying it as long as possible.

"So what are you doing instead, Joel?" she finally asked.

"Dr. Waterman's holding a symposium on AI. The venue was so small and crowded it was immediately sold out. But they decided to move it to the Civic Center in Kent so we were able to snag some seats. Want me to see if I can grab you a ticket?"

"Do you mean Introduction to AI Multi-Disciplinary Research?" Susan asked.

"Yes. Do you want to meet us? Hunter, Chad, Marlena, and Lindsey are trying to secure tickets, too."

"So you all are canceling on dinner?" Susan did her best to conceal an exasperated breath.

"We're sorry but Dr. Waterman's cutting back on his public appearances. We weren't sure we'd have another opportunity to do this."

"In case you forgot, I helped Dr Waterman create the syllabus for that symposium last year."

"Oh, that's right." There was another chuckle, then an awkward silence.

"So no, I don't want a ticket."

"If we have any questions, we'll know who to ask, right?" he added, as if that smoothed any ruffled feathers their cancelation created.

"He and I conducted this same symposium a few months ago. I offered you tickets then but you passed. I'm not involved this time, Joel, so if you have questions, I encourage you to ask Dr. Waterman. He usually has a Q and A at the end of his lecture."

"I meant, anything he doesn't cover, you could fill in the blanks."

"Again, I'm not involved in the presentation." If he wanted a capsulized version, after his inconsiderate indifference at canceling the dinner at the last minute, he could look elsewhere.

"I have to go, Susan. I'm glad I caught you before you sat down to dinner. We'll catch you another time for sure," he said dismissively and hung up.

Susan touched the phone to her forehead and closed her eyes, her nostrils flaring.

"Son-of-a-GD-bitch," she muttered venomously through a groan.

Val stood in the doorway with a spoon in her hand, gazing at her in concern.

"Before I tell you about the phone call, remember, don't blame the messenger."

"I'm listening."

"That was Joel on the phone. All of tonight's dinner guests have canceled. They're all going to a symposium on AI this evening. Artificial intelligence."

"What? All of them? All eight people I'm cooking fresh pasta and sauce for? They all canceled?" Val offered a lighthearted chuckle. "You've got to be kidding."

"I'm really sorry. I had no idea they planned to do this. Believe me. I was completely blindsided. I'm still paying you, of course. Absolutely." She offered a pained expression. "I'm so sorry, Val. I feel really bad about this."

Val stood staring at her for a long moment, then looked back at the sauce simmering aromatically in the pot. She tried to restrain herself but it was hopeless. She burst out laughing.

"All of them?" she asked through her laughter.

"Yes."

"Well, take a wild guess what you'll be having for dinner the rest of the week," Val said, finally able to bring herself under control. "I hope you really *really* like leftovers. At least you'll have wine to wash it down."

"Can't we freeze it or something?"

"Yep." Val reached over and turned off the burner with a flourish. "Fortunately, I haven't cooked the pasta yet." She opened the bag of bread, pulled out a slice and tore it in half. She dipped a piece in the sauce and handed it to Susan. "Here." She dipped the other half and held it up, ready to make a toast. "Say something deep and profound, Dr. Castle. Please!"

Susan accepted the bread, took a bite then thought a moment before slowly pulling a smile. "Yum."

"That's it? Just yum? That's your profound statement?" Val gave her a mock-puzzled look as if she expected more.

"I think it says everything that needs saying." She ate the rest of the bread with a satisfied look on her face. "Actually, it's mega yum."

"Is that for the bread or the sauce?"

"The sauce, of course. The bread is merely the vehicle to enjoy the sauce. By the way, how long does it take to cook the pasta? Not very long, right?" She peered into the large pot of water waiting to be called into service.

"Couple minutes or so. That's why I was waiting until your company arrived." Val pulled a box of freezer bags from the supplies she'd brought. "It'll be okay for a few months in the freezer. I'll package it in small batches so you can pop it in boiling water for about three minutes. Defrost it first." Val began filling baggies when Susan stepped to the stove and turned on the burner under the pot of water.

"My friends may have canceled and won't get to taste your exquisite cooking but who says we can't?" Susan cocked an eyebrow.

"You want some of this anyway?"

"I definitely want to enjoy it for dinner. Screw the rest of them. If I promise to not talk shop, will you have dinner with me?"

No way Val could say no.

"Okay. I can do that."

"Red or white?" Susan asked, opening the refrigerator door.

"Red."

As Susan stood at the counter wrestling the cork out of the wine bottle, Val looked down at the pan of water, watching it come to a boil. It was a diversion, a diversion she desperately needed. Here she was, Val Nardi, having dinner with Susan Castle. The attractive, intelligent and kind Susan Castle. It was a dinner date by happenstance only. Why not? She had made enough to feed an army. But something else was bubbling and churning up deep inside. She knew she couldn't help herself. If she looked up at Susan she wouldn't be able to stop herself. It was that real. She looked up anyway.

"Oh, what the hell," Val said, then turned to Susan, took her face in her hands and kissed her.

Susan stiffened and gasped, obviously taken back by Val's advances. She glared at her, then turned her back and stepped away. After a moment of hesitation, she looked back at her. Then reached for her, cupped her hand behind Val's head and drew her close.

"I told you. I'm too old for you," she whispered, then kissed her back.

It wasn't a long kiss but it spoke volumes. Confusingly surprising volumes. Certainly not what Val expected from the reserved and reclusive Dr. Susan Castle.

Susan rubbed her thumb across Val's smudged lipstick. "And there will be no more talk about it," she said emphatically.

Val didn't reply. She couldn't. Returning the kiss was somehow the last thing she expected. So what if Susan was older? She was caring, generous, practical and more intelligent than anyone Val had ever met. And she had a smile that drove her crazy.

"Susan," Val stammered, but the pasta water boiled over and sizzled on the burner.

"I think it's pasta time," Susan said, nodding at the pan, then she carried the wine bottle and two glasses onto the patio.

Val dropped a handful of pasta into the boiling water and gave it a stir, still processing Susan's kiss. Why had Susan kissed her then said the subject was forbidden? More than that, she desperately wanted another taste of those soft lips against her own, a taste that made Val's crotch moist.

Susan stacked another log on the fire, gave it a poke then added another. She kept busy on the patio while Val served up their dinner.

"I see we're dining al fresco," Val called, struggling to find an innocuous icebreaker.

"If you mean dining in the fresh air, yes. I thought we could. After all, you stacked the firewood. You might as well enjoy it. Is this all right?"

"Sure. Fresh pasta in the fresh air." Val carried their plates onto the patio. Two stemmed glasses of wine were waiting on the small table between the two wooden Adirondack chairs. "I added salad and some antipasto to the plates. I was going to use serving dishes for your friends and let them take what they wanted but this seemed easier for the two of us."

"Looks good to me." Susan seemed to have moved past the kiss. Her dry sense of humor and reserved demeanor were once again on display. She accepted her plate and waited for Val to take a seat then sat down. "These look interesting." She inspected the tidbits of antipasto on her plate. "Olives. Miniature cheese wedges. Salami. Almonds." She popped an olive in her mouth.

"The salty things awaken your taste buds and complement the pasta. *Buon appetito.*" Val held up an almond then ate it.

"I think we need to toast this amazing feast." Susan handed Val a glass of wine. "And I want to toast Joel for canceling." She propped her feet up on the rim of the firepit. "They're probably having a drive-thru hamburger on the way to the symposium and wishing they had time for a real meal." She hoisted her glass and smiled over at Val. "May their evening be a bust."

"Hear, hear." Val raised her glass.

"They can all go suck a lemon." She set the glass down and began her meal, a satisfied gleam in her eye as she took a second forkful. "I sure hope there's seconds."

Val laughed as she twirled a strand of pasta around her fork, using the crust of bread for assistance. The topic of the kiss seemed to have been put behind them.

After several more bites and a sip of wine, Susan said, "This is really good," and added, "Better than Nardi's."

"I'm glad you like it. Now you know what to expect for dinner tomorrow. And many days after."

"I'll buy a bigger freezer." Susan refilled their wineglasses.

They ate slowly, enjoying the meal but ignoring the elephant in the room. Val leaned back in her chair and took a deep preparatory breath.

"Are we going to pretend it didn't happen?" she finally asked.

Susan took a sip of wine. "I thought I would. Yes."

"How about the age thing?" Val said then turned a sideways glance to Susan. "Is that an acceptable topic?"

"Age thing?" Susan raised an eyebrow at Val. "Okay. If you want to discuss age, how old are you?"

"Forty-four. And what's a few years between friends?"

"A few years?" Susan chuckled.

"How old are you?"

"Older than you."

"How old?" Val studied her. How insistent would she need to be to get a straight answer?

"Sixty-three," Susan replied. She tossed a quick look at Val. "And in case you're struggling with the math, the difference in our ages is nineteen years. Nineteen is not equivalent to a few by any stretch of the imagination." She went back to twirling pasta.

"If you say you're old enough to be my mother, I'm going to smack you," Val declared.

"Nope. Never crossed my mind."

They ate the last of their meal in relative silence as if what happened between them was churning in their minds, clouding any conversation they might have. For Val, it was torture. She wanted to ask a million questions but knew from Susan's face and posture that that wasn't going to happen. At least, not today. Val carried her dishes into the kitchen. Susan followed. The silence was deafening.

CHAPTER TWENTY-SIX

Susan's phone rang.

"Hello, Claire," Susan said after glancing at the ID on the screen. She pointed to Val then to the dirty dishes and to herself, indicating she'd take care of the dishes later. Val ignored her and began rinsing, and loading the dishwasher. "How are you? How's Connor? Did he get the birthday card?"

Susan stuffed a hand in her pants pocket, leaned on the door frame and looked out onto the patio as she listened to the caller. Val watched her expression mutate from noncommittal and patient to worried and annoyed.

"How much?" she asked succinctly then listened, then repeated, "How much, Claire? One payment or two?" Susan straightened her posture and frowned. "That sounds more like five."

She closed her eyes and groaned, frustration spreading across her face. "Okay, Claire. Listen. Stop talking and listen. Yes, I understand what you're asking. You tell Ryan if he needs my help, he can call and ask me himself. He shouldn't make you run interference for him. *He* is my nephew. And I'm sure he knows what my answer will be. I told him I won't hand over cash. His track record is less than stellar. I'm not footing the bill for another cruise. I might consider a direct payment but not the entire indebtedness. We've been through this before. He knows my conditions."

Even from one side of the conversation, Val could tell it wasn't the first time Claire was eliciting Susan's financial help. If Ryan and Claire's money issues had anything to do with Covid, Val could well relate. But she had no intention of asking. Families usually considered financial matters private.

"Nope. As I said, he can ask me himself." Susan shifted her weight and ran her fingers through her hair. "He can man up, Claire. Yes, by all means. Tell him I said that." She ended the call.

She looked over at Val and saw the curiosity in her face. "Yes, that was Connor's mother. She's married to my nephew, Ryan." She released a small moan then forced a smile as if ready to put Claire's call behind her.

"Spider-Man's parents?" Val asked whimsically. "Cute little boy. He has your radiant eyes."

"I think you should take some of these leftovers home," Susan said, ignoring Val's compliment. She watched Val ladle sauce into freezer containers.

"Thank you. If you don't mind, I'll take a little to my grandmother. I'll remind her this is her recipe."

Susan received another phone call while Val packaged leftovers. It immediately turned technical. When Susan went into her office, Val finished loading the dishwasher then refilled the boxes with her cooking paraphernalia and carried them out to the car. She wiped down the counters, the sink, the stove and any trace of the meal she had prepared. She drank the last sip of her wine then added the glass to the dishwasher. She occasionally looked down the hallway but Susan sounded preoccupied with work.

Val wondered how best to let her know she was leaving. She was about to stick her head in Susan's office and whisper her goodnight when a text came through on her phone. Audra, inquiring about the rent on Val's building. There was a subtle hint she might have a possible renter if rent could be waived or lowered for the first few months. Half price seemed fair since it's been empty so long, Audra suggested. Val tapped out a terse reply, reminding her it hadn't been empty that long and no, she wasn't going to reduce the rent by half.

"Sorry that took so long." Susan strode into the kitchen. "You look like there's a problem," she said, noticing Val's furrowed brow.

"I own a small building. A drive-thru place on 410, ideal for a coffee kiosk or something similar. It's vacant right now and my sister-in-law is meddling in how I rent it."

"Is it the place that used to be Heidi's Coffee Cabin?"

"Yes. How did you know?"

"I stopped there several months ago. The coffee was okay. You own that building?"

"It was an investment years ago. We were going to base our cleaning service out of it but it was too small for all our equipment and supplies. I kept it but God only knows why. One of these days I'll probably come to my senses and sell it. Maybe I'm not cut out to be landlord material."

"Cute place and a great location. Are you having trouble finding renters?"

"No. I can find renters. Or rather they find me. But not suitable renters. They either want free rent in exchange for merchandise credit or partial rent for limited use. One lady wanted to know if I was zoned for a 'wink-wink' spa." Val held up her fingers as if making quotation marks. "I can guess what kind of spa she meant. And no, I'm not zoned for that nor do I want to be. Is it so terrible that I want to rent to a stable, mature individual on a long-term basis who will pay on time and not destroy the place?"

"I'm sure that's the dream of every landlord." Susan hoisted herself onto the counter and folded her hands in her lap. "By the way, who is the we you refer to? Was your cleaning service a franchise with several owners?"

"It wasn't a franchise. We looked into that but the franchise fees would have dipped so deep into the profits we'd be working for minimum wage. Kate and I started the business on a shoestring but it was ours," Val said reflectively.

"Kate was your business partner? Did she come work at Nardi's, too?"

"No, no." Val smiled fondly. "Three weeks after we closed our doors she came down with Covid. She was in the hospital for several weeks but her asthma gave her a compromised immune system." When Val didn't continue, Susan gave her a solemn look and waited. "She passed three days after her fiftieth birthday. She was more than my business partner." Val took a long resolute breath. "I was twenty-three when Kate came into my life and I will be forever grateful."

"I'm so very sorry, Val."

"She and I scraped together enough for the down payment on the little building and hoped to make a success of it. We knew pretty quickly it wasn't large enough for our cleaning service but we hoped to do something with it eventually. She was a dear, sweet woman. And I miss her."

"I can see why you haven't sold it."

Val shrugged, as if once again locking those memories away.

"May I ask why you don't do something with it yourself? Start your own business. You seem like a resourceful, intelligent woman. Why not reclaim your independence? Covid restrictions have been lifted. You aren't obligated to work for your brother indefinitely."

"My brother offered me a job when my business had to close. He didn't have to do that. I'll never be able to thank him enough. I might be homeless if it wasn't for him. I'm not going to turn my back on him." Val looked away, unable to hide the quiver in her voice or the moisture in her eyes.

"So you continue to work for him out of a sense of obligation?"

"As I said, I owe him." Val didn't want to discuss her financial struggles with this college-educated, highly successful professional.

"Val, Covid wasn't your fault," Susan said sympathetically.

"I know."

Covid wasn't her fault nor were the restrictions that closed her business. But hard as she tried, their failed business cut deep. Deep enough that she was still paying off the bank loans Kate convinced her they'd needed to keep their doors open. Friends had suggested Val file bankruptcy to clear those debts but she wasn't going to shirk her responsibilities. That wasn't in her nature. Every spare penny had gone to pay off the loan and she was close to being free of that burden.

"Instead of renting out your little building, how about opening something like Val's Palace?" Susan suggested.

Val looked over at her then laughed. "Palace? Have you seen my building? The only thing palatial about it is…Nope, there's nothing palatial about it. The most you could hope for is a table for two and it would have to be a teeny tiny table. We're talking dismal profitability."

But Susan was undeterred, staring at her seriously.

"Do you mean to tell me you've never considered opening a business of your own? Something new and different. Something you're passionate about."

"I've never owned a business by myself and I don't want anything to do with a drive-thru coffee shop."

"Okay but humor me for a minute. What could you serve from a drive-thru window?"

"Food I know nothing about."

"How about pasta?" Susan said it then fell silent, leaving it for Val to consider the idea.

It was true. Every now and then this fantasy crept into Val's dreams. Fresh pasta. Maybe three or four varieties. A similar number of sauces. Pomodoro. Alfredo. Olive oil and pesto. And of course, bolognese. Menu choices could vary. Weekly specials. Her menu. Her rules. Her profits. Enough to allow her a comfortable living without gouging her clientele. Simple menu but everything deliciously homemade and authentic Italian cuisine.

"You're thinking about it, aren't you?" Susan smiled over at her.

"Peanut butter and jelly sandwiches. How's that sound?"

"I can see it on your face. You're considering something else. You have a gift, Val. You are an expert at something people will wait in line to enjoy. Val's Pasta Palace?"

"Where did you dig up that idea?" Val laughed. "Mama Nardi's supplies enough pasta for the entire Bonney Lake area. I don't need to encroach on my brother's clientele."

"Apples and oranges. Mama Nardi's main income stream is pizza. You said so. Seventy-five percent? Eighty percent?"

"Something like that."

"And you said Joe prefers it that way."

"Maybe." Val had to concede that she served eight or nine pizzas for every pasta entree.

"Find your niche, Val. Narrow it down to the most popular items. Provide a consistent product. Make your fresh Italian food, serve it with a congenial attitude and they'll come back again and again. Keep it simple. Keep it authentic and you'll find success. I could create a program for you to track your inventory, expenses and profit margin. I've got one I could modify for you. Free of charge. This is what I do, Val."

"Thank you, Susan. But I don't think so." Val enjoyed the last fleeting image of what Susan suggested. How could she be so spot-on?

Before Val could steer the conversation in a different direction, away from those painful memories, her phone rang again and it was Audra.

"I better take this," Val said.

Susan walked out onto the patio, leaving Val a measure of privacy for her call.

Audra groaned deeply before she spoke. "Jackson's car got stolen right out of the parking lot. It was parked by the back door. He wasn't inside for more than five minutes."

"Oh geez. When did this happen?"

"Maybe an hour ago. The height of the dinner rush. He's got deliveries to make. How are we supposed to get orders out if his car is gone?"

"I assume he'll use your car, Audra." Val instantly knew why Audra called and it wasn't to solicit sympathy for Jackson's stolen car.

"Joe wants to talk to you," she said, cutting short their conversation.

"Val, where are you?" Joe demanded, skipping the pleasantries.

"Cooking dinner for Susan Castle's business meeting. I'm at her house." She had a feeling he was about to run roughshod over her plans for the evening.

"Are you done?"

"Joe, cut to the chase. What do you want?" She wasn't going to suggest anything. He was going to have to admit it himself.

"Did you hear? Some fucking asshole stole Jackson's car. What the hell? His car is a piece of shit. Probably one of his friends trying to get back at him for something."

"Did you call the police? You need a police report to submit to your insurance company."

"Yeah, yeah. We called them. They say it's Jackson's fault."

"How can it be Jackson's fault?"

"He left the engine running and the doors unlocked, so he enabled the thieves."

"He left the engine running?" Val couldn't stifle a snort. "You're kidding. My God, Joe. What did he expect?"

"Whatever," Joe snapped. "I need your car, Val."

She'd seen this coming like a runaway freight train from the moment Audra mentioned the reason for the call.

"Can you be here in fifteen minutes?" he added, assuming she'd agree without question.

"Joe, my car is still in the shop. It should be ready in a couple days."

"You're driving that woman's car, aren't you? You've got transportation."

"Susan allowed me to use her car in exchange for preparing her business dinner. Jackson may not use it so don't ask. He can use Audra's car or your truck."

"He can't drive my truck. You know that. It's a standard. Audra's car isn't here, we rode in together. Hers needs service, it's home in the garage."

"I'm very sorry, Joe. But he *cannot* drive Susan's car. Don't ask."

"What the hell, Val? This is an emergency. We need a vehicle and yours is the only one available."

"Use one of the server's cars. Ask Jolene. Or Owen."

"Is everything okay?" Susan asked, leaning on the doorway to the kitchen. Val had been speaking so loudly she undoubtedly had heard Val's side of the conversation.

Val shook her head and grimaced then spoke again into the phone. "Joe, this time you're going to have to look elsewhere for help. This is Jackson's fault. I hope he learns his lesson."

"Val!" he snapped. "I don't have time to argue with you. I've got orders backing up and no car. You're a Nardi. Get your ass over here and help. If Jackson can't drive your car, you do the deliveries."

"Joseph, don't talk to me like that. Jackson is the one you should be mad at. Not me. I've got to go. I'll see you tomorrow." Val ended the call before she said something she'd regret.

Susan folded her arms. "I take it they want you to bring them my car?"

"He is not driving your car. You've met Jackson. Do you really want an immature twenty-one-year-old schlepping greasy smelly pizza all over the county in your new and expensive Mercedes Benz? Once in a while I let him drive my car but it always comes back full of trash and sometimes with stains on the upholstery. He doesn't respect other people's property, which is why Audra doesn't let him drive her car. So this is *not* happening."

"I suppose you're going to argue with me if I say I really wouldn't mind?"

Val glared at her and shook her head adamantly. "You might not mind but I would. And now, if you'll excuse me, I think I'll go home, put my leftovers in the freezer and take a long hot soaking bath."

Val headed for the front door. Susan followed, opened the door for her and held it.

"It was an interesting evening, Dr. Castle," Val said, smoothing her hand down the shoulder of Susan's sweater. "I enjoyed myself. And I enjoyed your company."

"Dinner was wonderful. My friends don't know what they missed." She hesitated then added, "I had a very pleasant evening." She covered Val's hand with her own and held it against her chest.

"You may not agree with me but we definitely have a topic that needs discussion. An important topic that needs discussion."

"If you mean the kiss, that's all it was. A kiss. Nothing more."

"It may be but I'm reading a lot into that kiss." Val gazed into Susan's eyes. "A lot." She patted her chest. "Good night, Susan."

Val winked then headed to the car. Susan stood in the driveway with her hands in her pants pockets as Val drove away. The satisfied smile on her face was visible in the rearview mirror until Val rounded the bend. As Val reached down to adjust the seatbelt across her chest she noticed the middle button of her blouse was open, revealing a clear view of her pink bra. She chuckled to herself.

"Well, well, Dr. Castle. It seems I'm determined to flash you. No wonder you were grinning. Is that why you kissed me back? You wanted another closer look?" Val giggled softly.

"Thank you, little button."

CHAPTER TWENTY-SEVEN

Susan sat down at her desk, ready to sip her first cup of morning coffee and do a little work on the long list of projects that needed her attention, all of them screaming to be prioritized. She turned on her computer and scanned the email folder but before she opened anything, her phone chimed an incoming call. From Nardi's restaurant. Why wasn't Val calling from her personal phone?

"Susan Castle?" a man demanded. "This is Joe Nardi. Val's brother."

"Yes, this is Susan Castle. Is Val all right?"

"Yeah. She's okay. We've got a situation here at the restaurant and I'd like to discuss it with you. As I think you know, my son, Jackson, delivers orders but his car was stolen and until we can get that replaced, we're really short on transportation. I understand you're letting Val use your spare car while hers is being repaired. Is that right?"

"Yes, she has my permission to use it."

"Since she will be here the rest of the week, she won't need it once she gets to work. She didn't want to be the one to ask but would you allow Jackson to use your car to get these orders out? She really appreciates your generosity and so do we. I try to support Val as much as I can. She's had a rough few years. I thought we could work together here. I'll be glad to comp some meals while he uses your car. He's a good kid."

She was astonished by Joe's request. Val had made it clear she didn't approve of them asking. Maybe Val had acknowledged their need to use it and was too embarrassed to ask herself. Susan didn't owe Joe Nardi anything. But if Val couldn't bring herself to ask, forcing her brother to make the request, Susan could agree, for Val's sake.

"I don't have a problem with it," she finally said although she wondered if she should clear this with Val before she agreed. But perhaps that would embarrass her more.

"Great. Thanksgiving week is always hectic." He laughed as if she was now his new best friend. "I'll let Val know."

The call ended, leaving Susan with a confused look on her face as she leaned back in her desk chair. She opened the contact list on her phone and studied Val's number. Val had seemed so adamant and Susan didn't want to directly countermand her boundaries with her brother. She understood Val's devotion to family but she didn't like the way they repeatedly took advantage of her kindness. Still, that was Val's business. Not hers.

She closed the phone and carried her coffee cup into the kitchen for a refill. Okay, she thought. Jackson will be driving her car. Not a problem she needed to worry about. Val's car should be repaired and back in her possession soon, alleviating any concern Val might have with the arrangement. Nardi issues would once again be Nardi issues instead of Nardi-Castle issues.

There was that other situation Susan knew she'd have to deal with and probably sooner than later. The kiss. The kiss that reminded Susan she was indeed a woman with feelings. What she knew was best for Val was diametrically opposed to what she wanted and needed. Oh, my God, the kiss, she reminded herself. Val's soft, sensuous kiss from the most delectable pair of lips in the world.

It was exactly eleven o'clock when Susan's phone chimed.

"Dr. Castle," Val snapped caustically even before Susan offered a greeting. "I don't appreciate what you did. I made myself very clear and you went behind my back, completely ignoring my wishes. You had no right to do that."

"Hello and what boundaries do you perceive I have trampled?"

"I told you I didn't want Jackson using your car."

"Val, all I did was say I didn't mind if he used my car while you were at work. Joe asked and I agreed."

"I have to go. Please don't interfere with my family, Dr. Castle." Val hung up, leaving Susan to stare at her phone.

"I don't think I interfered, Ms. Nardi. After all, it is my car."

* * *

"Joseph," Val demanded, her hands on her hips as she glared at him. "Why did you call her? That car is worth more than your truck and car combined. You had no right to do that. You should have respected my decision." She followed him down the prep counter, continuing to glare at him.

"Look, Val. We needed another car. I took care of it. I asked her. She said sure. This is between her and me."

Jackson came hurrying into the kitchen, a broad grin on his face.

"Hey, I hear I get to drive the Mercedes. Damn."

She stared at him, her nostrils flaring, then slapped the keys on the counter.

"Please be careful with it, Jackson. Don't get grease on the upholstery and don't fill it up with trash."

Val walked away. She didn't want to see him take possession of Susan's car. She stopped and looked back at Joe. "Anything happens to her car, it's on you, Joseph. You'll pay for it. You. Not Susan."

"It's a goddamn car, Val. Not the crown jewels." He gave her a disapproving scoff.

CHAPTER TWENTY-EIGHT

Susan sat at her desk. She had several projects that needed her attention but guilt made concentration impossible. She'd stuck her nose in Val's family business and she should have known better. Allowing Jackson to use the car was Val's prerogative. She should have respected her wishes and told Joe no.

Usually, when something in her personal life tormented her, throwing herself at a software project blocked out the aggravation. It wasn't working. She could call her and apologize profusely. Then apologize again. But she needed to apologize in person, face-to-face and with as much sincerity as she could manage without stumbling and stammering over the words. Even then, it looked like a toss-up whether Val would forgive her.

She had been gone all day yesterday and when she returned she'd found the Mercedes parked in the driveway. Val had sent a cryptic text thanking Susan for allowing her to use it along with directions where she had hidden the car keys. Val hadn't tried the code to leave the keys inside. She hadn't looked up at the camera to offer a smile and a wave. The car had been thoroughly cleaned and vacuumed and the gas tank was full. A free calzone coupon was tucked in the visor but nothing was written on it. That meant Val hadn't forgiven her. The car looked fine. Unscathed from Jackson's use. She didn't give a flying flip if she got a thank-you from Joe or Jackson. It was Val's feelings she cared about. What she had intended as a helpful gesture had backfired spectacularly. And she was furious with herself.

She slammed the front door closed, stormed out to the garage, yanked open the side door, snapped on the light and crossed to her bicycle. She hadn't ridden it in weeks. A combination of nearly daily rain, business meetings and casual interactions with Val had made cycling outings less than inviting. Today she wanted a road trip, drizzle or not. She needed a road trip. She needed a diversion from the memory of Val's sweet face and warm lips.

She was halfway down the drive when she skidded to a stop and stood straddling the bicycle, eyes closed and her head lowered. This wasn't the answer. This was escaping and ignoring the issue. She needed to own her mistake.

Today, Friday, was one of Val's normal workdays. She could thank her again for cooking even though the meeting had been cancelled. Then she could apologize for sticking her nose in Nardi business and hope Val wouldn't toss her out on her ear. She'd order whatever the dinner special was, or ask Val what she recommended. Yes. Let Val have a say. Follow her recommendation and eat it even if she didn't like it. Every last morsel. Then apologize again. She wanted to be Val's friend. She feared she had irreparably damaged that friendship.

Val's car wasn't in the parking lot of Nardi's. Jackson was using Val's car for deliveries—that had to be it. He hadn't replaced his stolen car yet and Val's generosity was once again being called into family duty.

Susan parked and hurried across the parking lot, her shoulders hunched against the chilly rain. The lobby had several couples and families waiting to be seated. Friday was indeed busy.

"Franklin, table for four," Audra announced, taking menus from the rack on the podium. She escorted the family to a table. When she returned, she asked Susan, "Castle, right? Table for one?" She wrote something on the waitlist. "It'll be a few minutes."

"In Val's section?" She glanced around the room.

"Val isn't working this evening," she replied without looking back at her. "Jolene will be your server."

"Why isn't she here? She always works Friday. Where is she?"

"At home. Her grandmother died."

"*What?* Grandma Nardi?" Susan drew in a desperate gasp. "When?" she demanded.

"I'm not sure. Last night, I think."

"What the hell, Audra? You used my car to deliver pizza, the car I allowed Val to use until hers was repaired, and you didn't think it was appropriate to tell me a friend's grandmother passed?"

"I assumed you knew." Audra shrugged indifferently. "Didn't Val tell you? If you're her friend it seems like she would have told you herself. It was a blessing anyway. The old woman has been suffering long-haul Covid symptoms for months and months."

Susan resisted the urge to scream at Audra's apparent callous disregard for Val's feelings and stormed out the door, muttering, "Heartless bitch" under her breath. The famous Nardi togetherness didn't seem to include empathy for a grieving family member. She knew how much Grandma Nardi meant to Val. Susan sprinted to her car and roared out of the parking lot. Whatever misunderstanding she and Val had now took a back seat to the need to find her and offer sympathy. Hopefully she'd find a convenient moment to apologize and they could move on from the lapse in judgment. She wasn't sure how she planned to do that but she'd worry about it once she found her.

Twelve minutes. That's how long the GPS said it would take to get to Val's address, which Susan quickly located with an algorithm. She made it in seven. It was a modest frame bungalow at the end of a narrow street of similar size houses. She pulled into the driveway behind Val's Subaru. She rang the doorbell and knocked. She considered knocking again but hesitated when she heard the muffled sound of weeping coming from the side of the house. She followed the sound down the driveway to a side door that stood open a few inches. She peered through the screen door. Val stood at the kitchen counter, hugging what looked like a photo album and crying. She wore the tan slacks and the sky-blue button-up blouse, the one she'd worn during their shopping trip to Pike Place Market. But her hair, usually pulled back into a ponytail, was down and shoulder-length.

Susan hesitated, suddenly unsure if she should bother her in her time of grief. But why wasn't someone from her family here? Val needed someone, family or friend, someone. She tapped softly. Val didn't seem to hear and continued to cry, rocking back and forth as she clutched the album. Susan opened the door and stepped inside. Val didn't turn until the door closed with a click. Her eyes were red and swollen. Tear tracks ran down her cheeks. She drew a surprised breath and tried to smile but quickly succumbed to more tears. Susan didn't say anything. No words seemed adequate in the presence of such pain. The tragic Covid death of her partner and now this. Val continued to cry as she held tissues to her face. Susan took a step closer and held out her arms. Val dropped the album on the counter and rushed to her, her sobs deep and soulful. Susan gathered her in her arms, smothering her in a hug. Susan closed her eyes against her own tears of sympathy as Val huddled against her. This was what Val needed. Someone to offer support and understanding, and she was glad to offer it.

"I'm so sorry," Susan whispered as she gently stroked Val's hair. "I'm here." She continued to hold her and sway, hoping it was the right and adequate thing to do. Val seemed unable to speak through her tears. Holding Val in her arms, Susan desperately wished it was under different circumstances but she selfishly enjoyed the feeling of Val's body against her own.

"She's gone," Val finally said, choking back her tears, moving out of Susan's arms to look at her. "My Nana is gone."

"I'm so very sorry. You loved her and you will miss her. She loved you, too."

Val drew a deep replenishing breath and dabbed away the trail of tears as the chime of an incoming text sounded from the phone lying on the counter. She looked up at Susan with a pained expression and shook her head as if she couldn't deal with it. Susan reached for the phone.

"It's Joe," she said with a growing scowl and then an exasperated groan as she read it.

"He says, I'm sorry about Grandma. I hope you're going to be okay. Since you're home today, I'm sending Jackson over to pick up your car. We're really busy. Casey handled some of the deliveries but we're getting snowed under. We need another driver."

"Not today, Joe. Please," Val whispered painfully. She reluctantly reached for the keyring hanging on a hook at the end of the cabinet.

"Tell your brother you can't give Jackson your car because you aren't home." Susan covered Val's hand.

"But I am home. He'll expect me to hand it over." Val sounded resigned to it.

"You don't have to be."

Val looked up at her curiously.

"May I?" Susan asked, reaching for the phone.

"Okay. But, Susan, I don't want to be mean or vindictive."

"You won't be," she said as she typed, one arm still around Val.

I'm not home, Joe. I'm mourning my Nana.

Where Val was and what she was doing was none of his business.

"Grab your jacket. Lock up your house and your car. You're coming with me," Susan ordered.

Three minutes later Susan backed the Mercedes out of the driveway and headed them away from Bonney Lake, Nardi's restaurant and anyone who could add to Val's pain.

"Thank you," Val said. Susan had taken charge and she was relieved for her to do so. "I couldn't face that right now. It was too much."

"No problem. How are you doing?" Susan wanted to reach over and touch her. To let her know whatever she needed, she was there, eager to be supportive and understanding. She adjusted the rearview mirror instead.

"It was such a shock. I know. I know. We expect the older generation to go first but it came out of the blue." Val looked over at her. "She passed in her sleep last night."

"Peacefully then. She'll be with you forever, Val. Guiding and protecting and encouraging you. Trust that."

"I know." Val dabbed at her eyes as she once again quieted her sobs. She looked out the window at the darkness. "Maybe I shouldn't have run off like that. If they need to use it…"

"Val, I understand family devotion. I do. But you deserve a modicum of respect, too. You work double shifts whenever they ask. You provide transportation for their delivery service and without compensation. You go above and beyond at the drop of a hat. Yes, your brother gave you a job during a difficult time. But he reaps the benefits of you serving his customers. And it's all the damn time, Val."

"Not all the time," Val argued without conviction.

"Well, today isn't going to be one of them. Blame it on me if you want to." Susan reached over and patted Val's leg reassuringly. "Let's put Val Nardi first for a change."

Val reached for her hand and pulled it into her lap. She closed her eyes and leaned back against the headrest, her thumb caressing the back of Susan's hand as she cradled it in her lap. Susan drove along in silence, an evening drizzle splatting against the windshield and the occasional swipe of the wipers the only sounds.

"Val, I need to apologize," Susan finally said, then cleared her throat. "I need to explain why I did what I did. I'm so sorry about the car debacle."

"Debacle? You mean you telling Joe it was okay to use your car after I said no?"

"I honestly thought you changed your mind and wanted them to have access to my car but were too ashamed to ask. Rather than put you on the spot and embarrass you, I agreed.

I realize I should have consulted you but I didn't mind sharing use of my car."

Val turned her gaze back out the window.

"Am I at least partially forgiven?" Susan asked worriedly.

"Do you promise to do better in the future?"

"All I can promise are good intentions."

"Then we'll probably be having this conversation again. Right?" Val smiled over at her.

"Smart woman," Susan returned. "Keep your expectations low then you can't be disappointed."

"You know, if I was at Nardi's right now, I'd pour myself a glass of vino rosso and toast my grandmother. She loved a glass of red wine every now and then." Val's eyes were dreamy and reflective. "She said vino rosso was part of our Italian heritage."

"I'd have one with you. I'm not Italian and I never met your grandmother but I remember mine and she was absolutely worth a toast." Susan looked over at her expectantly. "Are you game for a little glass of wine?"

"I'd love to." Val lifted and kissed the back of Susan's hand. "What a great idea, thank you, Dr. Castle."

Susan turned off the highway, winding through the back roads of Pierce County toward her house. Val wanted to remember her beloved grandmother with a toast and Susan was pleased to help her do that. But something else tugged at her.

How could she make Valentine Rose Nardi, the beautiful Valentine Rose Nardi, see her as anything other than an over-the-hill computer geek with enough emotional baggage to stop a freight train? Could she ever see her as a woman with feelings and desires, age difference be damned? She desperately hoped so.

CHAPTER TWENTY-NINE

Susan keyed in the security code and held the door for Val. They stepped out of their wet shoes and left them on a mat inside the door. Val hung her jacket over the back of a chair then nodded toward the bathroom down the hall.

Susan went to the kitchen, retrieved a bottle of wine from the refrigerator, and poured two glasses for their toast. She then went out onto the patio to fill the firepit. She enjoyed the warmth and relaxing atmosphere and hoped it would comfort Val as well. She set a match to the kindling and blew across the embers, encouraging a flame.

"Better?" Val came outside, rubbing cream into her hands.

"You looked fine before and you look finer now." Susan smiled brightly and gave a thumbs-up. She handed her a glass of wine.

"Okay." Val drew a thoughtful breath then said, "Here's to Nana Nardi. The most wonderful, kind, generous, understanding woman to ever grace my life. I love you, Nana." Val held her glass up to the heavens in salute.

"Hear hear," Susan agreed and held her glass up as well. "And here's to Gigi Castle. Steadfast and benevolent rock during my childhood. You were, and are, loved." A tear glistened in Susan's eyes. "Definitely loved."

They clinked glasses then sipped, both of them silent with their memories.

"And here's to Nana Nardi for insisting I learn to cook pasta the Italian way. She's responsible for bringing us together. I wouldn't have met you otherwise."

"Sure, you would have. Of course, it would have ended with the be-my-date fiasco," Susan chuckled.

"True. And you'd still be backing away like I have the plague." Val sipped again, grinning behind her glass. "Thank you, Nana."

"By all means. Thank you, Nana Nardi." Susan sipped and saluted.

"Speaking of Nana, how did you hear the news?"

"I stopped by the restaurant." She wouldn't mention Audra's indifference to Val's pain and heartbreak. Perhaps she, too, was suffering from the loss of a family member and didn't know how to show it. She'd give her the benefit of the doubt. "When I heard what happened, I left to find you."

"So neither one of us had dinner this evening." Val poured another inch of wine in each of their glasses.

"I've got lots of leftovers if you'd like the bolognese and those little baggies of pasta. Or I can call in something and have Uber Eats delivery. Whatever you're hungry for, Val. I'll be glad to call."

Val opened the freezer and scanned the choices. "I'm sure we can find something we can enjoy. Hey, what's this?" She took out a baggie and examined the contents.

"Bacon. Thick-sliced, maple-cured, pepper bacon. I repackaged it after I used a couple of strips for a BLT."

"How about a breakfast dinner? Pancakes and bacon. You have pancake mix, don't you?

I love breakfast dinners. Pancakes, waffles, French toast, bacon, sausage. Anything breakfast-worthy works."

"How's this?" Susan pulled a box from the shelf and read the label.

"Perfect. We'll eat pancakes and bacon by the fire and remember our grandmothers."

"I think that's a great idea." Susan tucked a lock of hair behind Val's ear. "What can I do?"

Val pulled out a skillet and the griddle that fit over two burners. "You may arrange bacon in the skillet, after defrosting it in the microwave."

"I can do that. There's about half a package of blueberries in the freezer."

"Well, get them out, woman. We're celebrating with blueberry pancakes," she encouraged devilishly.

Val mixed up a bowl of batter. Susan dutifully tended the bacon in the skillet as Val prepared the griddle. Before spooning it, she did another whisking of the batter to make sure it was properly blended before folding in the blueberries. The more Val stirred, the more her butt shook, the natural reaction to vigorous whisking. Susan was watching. Val knew she was. And the more Val jiggled, the more Susan stared, seemingly frozen in place. It took a pop of bacon grease to restore her attention.

Val smiled to herself as she ladled the batter onto the hot griddle. She carefully spooned a few small round pancakes, then artfully drew pancakes in the shape of letters S and V across the griddle.

"I couldn't help myself," Val said, whimsically making a squiggle at the end of each letter. "Nana used to do that."

"I like it." Susan looked over Val's shoulder, grinning at the letters. "Restaurants make boring round ones."

They stood side by side, turning the bacon and flipping pancakes. They took up their plates and went out onto the patio to enjoy dinner by a crackling fire. It all seemed to lighten the mood although Val occasionally heaved a sigh and stared off into space.

"This is wonderful," Susan said, plucking a blueberry from her pancake and eating it with a piece of bacon.

They went back for seconds and laughed at the childhood memories the meal resurrected. Val was finally at a point where she didn't dissolve into tears at the mention of her grandmother. It might not last all evening but for now she was at ease and enjoying Susan's company.

Val took Susan's plate and her own and carried them into the kitchen. "I'm as full as a tick," she grumbled. "Shame on you for buying that delicious bacon."

"I'm so sorry for my transgression. I feel properly reprimanded." Susan followed, carrying the wine glasses. "May I make up for it with a cup of tea for dessert? I have that decaf pumpkin spice you picked out at the tea shop in Seattle. I haven't tried it yet."

"I'd like that, Susan. Yes, the perfect ending to a perfect meal. Would you like me to make it?"

"Nope. Tea, I can do." Susan winked, as if confessing a secret. While she made tea, Val loaded the dishwasher and tidied up the kitchen.

Susan handed her a mug of steaming tea and nodded toward the patio.

Val took a seat on the rim around the firepit, her back to the fire. Susan added another log, then sat facing her as she cradled her mug in her hands.

"This is so nice, Susan." Val scanned the patio, drinking in every detail. "If it was mine, I'd be out here all the time." She closed her eyes and drew a long satisfying breath, the cherry wood aroma filling the air.

"Would you mind sharing your perch with my feet?" Susan pointed to a spot next to Val on the rim of the firepit.

"Put 'em up here." Val guided Susan's feet into place next to her. She smoothed a hand over one of the comfy-looking socks. "I love your socks. I bet they're really warm. And they're so soft."

"I don't like cold feet."

"Me either. In the algorithm of life, cold feet are definitely last." Val grinned, knowing that would elicit a response from Susan.

"You love to throw that word up to me. I'm probably going to regret ever telling you about algorithms."

"What was that other word? Something about repetition."

"Iteration?" Susan suggested.

"Yes. Iteration and algorithms. If I know those two words does that make me a computer geek?"

"Absolutely. Iteration and algorithms. A finite set of steps performed in a precise sequence and repeated for a specific outcome. You don't need to know anything else." Susan laughed and tapped the side of her foot against Val's hip. "A computer savant."

"As soon as you have a few hands-on cooking lessons, you can be a pasta savant." Val set her mug down and moved Susan's feet between her thighs, gently caressing and massaging her feet, humming softly. "Warm feet are one of life's little pleasures," Val said coyly. A sparkle began to grow in Susan's eyes. It could be the flickering glow of the fire or it could be the wine. But maybe, just maybe, it was something else.

Susan's phone rang. She checked the caller ID then answered it. Val released her feet, stood and carried her tea into the kitchen. She set the mug on the counter and meandered down the hall so that she didn't appear to be eavesdropping. She stood in the doorway to Susan's office, arms crossed, admiring the handsome furniture and elegant detailing, exactly what she expected a successful professional's office to look like. Organized. Spacious. Well-appointed. Classy. Nothing like her cramped, cluttered and disheveled desk had been at the cleaning service. She rounded the large desk, drawing her fingers along the smooth walnut veneer. Not a speck of dust on it, exactly what she expected.

She could hear Susan talking about someone's program. The caller seemed panicked and Susan was doing her best to calm their anxiety.

"I already looked at it. Your conditional is wrong. It's an easy fix. Don't stress the small stuff. I wouldn't have used Java. C++ might have worked better in this case but you can correct the issue. How are you going to learn to do it if you pass it off to me?"

What was it like to sit behind an impressive desk where a software engineer created her magic?

"So, this is where you do what you do, Dr. Castle," Val whispered as she eased into the highbacked leather chair. She had learned the bare basics of computer knowledge to handle scheduling, inventory and payroll for her company but sitting behind Susan's desk with three large monitors made her feel even more computer illiterate than when she'd bought her first computer.

"We'll discuss it next week," Susan said, her voice louder as she drew closer to the office. "Yes. I'll perform CPR on your app if necessary." She appeared in the doorway as she ended the call. "I see the computer savant has found her office." Susan leaned on the doorjamb, slipped a hand in her pants pocket and smiled at her.

As Val rose from the chair Susan waved her back. "No, no. Sit. You wrangled it through the door. You deserve a turn in it."

"This is the Amazon behemoth?" Val smoothed her hands over the leather armrests.

"That's it. Assembled and adjusted. And I'm guessing your feet don't sit flat on the floor."

"Not quite. I'm not as long-legged as you." Val grinned and tapped her toes on the floor. "I feel like a kid in Grandpa's chair."

"It's easy to raise and lower. One of the reasons I bought this unit. Sometimes I spend more hours in here than my posterior likes," she mused then cleared her throat as if preparing for a new topic. "Val, I know you got your car repairs completed but if you need to keep the Mercedes for a while, do it. Let me help."

"Susan, that's sweet of you but I don't want to discuss it. Nardi's can figure out their own transportation issues. I refuse to allow them, or me, to take advantage of you."

"You did *not* take advantage of me." She reached over and squeezed Val's knee. "Please, never say that again. You did not."

Val stood and headed for the door. "Are you ready for more tea?"

"Wait a minute." She grabbed Val's arm. "Please don't walk away. Let's discuss this."

Val straightened her shoulders and said, "Okay. If you want to discuss something, tell me how I break through the crust that keeps you at arm's length. I want us to be friends but it seems like you put limits on our relationship."

"I'm not putting limits on anything. I want you to know I'm here. My car. My truck. Whatever you need." Susan hesitated then added, "I want to be the one you turn to. Is that wrong? You probably think I'm trying to interfere but I want to help. I know my age is a hurdle but can't we work around it? I'm not good at this but please, let me help."

"I need you to stop fussing over our age difference. It makes no difference. None. Am I wrong to want our friendship to be deep and meaningful?" Val felt tears welling. "You kissed me, Susan."

"I know." Susan stepped closer and lifted Val's chin, smiling down at her. "Yes, we are friends. You don't have to use my car. You don't have to do anything you don't want to do. But please, let me be part of whatever you do. Even if it's only lighting the fire to warm you."

"Be Susan Castle," Val said softly as her chin began to quiver. "That's all I want."

Val guided Susan's hand and held it over her breast. She stood staring into Susan's eyes. It was a long moment of silence, each of them swimming in the other's gaze. Susan combed her fingertips through Val's hair then lowered her lips to Val's. Then slowly drew her lips away and looked into Val's eyes, as if questioning the moment and how to proceed.

"Yes. Be the wonderful Susan Castle I know you can be," Val whispered then leaned into another kiss, wrapping her arms around Susan's shoulders. Susan seemed cautious at first then backed Val against the door, gently pressing her body against her. Her hands roamed down over Val's hips as their kisses became more insistent. Susan hooked a hand under one of Val's legs and lifted it, supporting it as she pressed into her. In an instant, Val leaped into Susan's arms, locking her legs around her and folding her arms over Susan's head as she moaned with delight. Susan wrapped her arms around Val's bottom and carried her to the desk all the while she hungrily devoured her lips and mouth. She set her down, pushing the keyboard and monitors aside before laying her back. Val kept her legs locked around Susan, refusing to let her go for even a moment, both of them kissing frantically. Val could feel Susan's breasts and pubic bone against her own. Insistent. Encouraging. Demanding. Satisfying.

"Is this okay?" Susan asked breathlessly as she kissed first one side of her face then the other. "Am I hurting you?"

"I love the feel of you against me," Val muttered emphatically. She threw her head back as Susan's kisses carved a path down her neck and into her cleavage. She locked her ankles around Susan's back, hungry for more.

Susan slid her hand down to cover Val's crotch, her fingers pressing against the seam of Val's pants. Val closed her eyes and drew a deep desperate breath.

"Oh, please. Again," she gasped.

Susan obliged as she kissed deeper into her cleavage, licking one side then the other.

"You are good. Yes. Like that. Just like that." Val arched her back and gave a guttural groan at the growing ecstasy and the anticipation of what was to come.

Susan unzipped Val's pants and worked her fingers inside, sparking a new and more intense sensation. Val immediately unlocked her legs, pushing herself up to Susan's touch.

"Here?" Susan gently but thoroughly massaged and caressed Val's tender skin.

"Inside. Please. Inside." Val writhed beneath her touch.

Susan delved deep, skillfully guiding Val toward an intense climax, her muscles straining at Susan's rhythmic strokes. She clamped her arms around Susan's neck, desperate to hold on as her body began to shake and twitch. Susan allowed her to ride the last exquisite moments until she lay breathless and satisfied.

"You are as soft as velvet," Susan whispered, withdrawing from her. She smiled down as Val enjoyed the smoldering afterglow. "My little Italian Rose petal."

"That's exactly the Susan I want." Val smiled adoringly then kissed Susan passionately.

She released a long, slow sigh, her body spent and exhausted. She couldn't help it but tears began to flow. Tears of happiness and satisfaction and relief. This kind, gorgeous and intelligent woman ignored their differences and concentrated on what they had in common. And it was beautiful. More beautiful than she could imagine. A few precious minutes that would forever be seared in Val's brain. Nothing could be more satisfying than Susan Castle making love to her. Susan wiped the tears from Val's cheeks then gave her a kiss of finality.

"That was absolutely magnificent." Val brushed her fingers through Susan's hair, admiring her lover. The two of them continued to lay together across the desk, oblivious to the hard surface.

Val cupped her hand over one of Susan's breasts, giggling and teasing her.

"Algorithms and iterations, Dr. Castle. Algorithms and iterations," she joked, her palm massaging Susan's nipple. She was unfastening Susan's pants when her phone chimed loudly. "*No*," Val exclaimed, grimacing.

"There are a million things I'd rather be doing right now and none of them involve my phone." Susan made no move to answer it, settling instead to kiss and lick at Val's cleavage.

"I know and I'd love every single one of them." Val tilted her head back, exposing her neck to more of Susan's kisses. "But why don't you answer the phone and I'll go visit the lotion room."

Susan gave one last peck on the lips, then reluctantly climbed off the desk and offered Val a hand up before pulling her phone from her pocket and reading the ID on the screen.

Val started for the door but looked back with a mischievous grin.

"I have a few ideas of my own, Dr Castle." She winked and sashayed into the hall.

CHAPTER THIRTY

When Val returned, Susan was sitting at her desk, phone to her ear and a scowl on her face.

"Jillian, calm down. No one is going to steal the contents of your hard drive. I can't understand your gibberish. Now, with your best big-girl voice, tell me what it's doing." Susan yanked the phone away from her ear and cringed as Jillian launched into a screaming harangue, part of which Val could hear as well. "Jillian. Jillian! Wait!"

Susan held the phone to her chest and whispered, "Apparently, Jillian's laptop is guilty of high mutiny." She held the phone to her ear again as something Jillian said caught her attention. "Where are you now?" Susan held her breath as her eyes widened. "That close?" She immediately rolled her eyes up to Val.

"She's coming over?" Val quickly combed her fingers through her hair, something she hadn't paid much attention to in the bathroom mirror since they had much unfinished business.

Susan nodded with an apologetic shrug.

Val rushed back into the bathroom. While she rebuttoned, straightened and combed, Susan reassured Jillian's fears that her problem couldn't possibly be as bad as she thought it was. Within a minute of ending the call, the toot of a car horn could be heard outside.

Rubbing her hand up and down Susan's arm as she joined her in the kitchen, Val asked, "Will she want tea?" She pulled another mug from the cupboard and opened the baggie of pumpkin spice tea.

"No, she'll want that." Susan pointed to the wine bottle then started for the front door. She was halfway out of the kitchen when she hesitated and looked back at Val.

"What?" Val asked.

"Oh, nothing. Admiring your glow is all." She smiled shyly and went to answer the door.

Val could hear muffled conversation before the voices grew louder coming down the hall.

"Hello, Val," Jillian said as she hurried into kitchen, her voice solemn with concern. She was dressed in stylish form-fitting jeans and a quilted vest over a deep V-neck sweater, a leather satchel draped over her shoulder. "Susan tells me your grandmother passed away. I so sorry to hear that, hon." She handed Susan her satchel then turned back to Val for a hug. "How are you doing? Losing family members can be absolutely devastating. I don't care how old they are. I remember losing my Aunt Vivian a few years ago. I was a wreck for weeks. We weren't super close but it's definitely a reality check when any member of the family dies."

Jillian didn't leave an opening for Val to respond but it didn't matter. It was too soon and her pain too raw to casually talk about her grandmother's passing. She'd only start crying again. Jillian took her hand and reiterated how terrible it was to lose family and friends and how Val should remember them lovingly.

"They say retelling stories and memories helps the grieving process. You're young, Val. I'm sure you'll move past the trauma with time but it's okay to be upset."

"Thank you," was all Val offered. She could see Susan standing behind Jillian, her eyes occasionally meeting Val's, as if acknowledging their time together on the desk. Val wondered if the blush she felt racing up her face was noticeable.

"Jillian, explain again what the problem is," Susan said, holding the strap of the satchel like it was a sack of potatoes.

"I told you. It died for no good reason." She looked back to Susan with an expression of desperation.

"It's your Lenovo?"

"Yes. I don't have the patience for problems this week. Could you take a quick peek? It's probably something simple but I'm ready to throw it out the window of a moving car. I need it for work tomorrow. Please, sweetheart," she whined. "Do that thing you do."

Susan opened the zipper and pulled out the laptop then handed the satchel back to Jillian. Balancing it on one hand while she booted it with the other, she tapped a few keys, a scowl deepening as she studied the screen.

"Did I fry it?" Jillian looked over Susan's shoulder as she continued to type and frown.

"We'll see." Her eyes narrowed as she studied the screen. "Have a seat and visit with Val. I'll be back." She nodded them toward the patio then headed to her office with the laptop.

"Do you need my password?" Jillian called after her.

"Nope."

"Can I make you a cup of herbal tea?" Val offered. "Or maybe a glass of wine?"

"Yes, wine. Thank you. If it wasn't tacky, I'd ask for a tumbler of wine instead of a polite glass." She shook her head. "I have a love-hate relationship with my laptop. Thank God for Susan. She's never intimidated by any computer problem."

"I know what you mean. I'm envious." Val handed her a glass of wine, then followed Jillian out onto the patio.

"Susan did a fabulous job of designing this outdoor living space." Jillian leaned her head back and closed her eyes, as if drinking in the ambiance. "The first time I saw it, I knew it was perfect for her. She loves quiet solitude when she works."

"Yes, it's very cozy." Susan's delicate and satisfying touch danced across Val's mind. She hoped Jillian didn't notice the blush she felt race up her face or her need to uncross and recross her legs at the sensation.

Jillian gave her a quick look, her eyes narrowed.

"Val, a word of advice. I know you and Susan have become friends. She's very proud and envious of your cooking talents. And I think that's great. You can never have too many friends. Susan enjoys her friends but only as friends, if you know what I mean." She reached over and buttoned the middle button of Val's blouse then patted it. "Anything beyond a simple friendship and you'll end up without a friendship at all. She has trouble saying no." She chuckled softly. "It's like a delayed kick of a mule. You don't realize you're in trouble until it's too late. Then you're lying in the dirt, bruised and bleeding." She squeezed Val's arm knowingly. "Just be her friend, hon. At her age, she'll appreciate you for it. Don't expect more than she can comfortably offer. And it won't come back to bite you in the ass."

Susan was right. Jillian was indeed chatty. Val was tempted to tell Jillian she might be right when she mentioned Susan avoided casual physical contact but there was another side to Dr. Castle. A gentle, giving side. Elemental and intense. One that turned Val on like no one she had ever met. It was none of Jillian's business. However, from her raised eyebrow and skeptical gaze, Val suspected Jillian was already making her own assumptions.

"I understand you spent several hours cooking for Susan's dinner party and then they canceled at the last minute. Damn. That's rude on so many levels. At least you got paid, I assume. If there's one thing I know about Susan, it's that she'd never stiff someone she hired to perform a service." She leaned her head back as if resurrecting a memory. "I remember a few years ago she hosted a bunch of clients at a swanky restaurant in Seattle. There were maybe twelve to fifteen people. She reserved a private room and ordered some top-shelf stuff. I wasn't there but what I heard from a couple of people who were that the food was bad and the service was egregious. Susan simply paid the check, left a generous tip and shook the manager's hand on the way out. The bill was huge. When the manager said he looked forward to hosting her events in the future, she smiled, patted him on the back and said *'When hell freezes the fuck over.'*"

"Really? She said that?" Val giggle-snorted.

"I understand she received profuse apologies from the owner plus offers of discounts but you don't screw with Dr. Susan Castle. Age has its benefits. She's been around long enough to know how to handle assholes."

"Her age definitely has its benefits." Val laughed, envisioning Susan putting that manager in his place. "I hope I'm as perceptive as she is when I'm her age. She has a way of explaining things without being aggressive or condescending. My grandmother was like that. The older she got, the less BS she took from anyone." Val nodded to herself as she remembered Nana's strength and resilience.

Jillian held up her glass, admiring the last half inch of wine. "You know, this is really good. I wonder what it is."

"Cabernet sauvignon," Val offered.

"Dago red wine," Jillian said with a chuckle and downed the last of the glass.

Jillian's remark was rude and Val didn't appreciate it. Before she could protest, Susan came out onto the patio carrying the laptop under her arm.

"Your Lenovo is ready. You picked up a boot sector virus. You need to stop accessing the Internet from the coffee shop Wi-Fi. Plus, your Microsoft update hasn't been run in a couple years. No wonder it wasn't detecting anything." She zipped the laptop into the satchel and handed it over with a stern expression. "Be kind to your computer if you want it to be kind to you."

"I thought it updated automatically." She stared up at her, still comfortably seated as if she was in no hurry to leave.

"Not the way you have it configured. When you get home, plug it in, turn it on and let it run. Give it an hour or so to rectify what you failed to do. Don't tinker with it until it's finished."

"Did it wipe my hard drive?" Jillian stood, slung the strap over her shoulder then dismissively handed her wineglass to Val.

"No. You're back in business, at least for now. And why aren't you using Linux instead of Windows? I explained that to you last year."

"Susan, sweetheart, you need to remember something." Jillian reached over, hooked her arm through Susan's and clutched it tightly. "You explaining technical stuff and me understanding it are two very different and separate entities. My nodding agreement does not mean I know what the heck you're talking about. Now, I'm going home before I refill that wineglass and become incapable of driving. Come walk me out, Susan. I want to hear how things are going with the port authority project in Olympia." She looked back and gave Val a patronizing smile, one only Val could see. "I'm so sorry about your grandmother, honey. You take care of yourself. And you be careful."

Val stood on the patio, Jillian's wineglass in one hand, her teacup in the other. She told herself that Jillian wasn't passing judgment or criticizing. She and Susan had been friends for years and she was merely relaying her personal opinion. She'd go with that. Val had more pressing things to worry about than one overly protective friend.

By the time the front door opened and closed she had washed the few glasses and cups and returned the kitchen to its pristine condition. Susan came into the kitchen, a strange look on her face. One that suggested she was worried about something.

"Val, I'm sorry about that. I didn't know she planned on coming over tonight. There always seems to be a detail someone can't figure out on their own. Usually a coding problem. Jillian's are more maintenance issues. If I don't rectify it right away, she'll screw it up so even MIT couldn't ferret out the problem."

"Everyone calls Dr. Castle because they know you can fix it." Val stroked her arm.

"You look tired, Val, and if you plan on working tomorrow, you'll need your rest especially after all the terrible emotion of today. How about I take you home?"

"You're right. I'm exhausted. But I had a wonderful time this evening, Susan." She slipped her hand in Susan's, as much for her own satisfaction as a sign of endearment. She wanted to feel her warm and wonderful touch one more time.

Val stepped closer and looked up at Susan. She expected a kiss or some small acknowledgment of their time together in each other's arms, albeit on a hard wooden desk. But Susan had turned and was heading for the front door, handing Val her jacket on the way.

It was a quiet ride to Val's house. Conversation seemed limited to weather forecasts, the Thanksgiving fundraiser and Val's expected hours working it. Susan avoided discussing their evening of passion. She pulled into Val's driveway and kept the engine running. Val placed her hand on Susan's thigh and smiled warmly. "I appreciate you rescuing me this evening. Thank you for being my rock through this craziness with Grandma Nardi."

"Are you going to be all right, Val?"

"With time." Val held tight to her emotions as she felt a knot rise in her throat. "I will with time."

"I hope so." Susan reached over and opened Val's door. "Good night, kiddo."

Val couldn't read Susan's expression. Something was wrong. They had only begun their sensory world of touch and taste and satisfaction. From the moment Jillian called and showed up at her house, Susan had withdrawn into her shell. But Val was undeterred. She leaned over and kissed Susan's cheek then stroked her face.

"Good night, sweetheart." Val patted her thigh then climbed out. She looked back at her through the open car door. "Sweet dreams." She closed the door and went inside. In spite of losing her beloved grandmother, Val knew she would indeed have very sweet dreams, in spite of Jillian's warnings.

CHAPTER THIRTY-ONE

Val loaded a few boxes into the back of her car. Many of Nana's possessions had been systematically distributed to family members over the years, but there were a few of her grandmother's mementos Val would treasure. Objects she remembered as a child or little gifts she had given Nana, including a pair of earrings. They weren't valuable but they had been her gift to Nana's for her eightieth birthday and Nana had enjoyed wearing them. Joe and Vinnie's selections seemed strongly influenced by their spouses. Audra wanted Nana's wedding ring. Since Joe was the eldest, she'd argued it should go to them. Val acquiesced to avoid an argument. Vinnie took a gold necklace with the small cameo. It had been worn by several brides in the family and Vinnie wanted Megan to wear it at their wedding. Val would have liked to have it but since she had no plans to marry in the near future, she reluctantly agreed to them having it. The one thing she was ready to go to war over was Nana's recipe book. Handwritten in a three-ring binder, with copious notes in the margins of the pages, the tattered remnants of a red-checkered tablecloth had been glued to the cover to reinforce the aging binder. It contained the recipes Nana had used for family dinners, church suppers and to teach Val to cook. Some pages had tiny splotches of pasta sauce or olive oil. A few pages had been taped and reinforced so they didn't fall out. Owning this bit of Nana's life was Val's hill to die on.

"Why the hell do you want that old notebook?" Joe had chuckled, giving Val a look of disgust. "Throw the damn thing in the trash."

"Touch it and die, Joseph," Val teased but she meant it. She didn't dare tell him what it contained or why it was so important to her for fear that would raise his or Audra's interest in it.

The graveside service had been modest, sparsely attended and somber, exactly what Nana requested. It lasted little more than fifteen minutes, crammed between Audra's morning spa treatment and Joe opening the restaurant. Megan didn't attend, supposedly suffering from a nasty bout of morning sickness. Val wore her blue blouse, the one Nana gave her, telling her how much she admired the way she looked with her hair down and gleaming.

The priest recited two prayers and mumbled something from the scriptures and left. Val was last to leave, standing in the morning drizzle a few minutes longer. She pulled a small bottle of imported Italian olive oil from her purse. She had purchased it at Pike Place Market to drop in Nana's stocking at Christmas. She kissed the bottle, and placed it on top of the casket, nestling it among the spray of red roses.

"Bye-bye, Nana," she whispered, her hand resting against the polished mahogany. "I love you." She turned and walked to her car without a backward glance as tears silently streamed down her face.

The next few days were tumultuous. Grieving the loss of her grandmother, she did her best to hide her emotions so she didn't have to put up with Audra's looks and Joe's indifference. She needed to work. She needed the distraction. And she needed the income since finding a renter for her building continued to be fruitless. It was amazing how many excuses people found to justify renting the building at a discount, or even free. The real estate agent from hell tried twice more to secure her signature on the dotted line so he could "relieve her of the burden." She thought it best not to call him a chauvinistic pig. She didn't want to lower herself to his level of rudeness. She allowed the two days Jackson needed to use her car to roll off her back. Taking issue with it wasn't worth the aggravation.

She'd be working a double shift for the Thanksgiving fundraiser. Long and tiring as it would be, it should be profitable for the servers, tip-wise. Customers attending a fundraiser were benevolent for the most part.

Susan had sent a well-worded sympathy card and a gorgeous bouquet of flowers as well as an apology for not attending the funeral. Val hadn't expected her to attend. She tried twice to call and thank her for the flowers and confirm a time to attend the fundraiser but both calls went immediately to voice mail.

"You are way too busy for your own good, Dr. Castle," Val muttered.

She finished a full shift and drove home exhausted. She sat in her driveway and sent a text, asking Susan again if she wanted a table reservation for the Thanksgiving event before going inside. She was nearly asleep when a text from Susan flashed across the screen. It was short, saying she was out of town and wasn't sure when she'd be back so attending the dinner was uncertain.

The next morning Val planned to arrive at the restaurant by nine. She settled into the driver's seat and started her car. While she waited for the heater to kick in and the defroster to clear the windshield, she called Susan's number.

"Hello and Happy Thanksgiving," Susan said, picking up on the fourth ring. She sounded distracted.

"Happy Thanksgiving to you," Val replied happily, pleased to finally talk to her. "You're hard to catch."

"I'm sorry about that. I've been busy."

"You're forgiven as soon as you tell me what time you're coming for dinner. I'm looking forward to seeing you."

"Val, I'm not sure I can make it. It'll be great, I'm sure. But I've got several projects that need my time."

"It's a holiday," Val argued. "Save the projects for tomorrow and come let me serve you water with lemon or a nice vino rosso with your pasta."

"I can't."

"Can't or won't?" Val asked carefully. Susan's reticence was worrisome.

"Val…"

"Do I need to come sit on the patio by a crackling fire so we can talk?" The memory of Susan's socked feet in her lap stirred a pleasant sensation. It had been the prelude to something tantalizing and exquisite. She hoped it had been for Susan as well.

"It would be better if you didn't," Susan said after a moment of hesitation.

"Better for who?"

"Val, I've got projects in the works and clients who need my undivided attention. This is a busy time of year for me."

"Susan, what's going on with us? Do you regret what we did? Have I crossed some kind of line? Be honest with me. What have I done or said? Please, tell me."

"Nothing. You haven't done anything. I need to go. Good luck with the fundraiser today. I'm sure it will be a big success." After a long, measured pause she finally added, "If I can make it, I will." There wasn't much enthusiasm in her tone.

Something was wrong. Something had Susan suddenly withdrawing to a time weeks ago when she'd had no time or patience for Val. A time before loaning vehicles or shopping Pike Place Market or cooking pasta. It was as if their intimate time together had been nothing more than a feather in the wind. Still, Val held out hope. Even as something was eroding those hopes.

Val clocked in, tied on her Thanksgiving apron and forced an amiable smile, ready to do this.

It was chaotic for over an hour as tables were moved, the buffet line was set up and preservice place settings were arranged. Signs on the door explained Nardi's was open as a reservation-only fundraiser though there were always a few who ignored the signs or insisted they had a reservation when they didn't. Audra did her best to accommodate but the one thing Joe refused to pardon or lower was the price since it was clearly advertised that one hundred percent of the revenue went to the Wounded Warrior Project. Lunch time was surprisingly busy and continued that way throughout the day, keeping the kitchen crew busy making a variety of pizza and pasta dishes.

On one of her trips to the kitchen with a bin of dirty dishes, Val noticed a man in the parking lot. He was dressed in a tattered hoodie, dirty jeans and sneakers that looked several sizes too large. He had a scruffy beard and was wandering the lot, staring at the ground, looking for cigarette butts. Probably in his fifties, he was thin, dirty, and had scraggly long hair. Val stood at the back door, watching him dig in the bushes for a cigarette. He blew the dirt off, straightened it then put it in his pocket.

"What's up?" Joe asked, taking a quick glance over her shoulder.

Val nodded toward the man.

"Oh, that's Burt. He's homeless." Joe shrugged dismissively and went back to the pizza oven.

"I hate to see that. And on Thanksgiving is even worse." She continued to watch him. "Doesn't he have family?"

"They cut contact with him years ago. He's harmless but he has PTSD."

Joe pulled two family-size pizzas from the oven, slid in two more and went about cutting up the ones ready for the buffet table. "Can you take these to the buffet? Bring back empty serving trays."

"Is he ex-military?" she asked as she prepared the pizza on the serving tray.

"Yeah."

Val carried the pizza to the buffet, collected three empty trays and headed back to the kitchen. Before she could ask anything else about Burt, Joe handed her a pizza box. He placed a bottle of water on top of the box then nodded toward the door, a knowing smile pulling at the corners of his mouth. She mouthed a thank-you, tucked a folded twenty-dollar bill from her tips into the corner of the box, and went outside to share Thanksgiving with Burt. He accepted the box, though he seemed embarrassed and shy. Val patted his shoulder and thanked him for his service and went back inside.

"You're a softie, sis," Joe said.

"You're a big teddy bear yourself," she said and carried a pan of meat sauce to the buffet.

By eight o'clock she accepted Susan wasn't coming. Disappointing as it was, she resisted the urge to call her. If she wasn't there, she wasn't there. Whatever the reason, Val hoped it was purely business. Not something she'd caused.

It was late and Val was exhausted from the long day on her feet at the fundraiser, and disappointed. At Joe's insistence, she had leftover pizza to take home but had little appetite for it. Sure, she'd spent Thanksgiving with her family. Vinnie, Megan, and Jackson all helped make the event a huge success. But it was bittersweet for Val. The one person she most wanted to see and enjoy Thanksgiving with hadn't bothered to return her calls or texts.

"Thanks for your help, sis." Joe was loading pans of sauce into the refrigerator as she headed for the back door.

"Your best fundraiser yet," she said, a hand on the door handle to the parking lot.

"Hey, Val," Audra called, hurrying into the kitchen. "I forgot to tell you. Your friend Susan Castle sent a donation for the fundraiser. An Uber driver dropped it off. Two hundred dollars."

"Two hundred?" Val was surprised. "That's very generous of her."

"A note with the check said she was doing it in memory of her grandfather who was wounded in the war. Tell her thank you if you see her. Well, good night, honey." Audra gave her a kiss on the cheek and closed the door after her.

Val headed home. At least that was the plan but, in spite of her fatigue, she found herself making a detour onto highway 410. She pulled into the parking lot next to her building. The security lights were on, including the one over the back door. She hadn't been inside in a couple of weeks. None of her potential renters had gotten past the discussion of price and expectations, so she didn't feel compelled to show it to them. She had no reason to go inside but there she was. Staring at a brown door and wondering why she stopped. She fumbled with her keys as she argued with herself. But finally unlocked the door and snapped on the light.

The building was exactly as she last left it. The air smelled like cinnamon and cranberries, thanks to the air freshener. She leaned back against the counter, fiddling with her keys as she slowly scanned the space.

"Oh, Nana," she groaned, closing her eyes. "What should I do? Sell it and end the stress? I'm no good at being a landlord." She heaved a long weary sigh. "I wish you were here to help me decide."

A gust of wind blew the door shut, startling her. A faint smell floated past her nose. Unmistakable. It was garlic. Fresh, sauteed and flavorful garlic. The aroma she remembered from Nana's kitchen and those early cooking lessons. She closed her eyes and drank in a deep quenching breath of it.

She was being silly. Her grandmother hadn't created the smell. The long tiring day working at an Italian restaurant caused it. Nothing more. She headed for the door, ready to go home and put her weary body to bed but she stopped in the doorway and looked back. Something was holding her, refusing to allow her to leave. Something floating around her, demanding her attention.

"What are you telling me, Nana?" she said, barely above a whisper as she scanned the room. "Could I really do it by myself? Is it the right thing for me? How do I justify it?"

Her palms instantly became sweaty as she wrestled with the idea. Susan's words of encouragement and support to free herself from working for her brother swirled around her, mixed with her grandmother's assurances that she could do whatever she set her mind to. Pasta in a box, she thought. Delicious, homemade, simple recipes. Created and served her way, to her customers. This had been her dream since childhood. All she had to do was seize the dream and make it come true.

She hugged her keys to her chest and closed her eyes tight. "You always said if I don't have confidence in myself, no one else will either. Oh, Nana. I may be crazy but I want to do this."

CHAPTER THIRTY-TWO

Val pulled into Nardi's parking lot and sat watching the rhythmic swipe of the wipers clear the drizzle interspersed with sleet. She left the car running and the seat heater gently warming her for a few more minutes before going inside. It had been four days since the Thanksgiving fundraiser. Enough time to think and plan without emotion to cloud her thinking. And time for her to stop wishing Susan would stop by for dinner or visit or something.

Joe's truck was parked in his usual spot near the back corner of the lot. Audra's car wasn't in the lot but it was early, earlier than she usually arrived, which was exactly what Val hoped for.

The near freezing temperatures and wind-whipped drizzle couldn't diminish the spring in her steps as she entered the restaurant through the kitchen door. She deposited her tote in the office and tied on an apron.

"Hey, sis. You're early." Joe was pulling ingredients from the freezer and refrigerator. She took the bags of cheese he handed her and placed them on the counter.

"Have you got a minute, Joe? I need to talk with you."

"Yep." His head in the back of the refrigerator, he pulled out a box of ground beef. "What's up?"

She waited for him to finish. She wanted his full attention for what she had to say.

"I'm giving my two-week notice," she announced, then shoved her hands into her apron pockets to let that soak in. As she expected, he laughed.

"Okay, I get it. You want a two-week vacation." He continued to remove more ingredients from the cabinets over the prep counter. He obviously wasn't taking her seriously. "Talk to Audra. She'll schedule it."

"Joseph, I'm not asking for vacation time. Since when have I asked for more than a day or two off?" She followed him down the counter. "I'm giving you my two-week notice." Once again, she waited for him to fully absorb her declaration.

"To do what? Work at McDonald's flipping burgers?" His tone had changed from dismissive to condescending.

"I'm going to open Pasta in a Box."

He gave her a sideways glance then turned to face her, scowling. "Pasta in a Box? What the hell is that?" He'd finally offered her his undivided attention.

"Remember when Nana visited Italy several years ago on that senior tour? She told me about little walk-up hole-in-the-wall places that served pasta in to-go boxes. Sorta like Chinese takeout boxes. They only had a few choices each day. But all of them were made fresh. Nothing fancy but the food was delicious. I want to do something like that. I want my own business in my own building making homemade pasta using Nana's recipes. Simple authentic Italian creations served to walk-up customers. Half a dozen or so choices. Served daily until I run out."

"You mean fresh egg pasta?"

"Yes. Things like bucatini carbonara or rigatoni with ricotta and sausage. Maybe gnocchi with parmesan and mushrooms. I might throw in mushroom risotto once in a while or linguine with clam sauce."

"Linguine with peas and prosciutto," he added, grinning at her.

"And occasionally tagliatelle alla bolognese," she said with a smile, thrilled with his participation.

"That'll be your big-ticket item. Charge extra for that one." He bumped her shoulder. She wasn't sure if he was taking her seriously or playing along with a joke. "Customers will let you know what's popular and what's not. Give them credit for weeding out the crap in your menu. No doubt about it. Some people will order something new so they can say they tried it. But the familiar standard dishes will be more popular."

They finally fell silent and stared at each other as if processing Val's news and the possibilities.

"What do you think, Joe?" She wanted to hear his honest opinion. She needed to know she wasn't completely crazy. "I'm still working out the details. I know it'll take some planning but I want to do this. I need to do this."

He adjusted his eye patch and the strap that circled his head as he thought. He blew an exasperated breath, moved a toothpick to the other side of his mouth.

"Just pasta? No pizza?"

"No," she said without hesitation. "That's Mama Nardi's Ristorante's responsibility. You do pizza better than any place in town. I won't cut into your business, Joe. My competition will be fast food franchises. Your customers want table service. They don't want to walk up and order a container of spaghetti with sauce. Your customers want restaurant cuisine and service. I'll be offering a quick lunch or dinner on the run. No seating. No reservations. No wine or beer. I'll make Nana's pasta dishes, served the way she'd want them served. With love and a little parmesan cheese." She smiled at her brother. "What do you think? Do I sound nuts?"

It took a minute but he finally slowly pulled a guarded smile. "I say good for you, sis. I figured you'd land on your feet someday. If you're sure about this, do it. Don't look back. We'll miss your help here but shit, you sound like you know what you want. Should I worry about how you'll feed yourself until you get things going?"

"I've saved a little so I should be okay for a while—that's assuming I don't have huge car repair bills again," she added.

"If you need an occasional evening shift to get you through, let me know. We can work you in."

"I appreciate that. You're a very kind man." She wrapped an arm around Joe's waist and smiled up at him. "You're my big brother and I love you. Hopefully I won't need to tie on a Nardi's apron once I venture out into the world but you never know." It was hard to hide a measure of trepidation. But only a small measure. She was jumping into the deep end, and logic said she should be scared to death. But she wasn't, at least not yet.

"I'll give you a list of a suppliers to contact. Some product brands are better than others. Inflation has grocery prices high enough without some of those jerks jacking stuff up."

"I know it'll be a learning curve for me. I want to serve good quality food at fair prices. My food. My way. I won't compromise on quality."

"I hope it works out for you, sis. You deserve it. And, Val, don't let Audra give you crap about your decision. When you're ready, let me know. If she gives you static, I'll take care of it. You do what you need to do. It might be hard for her to show it but she'll want you to succeed."

"I appreciate that, Joe. I don't want to cause waves."

"Hey, when waves hit you in the face, learn to surf." He laughed his big laugh.

"I'll remember that. You'll be doing the same when I'm not around for Jackson to use my car if he needs it."

"Didn't you hear? They found his car. One of his friends recognized the sailboat sticker he had on the back bumper."

"Really? That's great, Joe. No, I hadn't heard."

"Some eighteen-year-old kid stole it on a dare. His dad made a deal with Jackson. He agreed to fix the minor damage the kid caused, no questions asked, plus a little cash in Jackson's pocket if he didn't press charges."

"Did he agree?"

"Hell, yes. But Jackson told the guy he'd only agree if he got an apology from the kid, in person."

"Wow. That's very mature of him," Val offered, smiling.

"That's what Audra said. Surprised the hell out of her. Now, shall we get Nardi's ready for customers?"

Val threw herself into work, doing whatever Joe needed her to do. He seemed to recognize her giddy excitement and occasionally laughed at her for no particular reason. The lunch crunch faded and she was carrying bins of dirty dishes into the kitchen when Jackson came through the door with his backpack over his shoulder.

"Hey, Jackson. I heard you've got good news. Someone found your car."

"Yeah. Some little turd over in Yelm copped it. He side-swiped a mailbox and ripped off the outside mirror. The bastard even cracked the windshield."

"But it's drivable, so that's good."

"Yeah. I guess." He dropped his backpack on the counter and checked the refrigerator for something to eat. "Hey, Val. Would you tell Susan Castle something?"

"Susan? What is it you want me to tell her?" This request definitely grabbed Val's attention.

"Tell her thanks for the advice." He continued to rummage in the refrigerator.

"Tell her I'm taking a couple of online computer classes."

"Good for you, Jackson. I think that's great. What kind of computer classes, in case she asks?"

"I want to be a computer programmer. It's not nearly as sophisticated as what she does but I like it. In a couple years I'll be able to write code in C++ and Python. It's better than delivering freakin' pizza," he added.

"I'm very proud of you, hon. I'm sure you'll make a great computer programmer.

I'll tell her but you need to let her know yourself how you appreciate her advice. I'm sure she'd like to hear directly from you."

"Oh, I will," he said eagerly, clearly relieved she was willing to handle it this time. "Oh, and can I use your car today? Mine is getting the windshield replaced."

"Sure," she said, smiling as she carried plates into the dining room.

Val wanted to share her news with Susan. Both her business intentions and Jackson's online classes. But only in person. Not through a text or voice message. It was too important to her. Plus, she wanted Susan's input. They'd had only limited contact since their evening together and Val worried that Susan had withdrawn, as Jillian warned she might. If Val's advances did irreparable damage to a wonderful relationship, she hated herself for it. Maybe she should have left well enough alone. Allow Susan to accept her on whatever level she was comfortable with. If she was reticent to have anything more than a casual friendship, so be it.

"I'll be right back," she announced. She stepped out the back door of the restaurant and stood under the awning. As a cold rain darkened the afternoon skies, she called Susan's phone. Her voicemail picked immediately.

"Hello, Dr. Castle. This is your neighborhood pasta chef leaving you another message. You missed a wonderful Thanksgiving feast. It was very sweet of you to send a donation for the Wounded Warriors. I wish you could have been here to do it in person. Okay, so we didn't have turkey and cranberry sauce but we had a dozen kinds of pizza and several pasta dishes to die for. Joe did a great job this year. *And you missed it!*" She laughed. "I need to talk with you, honey." She added the term of endearment then thought better of it. But it was too late. She'd said it and meant it even if Susan didn't necessarily want to hear it. "Jackson asked me to call and thank you. He took your advice and is taking online computer classes. He seems excited about his future. He wants to be a programmer. He's still delivering pizza so he has an income while he takes the classes. Anyway, he asked me to thank you. I think you intimidate him, Dr. Castle." She thought a moment then added softly, "You intimidate me, too. But on another level. Please call me. I need to hear from you." Val was ready to hang up but she hadn't said everything she needed to say. She took a deep breath and continued.

"Susan, you don't seem to have time for me right now and that's okay. I understand you're busy. I feel like I forced you into something that made you uncomfortable and I'm sorry. I promise I won't do it again. Jillian warned me I shouldn't force a relationship. She said you prefer friends with no strings attached. I won't push for more than that. Jillian said you dated her sister, Dallas. Did she trample your boundaries, too? I want to be your friend, Susan. That's all. I don't expect or want more. Just friends." She ended the call and clutched her phone to her cheek, her eyes closed against the tears threatening to spill out.

The next week was hectic. She worked several double shifts, something she suspected was Audra's underhanded punishment for her decision to leave Nardi's. But she needed the income. She wasn't sure how long it would take to open her pasta business and turn a profit. When she wasn't working at the restaurant, she was planning and mapping out her business decisions.

Susan's only contact with her were text replies that she was out of town and busy finalizing projects or repairing client-created glitches before the end of the year. Nothing on a personal level. No comments about their time together. No teasing messages about how much she missed Val. It was as if those precious moments never happened. Susan did offer congratulations for Jackson and wished him success. Val hadn't yet told her about her plans to open Pasta in a Box. She wanted to tell her in person and see her reaction. With luck, she'd get that opportunity. And hopefully Susan would be as excited about the future as Val was.

* * *

"Val, could you help Owen for a few minutes?" Audra asked, following Val into the kitchen as she carried a bin of dirty dishes. "He's got a big takeout order for the VFW and he's having trouble keeping up."

"Sure." Val washed her hands and pulled on plastic gloves, ready to help.

Afterward, she dropped the plastic gloves in the trash and washed her hands, ready to return to serving customers but Audra intercepted her before she made it out of the kitchen.

"How are your plans going?" She sounded more judgmental than curious.

"I'm still in the planning stage but I'm working on it." She didn't need or want Audra's advice.

"The rich lady with the Mercedes. She's helping you get started, right?"

"What are you talking about, Audra?"

"Oh, come on, Val," she said, giving her arm a playful bump. "That woman is loaded. She could buy and sell that little building of yours a dozen times over and not break a sweat. It's okay, honey. I understand. You accept help wherever you can find it. If Susan Castle can help, good for you. Money is money."

Val's temper flared at her sister-in-law's insinuation.

"First of all, Susan is *not* helping me. How dare you suggest such a thing?" Val stepped closer and glared at her defiantly. "Any financial assistance I need I'll get from a small business loan. And I'll pay it back, on time, in full. I'd never ask Susan for the kind of help you're insinuating. Yes, she encouraged me to open my own business if it was something I wanted to do. Shame on you for suggesting I'd ask her for money. She loaned me one of her cars while mine was being repaired. She's a friend, Audra. That's all. She's not my bank."

"Val, order up," Joe called, plating a pair of personal pan pizzas. Audra grumbled something and returned to her duties in the dining room.

"Hey," he said under his breath before Val headed to the dining room with the order. "I'll take care of it." He nodded to where Audra had gone. "She's pissed right now. Jackson is talking about moving out and getting his own place with a couple of friends. They're all taking computer classes together. She's mad she hasn't been able to talk him out of it."

Val gripped his arm and said, "Don't let her, Joe. Encourage Jackson to be his own man. She'll thank you in the end."

"Yeah," he said then gave a guttural groan. "She'd make a hell of a drill sergeant."

They both laughed as Val headed to the dining room with the tray of food.

CHAPTER THIRTY-THREE

Susan wasn't mad. She was furious. She took a deep breath, hoping to lower her stress level and quell her festering anger. It wasn't working. The snarled commuter traffic on Highway 5 north of Seattle wasn't helping. She touched the Bluetooth on the steering wheel, knowing this call couldn't be postponed any longer.

"Call Jillian Ramsey."

"Hey, there, Susan," Jillian said happily. "Yes, I allowed the updates to finish and I even installed Linux like you told me. All is well. Where are you? You sound like you're in the car."

"I'm driving back from Vancouver."

"Vancouver, Washington, down by Longview?"

"Vancouver, British Columbia."

"What the heck are you doing in Canada? I don't remember you developing a project for anyone up there."

"Working on a proposal. Jillian, what did you say to Val Nardi?" she asked pointedly.

"Say to her? You heard me. I told her I was sorry about her grandmother."

"What else? What else did you say to her?"

"Susan, sweetheart, I've had several conversations with Val. I can't remember everything I ever said to her. You need to be more specific."

"A couple of things have come to my attention."

"Like what?" Jillian laughed as if this were some kind of guessing game. "Tell you what. Give me a topic and I'll see what I can come up with."

"Val told me you said I dated your sister. Did you tell her I dated Dallas?" Susan demanded flatly. Susan heard her gasp. "Did you, Jillian?"

"I don't remember."

"You don't have a sister, Jillian. You are an only child and your full name is Jillian Dallas Ramsey. Why did you tell her differently?"

"Sweetheart, I honestly don't remember. She might be mistaken."

"She mentioned Dallas on two different occasions. My guess is you made up some convoluted scenario about me dating a nonexistent sister to make a point. What was it? Were you trying to scare her off? Jillian, you and I will never have a relationship. Not the kind you want. I told you that years ago."

"She's taking advantage of you, Susan. You know she is and you won't do anything about it. I'm trying to help," she bristled.

"Since when is my friendship with Val Nardi or anyone else any of your business?"

"She needed to know some things. Things you certainly aren't going to tell her. Things like you have an anxiety attack every time a woman stands too close or hugs you or, God, forbid, kisses you. Admit it. You don't process intimacy, Susan. You never learned how. If you knew how to handle women's advances, your past girlfriends would have lasted more than a few weeks. What was it you said about that woman, Tricia? The blonde with the sailboat. You said things went from zero to sixty in less than a week." Jillian chuckled. "And you were stomping the brakes after day two. You know everything there is to know about computers and software but you are completely illiterate when it comes to love. You are defenseless. It's the reason you haven't been in a meaningful relationship in like ever."

"This is a completely different situation."

"You had sex with Val, didn't you?"

"Jillian," Susan snapped. She couldn't imagine Val had confessed their evening of pleasure but Jillian was very perceptive. She could be fishing.

"You did. She talked you into it and now you don't know how to unravel the mess you caused. You're a woman in her sixties, floundering and drowning in what you can't handle," Jillian insisted. "You know you need my help to get out of this, Susan."

"No, I don't. What I need is for you to butt the hell out," Susan demanded through gritted teeth, her blood pressure escalating by the second. "It's my life. And I'll conduct it on my terms. In my own time. My way."

"My God, Susan. There's a whole generation between you two. Believe me, honey. Val is very aware of your age difference. She said so. We're talking blinking light, screaming siren aware. She's grieving the loss of her grandmother. She sees you as a substitute for what she lost."

"Goodbye, Jillian." Susan ended the call. Jillian's remark stung like a slap across the face. It was true. Sure, she was nearly two decades older than the most attractive and endearing woman she had ever met. But could Jillian be right? Was Val subconsciously attracted to her as a replacement for her grandmother? Susan was exasperated with herself for not considering it.

"Son of a bitch," Susan shouted and smacked the steering wheel. Then smacked it again.

CHAPTER THIRTY-FOUR

Susan stood in the lobby, hands in her pockets, nervously jingling her change as she waited her turn. Audra was busy seating customers during what looked like the height of the lunch rush. Susan made a quick scan of the dining room, hoping to flag down Val so she could be seated in her section. She needed those extra few moments to quiet her anxiety and clear her thoughts.

"Audra, could I have a table in Val's section please?"

"Val doesn't work here anymore," was all she said and it seemed an effort to admit that much.

Susan stood frozen in shock, her eyes following Audra as she walked away to seat a family. Why hadn't Val told her she wasn't working for her brother anymore? Now she was even madder at herself for not interrupting her meetings and office work to return Val's calls.

"Audra, where is she?" she demanded as soon as Audra returned to the podium.

"I'm sorry, Ms. Castle. I'm not at liberty to say."

Susan knew nothing would be gained by playing twenty questions with this woman since whatever caused the end of Val's employment obviously didn't sit well with Audra. Susan wanted to hear the facts directly from Val. Not from a woman with a chip on her shoulder. She turned and trotted out to her car.

"Call Val Nardi," she said after activating the Bluetooth. The call immediately went to voice mail. Susan contemplated leaving a message but hung up instead and roared out of the parking lot. She headed to Val's house. But neither Val nor her car were at her house. She peeked in the window. Nothing looked out of place.

She called her again, but again it went to voice mail. This time she left a message.

"Val, where are you? I went by Nardi's and Audra said you don't work there anymore. Explain, please." Susan paused, deciding what else to say. "You're right. We need to talk. And no, you did nothing wrong."

Susan ended the call. She sat staring at the Bluetooth. She closed her eyes and waited but there was only silence and her desperate breathing.

"Call me, please. Call me, you wonderful person you. Call me and tell me I didn't royally screw this up."

She'd keyed in the security code and stepped inside her house as her phone chimed. She nearly dropped her briefcase when she saw it was Val.

"Hello," she gasped. Whatever the problem, at least she had Val on the phone.

"Hello, your own self." Val chuckled happily. "If I didn't know any better, I'd swear we were playing phone tag."

"I agree. It's been far too long since we spoke."

"Before you say anything else, I completely understand busy."

"Val, what's going on? I stopped by the restaurant and Audra said you don't work there anymore. What happened?"

"That's true. I'm not working for Joe anymore. And I have a confession I didn't want to tell you in a text or leave a voice message, but I took your advice."

"My advice? What advice is that?"

"Okay. I wanted to tell you in person but I'll tell you now. I did a lot of thinking and weighing my options and soul-searching and I decided it was time for me to spread my wings and be my own boss. I've decided to open Pasta in a Box. Joe and I talked about it and he agrees it's doable with a little planning and patience. You were right. I was bogged down in Nardi's restaurant. It was a safe place to hide away from being independent. But thanks to his support and your encouragement, I am going to do this. My recipes. My way. I need to be my own woman again."

"I think that's great, Val," she said fervently. "And yes, you absolutely can and should do this."

"I think it's fair to say I'll be super busy for a while but I'm looking forward to it. I apologize if we don't talk as much as we used to but like you said. You're busy and I will be too."

"Pasta in a Box, eh?" Susan was still absorbing Val's news.

"Yes. I thought about Val's Pasta but I think the box idea better fits what I'm offering. Authentic Italian pasta dishes taken from my grandmother's recipes. I'll tell you more when I see you."

"Your grandmother would be very proud of you. I am. This is exactly what you need to do for you."

"I think Nana would approve," Val said reflectively. "I hope she would."

"Val, I need to explain a few things," Susan began.

"Susan, you don't need to explain anything. I understand. You were my savior during a difficult time. I didn't respect your boundaries. If you can forgive me, I promise we can be friends. The kind of friends who talk on the phone or meet for lunch once in a while. Of course, it might be a few weeks before our calendars mesh. Tomorrow the electric company is coming out to see why the electric meter isn't running correctly. Oh, and I'm having the locks changed. Who knows how many keys Heidi shared with her friends. I don't want unexpected guests in the middle of the night eating the profits. And I'm sure we'll both be busy during Christmas. It's always crazy at Nardi's." Val was babbling and couldn't stop herself.

"Val." Susan tried to interrupt.

"Susan, I'm sorry but I need to go. An inspector from the Health Department is here and if I don't keep this appointment I'll have to wait until after the first of the year for another one. I'll talk with you soon. Bye-bye." Val ended the call before Susan could stop her.

Susan walked out onto the patio and sat down, mindlessly staring at the firepit. There was no fire, only a small pile of silver ashes from the evening she and Val had spent together. Remnants of a wonderful evening. Susan stepped out of her shoes, sat down and propped her feet up on the rim as she remembered Val gently caressing and massaging her feet. She slid her feet over to where Val had sat cradling Susan's feet in her lap.

"Come back to me," she whispered. She closed her eyes and leaned her head back. "How do I tell you how much I want you and need you?" She finally put her feet down before the sensation growing between her legs had her groaning over what was left unfinished.

She stood, needing a diversion from the sensations those memories stirred. She wandered through the house, hands in her pants pockets. She looked in the guest room where Val had admired the handmade quilt and enjoyed the bouquet of flowers on the dresser. She went into the bathroom and touched the bottle of hand lotion Val had liked, smiling to herself. She squirted a small glob on her hand and held it up to her nose, reliving how wonderful Val smelled wearing it.

"Damn, woman. You smell good even without lotion."

Susan meandered back up the hall and stopped at her office door. She looked in, leaning against the doorjamb. One of the monitors on the desk was slightly askew and she moved to straighten it. Once she had it perfectly arranged and satisfactory, her hand lingered on the desk where she had placed Val's body, her exquisite and supple body. She threw her head back and groaned at the memory of Val's sweetness and her kiss. She closed her office door and sat down at the desk. She opened the drawer, pulled out a red flash drive and inserted it into the

USB port. She needed work to take her mind off Val or she was going to scream. It was two-twenty in the morning when she removed the flash drive, shut down her computer and went to bed. Maybe a few hours sleep would settle the anxiety.

* * *

It was 8:20 the next morning when Susan observed Val's car pull into the parking lot behind her building and saw her run inside through the rain. Susan had been sitting in her car since 7:10, watching and waiting. Lights came on inside the building. Susan's cue. She ran her hands down the legs of her jeans. It was a different look but maybe a different look was a good thing.

When she opened the back door to the building, Val was kneeling on the floor, sorting through a large box of kitchen gadgets and accessories. She immediately snapped a look up at Susan.

"Hello," Susan said then swallowed hard.

"Hello," Val stammered in surprise.

"I'd like to discuss a business proposal with you, if you have a minute."

"Business proposal?" Val sat back on her heels. "Hey, you're wearing jeans."

"I thought I needed a new look. Now, if you'll allow me to explain," she said, offering Val her hand and helping her to her feet. "You may not need what I have to offer but I thought I'd make it available." She pulled a red flash drive out of her pocket and held it up. "You may have already made arrangements for your programing needs for your new business but I'd like to offer this."

"I was thinking I'd adapt the program we used in the cleaning service. It wasn't perfect but I thought it would be a place to start." Val looked like she was still processing Susan's surprise visit. "I haven't taken a close look at it yet. Some of that stuff is way over my head. What exactly are you suggesting?"

"I already had something that was easily adaptable to what I think you'll need. I didn't want to overwhelm you but this will do the basics. Track inventory, expenses, point of sales, that kind of thing. I'll be glad to assist in getting it installed and functioning." She took Val's hand and placed the flash drive in it then closed her fingers around it.

"Susan, you made a software program for me?"

"This is what I do. It's my gift for Pasta in a Box."

"What a wonderful business proposal. Thank you." Val touched Susan's arm, much like she had done many times before but withdrew it.

"Let me know when you're ready and I'll help install it for you." Susan scanned the counters but didn't see a computer or laptop. "Well, you look like you're busy so I'll leave you to your work," she said, feeling her anxiety dictating her next move.

Val released a small desperate gasp as Susan turned to leave. Susan stood frozen, her fingers gripping the doorknob hard enough to turn her knuckles white. She opened the door then slammed it shut and turned around.

"One more thing," Susan said with a suddenly devil-take-the-consequences smile on her face. "My name is Susan Castle. I'm single, sixty-three years old, and I'm a computer geek. I hope you won't hold that against me. Valentine Rose Nardi, you are the most charming woman I have ever met. And I'm in love with you. I'm in love with you so deep even a ladder couldn't rescue me. Only you can do that. If you are willing to undertake the Susan Castle challenge, I would be extremely appreciative." She stepped closer and took Val's hand, swimming in her big brown eyes.

"Oh my God, Susan. You love me?"

"Yes." Susan kissed Val's palm. "Most definitely, I do. I was in love with you before our first kiss." With that, she gathered Val in her arms and kissed her tenderly and completely. "I've cleared my calendar for the next few weeks if you are available."

"I would love to take on the Susan Castle challenge. I've been waiting and wishing and praying for this." Val's chin quivered as she slipped her arms around Susan's neck. "I love you, too. And I mean really, truly, deeply, love you." She lay her head against Susan's shoulder.

"You are a very patient woman." Susan smiled down at her adoringly as they swayed ever so gently.

"You are so worth the wait, Dr. Castle. More than you know, you are worth the wait."

"I have one more little thing I hope you'll accept from me." Susan slipped her hand in her jeans pocket. "I've been carrying this around and wasn't sure when I'd get a chance to give it to you."

She took Val's hand and slipped a ring on her finger. It was a gleaming gold strand spiraling around her finger like a single piece of spaghetti delicately sculpted precisely to fit.

"Oh, Susan," she gasped. "It's gorgeous." Val squealed as she stared wide-eyed at the ring. "It's pasta on my finger. I love it." She pulled Susan's face down and kissed her repeatedly. "It's the most wonderful gift you could have given me."

"I think they call it a promise ring. And if you wouldn't mind wearing it, I promise you I will forever be yours and you will forever be mine." Susan kissed her hand. "That's assuming you need a woman who loves you dearly."

"Oh, yes. I do. I need you terribly." Val pressed her newly ringed hand against Susan's chest and leaned into her. "And I need you to kiss me like you'll never let me go."

"My pleasure."

And she did.

Bella Books, Inc.
Happy Endings Live Here
P.O. Box 10543
Tallahassee, FL 32302
Phone: (850) 576-2370
www.BellaBooks.com

More Titles from Bella Books

Hunter's Revenge – Gerri Hill
978-1-64247-447-3 | 276 pgs | paperback: $18.95 | eBook: $9.99
Tori Hunter is back! Don't miss this final chapter in the acclaimed Tori Hunter series.

Integrity – E. J. Noyes
978-1-64247-465-7 | 28 pgs | paperback: $19.95 | eBook: $9.99
It was supposed to be an ordinary workday...

The Order – TJ O'Shea
978-1-64247-378-0 | 396 pgs | paperback: $19.95 | eBook: $9.99
For two women the battle between new love and old loyalty may prove more dangerous than the war they're trying to survive.

Under the Stars with You – Jaime Clevenger
978-1-64247-439-8 | 302 pgs | paperback: $19.95 | eBook: $9.99
Sometimes believing in love is the first step. And sometimes it's all about trusting the stars.

The Missing Piece – Kat Jackson
978-1-64247-445-9 | 250 pgs | paperback: $18.95 | eBook: $9.99
Renee's world collides with possibility and the past, setting off a tidal wave of changes she could have never predicted.

An Acquired Taste – Cheri Ritz
978-1-64247-462-6 | 206 pgs | paperback: $17.95 | eBook: $9.99
Can Elle and Ashley stand the heat in the *Celebrity Cook Off* kitchen?